FAMILY SECRETS

The stick. Outlined against the light. Raised, ready to strike. The punishment stick. The stick for beatings. Dad's stick.

It happened so quickly that Jonathan had no time to fight, no time to hum or recite or sing. The suckers whipped around his brain, squeezing and wrenching until the foreigner was in control. Dread burned like acid in his stomach. He'd broken the rules, done the forbidden, and now he knew what was coming.

He yelled out a foul curse. He felt wild, untameable, feral. He rose to a crouch. A black dog (whose dog? Not one of Dad's Patterdales) was growling at him, its ears flattened, the hair on its spine erect, its teeth bared and ready to snap. He knew what you did with dogs: you went for the muzzle with your metal toecap. Then the man rushed forward and tried to grab him. He fought back, hammering his boot into the man's calf and slashing up at his face with clawlike hands. In this mood he would kill.

FAR CRY

Also by Michael Stewart

MONKEY SHINES

FAR CRY

Michael Stewart

PaperJacks LTD.

TORONTO   NEW YORK

PaperJacks

FAR CRY

PaperJacks LTD

330 STEELCASE RD. E., MARKHAM, ONT. L3R 2M1
210 FIFTH AVE., NEW YORK, N.Y. 10010

Freundlich Books edition published 1984
PaperJacks edition published February 1988

ISBN 0-7701-0785-0
Copyright © 1984 by Michael Stewart
All rights reserved
Printed in the USA

this is for
Katherine Stewart, my mother

ACKNOWLEDGMENTS

Especial thanks are due to: Dr. Henry Campion; Dr. Christopher Dare, Consultant Child Psychiatrist, Maudsley Hospital, London; Dr. David Geaney, Radcliffe Infirmary, Oxford; Dr. Paul Harris, Department of Developmental Psychology, University of Oxford; Dr. Robert Lefever; Dr. John Marshall, Neuropsychology Unit, Radcliffe Infirmary, Oxford; The Warneford Hospital, Oxford; The Westminster Coroner; and, above all, James Hale.

FAR CRY

1

Now that he'd left the town behind the boy broke into a run again. He ran towards the open country in the wintry dark and drizzle. His jacket was drenched and the wind bit numbingly through the jersey sleeves he'd pulled down over his hands. He didn't know where he was or where he was heading, only that he had to carry on, on along the same straight line he'd taken all the way from home. He was following the call, the far cry for help.

His ankles were raw where he'd kicked them and the wind had turned his sodden trousers to sheaths of ice that cut at his legs. He had to keep on. He was on a knife edge: if he stopped, if he merely let up for a moment, he would lose it, he'd stray off the beacon's course and sideslip into one of his mad times. Already the bitter almond taste filled his mouth and he had to force himself to stave it off. He *mustn't* become Tommy now!

Hold on, hold on, hold on, he chanted in rhythm to his step.

He struggled across a plowed field, his stomach aching with a stitch and heavy clumps of mud weighing down his track shoes. He tripped and fell, but gathered himself up and stumbled on. How long had he been going? Would his mother have found his note yet? Would they track him down before . . . before he got to the end of the line?

Help, came the whispered cry again, full of anguish and bewilderment.

The field flowed into a darkening wood which reared up tall and dense against the glowering evening sky. The line led through the middle. He shivered, afraid. Tommy wouldn't be: *he* enjoyed being taken out into the fields and woods; foxes and badgers and the spirits of the night were his familiars. The boy bit his lip and plunged into the wood. He tore his hand on a barbed-wire fence and called out in pain. An owl echoed him from deep among the trees.

The wood opened abruptly onto a winding country road. Exhausted, he slumped over a fence-post for a moment. He fumbled for the bar of chocolate in his pocket but his mouth was too full of saliva and his stomach too tight to eat. As he fought to regain his breath he suddenly became aware he'd lost it! He couldn't feel the pull any more—there was nothing but a strange, dull, humming sound. He looked about him in alarm and saw, above, a tall power pylon that reached towards the dark rainclouds, its thick corded cables looping low alongside the road. He scrambled through the fence and onto the clear open road. And then the faint signal in his inner ear returned and the pull began to tug once again deep inside his head.

He broke into a jog and followed the wet road up a low hill. As he reached the crest he saw, in the shadows of a bus shelter some yards ahead, the glowing pinpoint of a cigarette. Quite suddenly a figure in a raincoat, his features hidden in darkness, stepped out into the road and swept out an arm to halt him.

"Bus ain't due for five minutes, son."

He drew up, his heart thundering. Could he get past?

"My dad's collecting me."

"His dad's collecting 'im." The man laughed shortly. "Come in out of the rain. In 'ere, with me. I could show you something."

The man took a step forward as if to herd him into the shelter, then snatched him fast by the wrist. The boy yelled out, kicked him hard on the kneecap, broke away and tore off back down the road.

Pursued by shouts he ran for his life, skidding and slipping and not daring to look back over his shoulder. He dodged to the left and right, speeded by terror, abandoning the pull and heedless of the dim inner cry.

He didn't see the car's headlights until it was already rounding the corner. He didn't hear the engine until it was yards away. By then he was in the middle of the road and running headlong into it.

The blow caught him on his side and flung him off balance. The sky cartwheeled above him and gravel bit deep into his hands and face. And the next moment he was sliding down into a ditch, a damp and slimy coffin at the bottom of a black world.

2

Frank Fuller was driving slowly back towards Bedford in the drizzling September twilight. Today he felt older than his thirty-nine years, older and scraggier. He'd never regained the weight he'd lost when his wife Cathy died, two years before. His suits were baggy and the wedding band she'd given him had fallen off and was lost. He rubbed a hand over his aching temples. He needed some hard exercise to get the week out of his system.

Though the territory he covered as a sales representative with the publishing firm of Strang and Longley spanned several counties, Frank knew most of his customers intimately; he had a special fondness for the bookseller in Deanshanger, where he'd paid his last call of the day. The man was going slowly bankrupt. Drinks lengthened into supper as they discussed ways of keeping the shop going. Frank set off for home late.

"What a business," he murmured to himself, and leaned forward to depress the dashboard lighter.

How the hell did anyone make publishing work? How did the business survive? Did the bestsellers *really* pay for the books that didn't make it? No one really knew, whatever the accountants made their ratios say. And so long as there was a good list to sell, most didn't care.

He wasn't driving fast. There was no particular hurry to get home. Except for his Labrador spaniel named Dog, the house would be empty. Once again he felt remorse that he and Cathy had decided, because of her condition, not to have children. With *that* hanging over their heads, they'd thought it irresponsible to bring children into the world. The folly of overcaution! Otherwise there might now be children waiting for him at home —small faces at the window, a girl with Cathy's complexion or a boy with her quick humor. In the first months after she died Frank left the radio on to come home to. Even now he set the lights to come on by a timer. Before she'd died he had always considered himself tough, in the way he was tough climbing on the rock faces of Wales where he spent his holidays. But afterwards he'd had a minor breakdown. It had taken him every ounce of his toughness to piece himself together. That, and of course Lawrence's help.

The thought of Lawrence made him smile. He'd had to cancel supper at Lawrence's house that night so as to be with the bookseller. He pictured his friend at that moment, sitting like Einstein at the head of the refectory table in their large, chaotic house near the hospital; his wife, Fiona, pregnant again, extricating a cat before filling up the dishwasher; Benjamin, their eldest at thirteen, playing mother against father to postpone his bedtime.

He sighed and stubbed out the cigarette. His body ached from a long day's driving. His eyes were strained from peering through a smeared windshield. The radio offered nothing but news of strikes, higher inflation, a cold front on its way. He found his favorite cassette, Elgar's *Dream of Gerontius*, and settled back to the music. The road was wet and slick. Gusts of wind scoured the black hedgerows and contorted the trees lining the roadside. He'd soon be home. Home to Dog and a good strong whisky. He slipped into a lower gear as he turned a bend at the foot of a low hill.

Then he saw the boy.

He was running in the middle of the road, running right at him, right into the car.

Frank stamped on the brakes and wrenched the wheel. The car lurched to the side. There was a brief crumpling sound and the boy sheered off the fender. The car skidded, slewed around and finally came to a stop broadside across the road.

He threw open the door and ran back. From the ditch he could hear choking. He jumped down and gently hoisted the boy to the side of the road, where he knelt over him.

Even in the half-light he was taken aback by the brilliant blue of his eyes. From a cut in his head blood streaked his fair hair. It was a handsome, strong face. The eyes stared unseeingly and began to roll upwards. His lips twisted and suddenly he threw up his hands as if to claw something off his face. Then, as Frank tried to calm him, he started yelling. A stream of rough oaths poured from his clenched mouth. And the first tremblings began. It was as if a violent inner force had taken over his body. He shook from head to foot. As Frank watched in horror, the shaking developed into a series of rhythmic convulsions—wave upon wave of spasms that racked the stocky little body. Snatching a pencil from his pocket, he rammed it between the boy's teeth and struggled to hold him down until the crisis subsided.

Gradually the boy grew limp and still. Fearful of broken bones, Frank carried him gently to the car and laid him on the back seat. He was in bad shape; his chin was bloodstained, his jacket was ripped apart and one of his track shoes was missing. But his face had begun to relax from the strain and, behind his bewilderment, Frank saw an expression of desperate helplessness.

He leaned over to soothe him. How did he feel? Where did it hurt? What was his name?

At this question a light frown came over the boy's freckled face and he blinked rapidly several times. Now he spoke in a clear, well-brought-up voice.

"Jonathan," he said. "Jonathan Hall. Not Tommy." Then he slipped into unconsciousness.

3

At five to seven that evening, Sarah Hall went to the foot of the stairs in her small modern house and called her son Jonathan to supper. There was no reply. She listened; maybe he was on his CB radio, helping William with his maths homework. There was silence, so she assumed he was playing with his small desk-top computer, finishing off the random-number generating program he'd been telling her about. The boy was computer-mad, as they all were these days. She made a mental note to find out from his teacher at Brickhill Middle School what she could get him to add to it. Jonathan had been talking about a dot-matrix printer, whatever that was. With the little spare money she had from her teaching job she liked to buy him educational presents. She particularly encouraged his interest in the computer and CB radio, as well as books and chess—home occupations where she could keep him under her eye.

She sat down at her desk in the small alcove she used as her study and checked the diary for the next week's engagements. On the top of the desk stood framed photos of Jonathan at different ages and in their different houses. The color ones—appropriately, she considered—had been taken since they'd moved to Bedford and their life had grown brighter. Beside them a silver carriage clock, a family heirloom her mother had discreetly given her without her father's knowledge, now struck seven. Normally she liked to have supper with Jonathan. She'd make them both the same food and they'd sit down opposite one another at table. Though he was only eleven she treated him as an adult, and she made something of a ritual about these moments together at the end of the day. It was a time when they could talk, and she could check.

Maybe tonight, if he was busy on his computer program, she'd let him have his supper upstairs on a tray. She'd give it another fifteen minutes.

Ever since her husband walked out, three months after Jonathan was born, she'd coped alone with her troubles. She was slim, with penetrating pale blue eyes and a strong, active face that lit up when she spoke. She kept her hair a mid-brown; few people realized that it was in fact gray. Her looks were what other women called striking. She knew she was attractive to men, but most of those eligible were either too self-opinionated or too weak. In days gone by she had tormented herself with the guilt of Jonathan's lack of a father. Now she believed that, whatever his problem was, it wasn't paternal deprivation. He was doing well at school and her job in the adjacent building at Brickhill Lower School meant she could keep a close watch on him. In the staff room they were forever telling her to remarry, but what man would really understand and accept the situation?

She wrote a letter to one of her parents and went back to the foot of the stairs.

"Darling," she called again. "Supper's ready. Are you coming down or do you want it upstairs?"

There was still no reply. She took the casserole out of the oven and put it on a tray, along with the pill and a glass of milk. She carried it upstairs and tapped at the door.

The room was empty. A note lay propped up against the computer keyboard.

Dear Mum, it read, *I had to go, but don't worry—I won't get caught this time. I promise. J.*

Oh God, she thought. He's gone against the pact. They'll catch him. In *that* state. The police will be around and it'll start all over again.

Frank paced up and down beneath the cold strip-lighting in Casualty. Unnerved still by the shock of the accident and the boy's alarming seizure, he reached for a cigarette. The woman at the admissions desk tapped her pen against a No Smoking sign. He left it in his mouth unlit. What had he done? Had he been driving too fast? What had the boy been doing running like a madman down the center of a country road in the dark? *Was he all right?* Frank went over to the desk again.

"I can't keep phoning through just for you," the woman said, looking up at him over thick-framed spectacles. "This is Friday night, in case you hadn't noticed."

He turned back and continued prowling the room among the desolate knots of ashen-faced people nursing home-made bandages. He felt trapped. He hated hospitals, with their abattoir smell and their conveyor-belt system of cure. What had they done for Cathy? They hadn't even allowed her the dignity of dying when it was her time.

The battered heavy plastic doors leading into the body of the hospital swung open and a familiar young nurse came in carrying a clipboard. Frank went over to her at once.

"Can you tell me: how's the boy I brought in?"

"His mother's been notified. She's on her way." The nurse turned aside to move past him.

"I'm sorry, but is he all right? I mean, is it anything serious?"

The nurse straightened. "We'll be doing X-rays in the morning. Now why don't you get on home. . ."

"You're keeping him in overnight?"

"Look, you can see we're very busy. The boy's going to be all right. Phone in the morning, please. And now excuse me."

Frank went outside onto the porch and lit his cigarette. Rain still fell lightly; from the fallen chestnut leaves on the carpark rose the smell of damp humus. As he stared out over the rooftops at the bruised purple night sky an idea suddenly struck him. He trod out the cigarette quickly and went back in. Where was the telephone?

"Phone's over there." The admissions woman pointed her pen towards a pay phone booth without looking up.

"It's internal."

Now she raised her head. She put a hand on the phone beside her. "This isn't for the general public."

"I'm a friend of Dr. Miller's, in Psychiatry. I'd just like a word with him. Do you know the number?"

The woman released her hand from the phone with some reluctance. "Dial zero. Ask the operator."

But as he dialled the number he was given he remembered that Lawrence wouldn't be in the hospital. They were giving a supper party; he should have been there. If only he hadn't cancelled. If only he'd left Deanshanger five minutes earlier, or five minutes later. Or gone a different way, by a different road. If only.

He put the phone down and turned to see a woman in a gray raincoat talking quickly to the nurse. He knew at once it was the boy's mother. But the nurse led her through the plastic doors before he could speak to her.

. . .

Twenty minutes later she returned accompanied by the nurse and a doctor. Frank could hear some of what they were saying. She was clearly angry but was trying hard not to show it.

"You tell me you only *suspect* a fractured rib," she said to the doctor. "Otherwise it's just cuts and bruises. I really think that's no cause to keep him in."

"Mrs. Hall, as I've said before, I won't take responsibility for discharging him," replied the man.

"Then, as his mother, I will. Don't worry: I'll bring him back for the X-rays in the morning. I'd far rather Jonathan woke up in his own bed after the shock of the accident."

"Listen, Mrs. Hall, he's been given a sedative. It's better he. rests where he is. I'm going to insist he stays in."

She seemed to weigh up the situation. Then, with a sudden flash of charm, she smiled. "Very well, I'll leave him in your care. I just hope he behaves."

She turned quickly, decisively, and walked out into the drizzle. Frank followed and caught her up as she was getting into a small battered car. She looked up at him from the driver's seat; anger and determination sharpened her features.

"Mrs. Hall?"

"Yes."

"My name's Fuller. Frank Fuller. I was driving when your boy . . . when I ran into him. I couldn't have done anything to avoid him. I just wanted to say how sorry I am. Is he all right? I see they're keeping him in."

"Yes, he's being kept in for X-rays. It's quite routine." She reached forward and put the key in the ignition.

He hesitated, surprised at her manner. "I was pretty alarmed when I got to him. He was having some kind of epileptic fit. Does he get them normally?"

She withdrew her hand from the key and looked up quickly. Her pale blue eyes bored into his. "Did you tell them about that?"

"Tell the hospital? No. As it happens, I could scarcely get to speak to the nurse at all."

Her face relaxed. "Well, small boys go through these phases, but they grow out of them. There's no reason for you to worry, Mr. . . ."

"Fuller. Here, please take my card. Let me know if there's anything at all I can do."

She took the card without looking at it and put it among the road maps under the dashboard. "It was an accident. Don't think any more about it."

"Anything at all," he repeated.

"As I said . . ."

"No, but I mean it," he persisted.

She flared up suddenly. "Look, haven't you done enough already? You could have killed Jonathan. Let's leave it at that. Now, please, if you don't mind, I want to get home."

Abruptly she started the engine, wound up her window and, looking beyond Frank to check the way was clear, moved off out of sight into the wet street and the scanty late-night traffic.

Frank stood rooted to the spot and watched her go. An ambulance had to flash its lights to move him out of its path. Sitting in his car he lit another cigarette. It burned down to his fingers before he realized he hadn't started the engine. He needed a drink.

When he got home he found Dog whining with hunger.

4

Frank's weekend began with the Saturday-morning jog. Like a somnambulist he climbed into his tracksuit and, with Dog at his heels, stumbled out into the cold September mist. He ran through country lanes; his village, Oakley, was a mere five miles from Bedford but was entirely rural. Just last week he'd come upon a fox cub that had bled to death, impaled on a barbed-wire fence, and earlier in the year there'd been the cow that had drowned in the floods just as it was giving birth.

Doubling his pace on the home stretch, Frank was pleased to find his body holding up well. Tall, lean and darkhaired, he wasn't good-looking in the classical sense; silver threaded his temples and deep lines scored his rugged face. But for a man nudging forty he felt fit and in good shape.

He stopped beside his car to recover his breath. As he straightened up he caught sight of the dent in the front fender and all of a sudden he saw the image of the boy caught in his headlights. A wave of nausea swept over him and left him chilled.

A hot shower did nothing to relieve it. In the mirror, as he shaved, the stain of shock in his dark eyes stared back at him. He dressed absent-mindedly. As he swept up the loose change from the dressing-table Cathy's photo, in its thin gilt frame, was just another ornament.

After breakfast he took the mail and the newspapers up to his study, an attic conversion with generous views over the fields to the west. He sat down to read: mail from head office, circulars, advance publicity notices, press cuttings; the week's *Bookseller*, a padded envelope containing book samples, a ski-holiday brochure—nothing important. He couldn't concentrate. He paced around the room and let his eyes wander absently along the lopsided bookshelves that ran the length of the walls, housing at one end tiny pocket dictionaries and at the other large-format art books. The old mill-house had been built without knowledge of the right angle.

With sudden decisiveness he reached out and dialled Lawrence Miller's number.

Lawrence answered from the kitchen. In the background Frank could hear the babble of squabbling kids.

"Morning, Lawrence," he began cheerfully. "How did the supper party go last night? I was sorry to miss it."

"You bloody wouldn't be if you had my head right now. What do you want? I know when you're after something."

Frank laughed. There was a crash at the other end and Lawrence's rich voice bawled, *"Bennie, do that again and I'll thump you!* Frank, take a word of advice: don't ever have kids. Look, why don't you come over this evening? I've got a hell of a day."

"You're going in to work today, then?"

"Come on, Frank. People aren't just ill Mondays to Fridays."

"No, I'm serious. I want you to look in on a boy in Casualty. His name's Jonathan Hall."

Frank told his friend about the accident.

"Feeling guilty, are we, Frank?"

"No, it's not just that. He didn't actually break anything. At least I don't think so." Then Frank told him about the seizure.

"Interesting, that," replied Lawrence. "But you're not to blame yourself, it's counterproductive. Remember what we used to say about that? Accidents are just what they say: accidental. Okay, I'll take a look at him. On condition you come this evening."

"You've got a deal. Thanks, Lawrence, I appreciate it."

"Stuff it. See you later."

With a lighter heart Frank prepared for the next ritual of the weekend—the shopping expedition to the supermarket. On the way home he stopped to buy a pair of track shoes. As he tried to guess the boy's size he remembered him in his mind's eye— the shock of fair hair, the blue eyes, the face strong, alert, inquisitive. And then in a flash that other face: the mouth contorted in the rictus of a snarl and the harsh, vile language he'd used.

Lawrence spent the morning doing the rounds of the psychiatric wards. He discharged one old recidivist on impulse, interested in how long he could cope with the world, or it with him, this time. Then he left his small office to look in on the Hall boy. A few yards down the corridor he stopped and went back for a white coat. That was the uniform more suitable for Casualty; in his own department he encouraged informal dress.

Briefly he ran a hand through the thick black hair which, however Fiona cut it, always sprang back from his large balding forehead. He was a short man who radiated size and energy. His arms were long in proportion to his legs; his eyebrows jutted out above baby-smooth cheeks, and his mouth was small and ridiculously delicate for a man with such a voluminous laugh. He inspired love in his ex-patients; he infuriated colleagues with his disdain for red tape. No one who knew Lawrence Miller reacted with indifference.

The sister in Casualty led him into her cubicle and handed him Jonathan's chart and X-ray results. "Nothing wrong there," he said.

"Just local bruising," she agreed. "And a nasty scalp cut we stitched up. But he's all ready to go home. His mother's in there with him now."

"Mind if I look in?"

"Of course, doctor. It's not often we see you down here."

"I hate the sight of blood," he said. She smiled uncertainly.

He introduced himself to Sarah and Jonathan Hall and was at once struck by the piercing blue eyes they had in common. The mother's hair was darker than the son's but they were very alike. And there was another quality he couldn't place right away: perhaps it was a kind of complicit *understanding*. They made a strikingly attractive pair.

"You'll be home in no time, darling," Sarah was saying reassuringly as the sister came forward to change the broad white head bandage.

"Mrs. Hall," said Lawrence, "Frank Fuller's a friend of mine. He asked me to look in on Jonathan. He'll be relieved to know all's well. He was anxious." He hesitated. Something in the boy's manner had alerted his professional eye.

Sarah's tone grew suddenly cooler. "So he said last night." She turned to her son. "What shall we have for lunch?"

The boy was holding one hand tightly in the other, trying to cover up its shaking. For a split second his eye caught Lawrence's, then continued darting anxiously to and fro. When he spoke he was clearly making an effort to sound normal.

"Oh, a cheeseburger, please. And large fries. Large fries," he repeated, nodding and blinking.

"Are cheeseburgers your favorite, Jonathan?" asked the psychiatrist carefully.

The boy looked up again. But his expression was blank, as if he hadn't heard the question or didn't know what the word meant. As the nurse finished fastening the dressing, his face underwent a slight but distinct change. The pupils of his eyes dilated and his lips swelled into an ugly pout. His head was shuddering in small spasms. Lawrence's eye went swiftly to his hands: a disproportionate amount of the brain's motor cortex was concerned with mouth and hands. They had curled in on themselves to form arthritic, contorted claws.

Sarah reached over quickly and took his hands in hers. Her voice was controlled but full of warning.

"Jonathan, *Jonathan!* Be good!"

It was perhaps two seconds before the boy responded to his mother's quiet command. His face softened, his eyes and lips returned to normal and his hands relaxed. He blinked and looked around anxiously as if he had just woken up.

"I am, Mum. I haven't done anything wrong," he said reproachfully.

"I know, darling. Let's keep it that way. Now how about you getting dressed?"

"All right," he said mildly.

Lawrence was puzzled and alerted. He touched Sarah on the elbow and drew her to one side.

"Might I have a word with you?"

She followed him down the ward to the sister's small office.

They stood facing one another in the small cubicle. A glass wall looked out over the ward and the desk was piled with neat stacks of files and trays of medication. Lawrence offered Sarah a chair but she declined. He smiled to put her at her ease, all the while keeping a sharp eye on her.

"Well, what was *that* all about?"

She smiled back. "That? Jonathan always gets nervous in strange surroundings."

He hesitated. "Mrs. Hall, does he ever have funny turns, possibly mild seizures?"

"Does he have fits? Good gracious, no!"

"I understand he had one last night, at the time of the accident."

Sarah held the doctor's eye. "I'm sure not," she replied after a pause.

A tense silence fell between them, broken only when Lawrence's pocket pager bleeped. "Excuse me," he said. He reached for the intercom on the desk and depressed a knob. "Dr. Miller here."

"Oh, Dr. Miller, you're wanted back in Psychiatrics please."

"OK. Tell them I'll be right along."

He released the knob and turned to see Sarah with her handbag clutched tight against her stomach. She had gone pale, and when she spoke her voice was contracted.

"Don't let me keep you any longer, doctor. Anyway, it's time Jonathan went home."

Lawrence moved to the doorway, blocking her exit. "Mrs. Hall, I'd like him to stay in a little longer. Just for observation. The accident may have affected him in ways that aren't immediately apparent."

"Nonsense! There's absolutely nothing wrong with him, just a few cuts and bruises. I'm here to collect him and take him home."

"I'm serious. My advice is . . ."

"Dr. Miller, I appreciate your concern and it's very kind of you. I can assure you, I'd be the first to know if there was anything amiss."

She moved purposefully towards the door and Lawrence was obliged to stand aside. He strolled after her as she went to claim her son.

Jonathan was fully dressed by now, the bandage comfortably stretched across his forehead. Sarah put her hand on his shoulder and looked carefully into his face. "How do you feel, darling?"

"OK. Just hurts a bit."

"All right, then," she said cheerfully. "We'll be off."

Lawrence stared for a moment, then caught sight of the ward clock. He turned and walked briskly back upstairs, taking off his white coat as he went. When he reached his own floor he stopped. He was not a child psychiatrist but it was startlingly clear that there was something wrong with this boy. Maybe he was already receiving help: mothers were often too ashamed to admit that kind of thing. If he had time he'd check the boy's name in the records. But first there was a consultation in his own department to deal with. Oh God, he thought, here we go again.

Mother and son sat in their car in the hospital carpark, the windows closed against the fine autumn drizzle. Sarah still felt tight in the stomach. It was that word: *Psychiatrics*. So Frank Fuller had lied to her. He *had* told the doctor in Casualty, and the man had brought in someone from Psychiatrics to look at Jonathan. This Dr. Miller probably hardly knew Frank and the whole thing was a trick.

She reached into her handbag for the bottle of Luminal. Jonathan had missed the night before's, too, and she'd only just stopped him that morning from having another spell in front of the doctor. He swallowed the pill, without water, in silence.

"Let's go, Mum," he said finally. "What are we waiting for?"

"Look at me, Jonathan."

"Oh, come on, Mum. I'm hungry."

"Look at me! I've got something serious to say."

The boy turned, reluctantly. She knew he understood.

"Darling, you weren't running away because . . . you're unhappy in some way, were you? If so, you must tell me what it is."

Jonathan shook his bandaged head.

"You did it because you were being Tommy, weren't you?"

He looked at the floor and scuffed the rubber mat with his shoe.

She went on, "And just now. It nearly happened again. You remember our pact, don't you? Well, don't you?"

He sniffed but said nothing.

"Tell me our pact. Tell me what we agreed. Go on."

Without raising his eyes he replied sullenly, "I mustn't be Tommy outside. Only at home. But, Mum, I couldn't help it. I just felt it coming."

"You know what you have to do when it comes."

"I did try."

Sarah leaned forward and kissed his cheek. Tears welled up in his eyes and his chin was thrust forward in an effort to contain them.

"Anyway, whatever's done is done," she said more brightly, and started up the engine. "Let's go and get that cheeseburger."

"And large fries," he said firmly. The glint in his eye was for things left unsaid.

Her heart almost broke. As they joined the street traffic Jonathan looked across at her and said in a grown-up voice, "I'm sorry, Mum. I'll try harder."

"You can do it, darling," she said, squeezing his hand. She corrected herself. "We can do it."

5

Lawrence brought the subject up first, at supper that night. They were sitting in the kitchen at a stripped pine refectory table scarred with candle-wax and children's scribblings. It was a homely, untidy room. A fight was going on upstairs and the red enamel pans on the kitchen range shivered with each thump. He reached out to fill Frank's glass from a two-liter bottle of Italian wine.

"Epilepsy," he said, "is an electrical hiccough in the brain. In small children it's sometimes brought on by abnormally high temperatures. Hormonal changes at puberty can also be a cause. But Jonathan's too old for the first and too young for the second."

"What about a sudden shock, a knock on the head?" Frank asked quickly. He was leaning forward with his elbows on the table; the bushy eyebrows on his rugged face were stiff with anxiety.

Lawrence didn't answer at once. "From your description, what he had when you found him was what we call a primary *grand mal*. That's a seizure involving the whole brain. In the first phase you get generalized convulsions and loss of consciousness; the muscles go into spasm and the body goes rigid. That's called the tonic phase. In the next stage the muscles relax and contract in rhythm as the brain cells discharge. It can be an unpleasant sight. After a while the person's color and breathing return to normal but they can stay unconscious for a few more minutes. When they recover they won't have any memory of the fit. Or feel any pain. They'll be exhausted and probably want to sleep. That's pretty much how it was, didn't you say?"

"It's exactly how it was."

"Curious, then."

Lawrence reached for the fruit salad. He frowned. "Sweetheart," he said to Fiona, who was at the sink washing out the coffee percolator, "Olivia's been at the strawberries—I can tell from the teeth-marks on the ones she spat back. I'm going to try some aversive conditioning on the brat. Like a clip round the ear."

Fiona addressed her thirteen-year-old next to him. "Benjamin, say goodnight to Frank."

"Dad, what's aversive conditioning?" asked the boy.

"Take this milk up with you," continued his mother. "And tell Mattie and Olivia up there to stop that din at once. Now get along. No, Lawrence, don't distract him or he'll never go to bed."

"An hour or two's sleep, that's all the body needs," responded her husband, routinely argumentative. He speared a strawberry with a fork. "We only sleep to dream."

"Well, he needs his dreams, then."

Fiona, an oval-faced beauty with graying hair and a complexion worn smooth with childbearing, steered her stomach towards the door and shepherded the boy out. "Night, all," he called back.

Frank waited till he'd gone, watching Lawrence eat with gusto, obviously relishing the suspense he was causing.

"What do you mean, *curious?*" he asked at last.

Lawrence sat back, replete, and eyed his friend. "When I was in Casualty this lad Jonathan seemed to be about to have a *petit mal* seizure. What's sometimes called an 'absence.' They're epileptic fits of a very minor kind; children seem to have them quite often. You get a loss, or more a clouding of consciousness, lasting a few seconds, that's all. It often looks just like daydreaming. Except . . ."

"Except what?"

"Except it isn't." He paused. "His mother tried to make out it was perfectly normal."

"Maybe it was."

Lawrence went on, reverting to the original question. "No, it's curious because very often a *petit mal* heralds a *grand mal.* The patient must be very closely watched. She seemed to stop him before that happened."

"I don't like the word 'patient,' " said Frank.

"It would be interesting," continued his friend, ignoring the remark, "to know if the boy had a history of myoclonic seizures in earlier childhood—that is, infantile spasms. I can't believe he didn't."

"Lawrence, you're getting me worried. I asked you a straight question: did the accident cause the fit I saw?"

"OK, Frank. I'd say it's possible it did."

"Oh, God."

"Now, wait; don't start that again. Remember how you convinced yourself you were responsible for Cathy? You thought if only you'd given her more love, more time, more of this, more of that. No man could have devoted more to his wife than you,

Frank. But her condition was chronic. It may be the same here, with Jonathan. What I mean is, it's just as possible he has a history of seizures. There's nothing on the hospital files: I checked. Look, I'm not his doctor, I'm not even a pediatrician. I only deal with adults."

Frank swirled the wine around his glass. More quietly he said, "Sorry. I didn't mean to go overboard."

His friend's manner relaxed. "If you're anxious, why don't you go and visit the lad at home? They live on the Putnoe estate. I don't think there's a Mr. Hall, just the mother, Sarah. Offer to dig the garden or build her some bookshelves."

Frank smiled; it was a private joke. Lawrence had just moved to this house at the time Frank went to see him for treatment. Instead of admitting him to hospital he took him home to lunch and Frank stayed two weeks. The vegetables they'd just eaten came from the kitchen garden he'd laid out; even the table they were now sitting at had been stripped by his own hands. He would never forget what Lawrence had done for him during that time.

"Come on, I'll give you a game of backgammon. A penny a point."

"You can't afford it, son, not on a rep's salary," replied Lawrence, and cleared a space for the board.

Frank found the address from the phone book. He didn't call Mrs. Hall in case she put him off; he knew she wouldn't be greatly pleased to see him. He chose tea-time on the following day, Sunday, and took with him the new track shoes for Jonathan.

The housing estate was made up of small identical pale-brick homes, all looking as if they'd been designed by a five-year-old: large square windows on either side of the front door, two smaller bedroom windows above and a shallow pitched roof supporting a chimney and a television aerial. On the left of the

25·

Halls' house a double concrete strip led to a small garage and, to the side, a narrow alley to the back garden. In front, a small garden was enclosed by a low block wall with an ornamental metal gate set into it. As Frank drew up Jonathan and another boy, encumbered by fishing-rods, skidded their bicycles to a stop.

"Hello, there. Catch anything?" he asked as he got out of his car.

"Oh, hi, it's you," said Jonathan. He turned his brilliant blue eyes on Frank and touched his bandage. "Not much, just a few tiddlers. Didn't we, Willy?"

"Sometimes you know just where to find them," said the other boy, plump and shy. "Today it was hopeless. You weren't trying."

"It doesn't work every time, you know that. It wouldn't be fun if it did. You're not coming in? OK, then. Give me a one-four later if you get stuck with math."

"I did math this morning," he said mournfully, getting onto his bicycle. "It's the history that bothers me. See you, Johnnie."

Jonathan opened the gate and wheeled his bicycle up the concrete path. "Have you come over to meet Mum?"

"I've met her already, but yes. And to see how you are, too. By the way, I bought you some new sneakers. I hope they fit."

"Hey, thanks." The boy leaned his cycle against the garage door and opened the bag. He bent down and measured one shoe against his own. "They're great."

As he straightened up the front door opened and his mother appeared on the step. When she saw Frank her expression hardened. She looked at the shoes in Jonathan's hand. "Where did you get those, darling?"

"He's just given me them," said the boy proudly.

Frank stepped forward. "I just thought . . ."

"We really can't accept them," said Sarah.

"Oh, Mum, they're terrific," said Jonathan.

"It's really nothing," said Frank. "It's the very least I could do."

Her manner changed. "Well, it's very thoughtful of you. Jonathan, have you thanked Mr. . . . . ?"

"Fuller. Frank Fuller," he said. She hadn't remembered his name.

"I already have," said the boy.

There was an awkward, uncomfortable silence. Then Frank turned to Jonathan. "Well, you're looking a lot better, I'm glad to say. I'll be off, then."

"Do you have to go? Can't he come in, Mum?"

"He's probably got things to do, darling," she said.

Jonathan turned to Frank. "Don't you want to see my Spectrum?"

"His mini-computer," Sarah explained. "I'm so sorry, I'm being very inhospitable. Would you like to come in for a cup of tea, Mr. Fuller?"

"It's Frank. Well, I wouldn't say no."

The front door opened directly into the living-room, a single large T-shaped area. Along the left wall rose the stairs to the upper floor; the alcove beneath had been made into a study. Beyond lay the kitchen and utility room extension. The right wall had been stripped to the brick; around the gas-log fire in the center stood a comfortable three-piece suite upholstered in burgundy corduroy. On the walls hung reproduction Russell Flint watercolors and Jonathan's school photos and certificates. Magazines and newspapers spilled off the low coffee-table onto the slate gray carpet. It was a masculine kind of room, yet there were no signs of a man about the house. All the photos on the desk under the stairs were of mother and son, or of Jonathan alone. This was a self-contained, private world of two people who received few visitors. There were no ashtrays.

Jonathan came down the stairs with his home computer and plugged it into the television. He was at home with the machine; his movements were swift and economical. He motioned Frank to the sofa and knelt on the floor beside him, tapping instructions into the keyboard to demonstrate a card trick he'd taught it.

Frank played along, then laughed. "It's very clever. How long have you had it?"

"Oh, Mum got me it just after we left Warwick."

"You haven't been in Bedford long, then?"

Sarah intervened from the kitchen before Jonathan could answer. "Do you take sugar, Mr. Fuller?"

"No thanks."

She quickly brought in the tray and sat beside Frank, facing him directly, engaging his attention so that Jonathan was excluded. With deliberate civility she asked about his job. He told her.

"I do a lot of driving," he said. "I get about a fair bit."

"Yes, I can see that," she said coolly.

She told him she was a teacher but didn't encourage further talk about it. More than once she seemed to glance at her watch. When she offered to refill his cup before it was empty she declined and rose to leave.

"Where's your house?" Jonathan broke in, trying to prolong the conversation.

"Oakley," he replied. "It used to be the mill-house, though the stream doesn't go past it any more."

"Any fish there?"

"Sure: perch, tench, sometimes trout. It's quite a favorite spot for anglers."

Sarah was by the door, holding it open. She surprised Frank with a brilliant smile and held out her hand. "Well, it was nice meeting you properly," she said with finality. She laid a gently restraining hand on Jonathan's shoulder.

" 'Bye," said the boy ruefully.

" 'Bye," responded Frank with a wave. At the gate he looked back. In the frame of the closing door flickered an expression of anger and concern on Sarah's face as she turned to speak to the boy.

In the late afternoon sunlight Frank took Dog for a long walk. The air was sweet and cool. Dog would lope away and return, nose his hand and lope off again. Frank suddenly felt weary. There was nothing wrong with the boy; this afternoon he could not have been more normal. He was an attractive, intelligent child with a healthy outdoor interest—fishing—and an organized, bright mind fostered, no doubt, by the attention of his mother, a teacher, of whom the child was clearly very fond and who gave him all the love and attention he needed. He may have seemed eager for Frank's approval, but otherwise the lack of a father had had no obvious effect.

Was this really the same boy Frank had seen in that roadside ditch two nights before, a violent, possessed child? Yes, he had to admit. If you'd been knocked down by a car you wouldn't be at your best, either. But *why* was he running down that road, at that time of night, so far from home? And what was he running from? And why that look of anger on Sarah's unguarded face just an hour before? Had Jonathan been running from Sarah?

An idea occurred to him. Lawrence had said there was nothing on the boy in their hospital files. But the family had only recently moved to Bedford. Calling Dog he strode purposefully home and rang Lawrence. Warwick, that's where the Halls had been. If there was going to be anything on file about Jonathan, that's where it would be.

Sarah closed Jonathan's bedroom door gently. He seemed to be asleep; he needed all he could get. She lay on her bed without the energy to undress. Perhaps she had been too hard on Frank Fuller. At times she longed for somebody to take this burden from her. Day by day she lived with the weight of uncertainty: when would Jonathan's spells strike next? And the frightening suddenness when they did. Over the years it had worn her nerves down. How much more could she take? And now there was this latest incident: did it come as a harbinger of new bad times?

She stroked her finger-tips over the satin eiderdown and looked across at the pillow beside hers. Was it unnatural to eschew the life most women of her age took for granted? Would she regret it later, when her womanhood had dried up and her son had left home? She reached for a book to take her mind off the endless questions. It was better not to dwell on such things.

Jonathan was not yet quite asleep. He'd grown more and more afraid of the moment of sleep. He'd never told anyone, not even his mother, what it was really like. He couldn't do it quickly; he had to tiptoe into it, very carefully, inch by inch. At any moment he might be invaded, for that was the time when his defenses were at their weakest. It felt as if something, some glutinous evil polyp, had made its lair on the inner surface of his skull, from where, when stirred, it would flash out its tentacles and take over his mind. And then he would stop being *him*. He'd become host to someone else. He'd become Tommy. He'd become mad.

Why him? Why had he been born that way? Why couldn't he get better? Why wasn't it enough to try really hard? For he *did* try. He fought as hard as he could. Sometimes he'd go on and on for an hour, reciting to himself the things that seemed to stave it off. He tried to be brave and he hardly ever cried. Why wasn't that enough?

That night he fell asleep biting his lip so hard that it was swollen in the morning and whispering to himself, over and over again, *please, please help me*. But no one heard him.

6

MEMORANDUM

To: Case File
Date: 19 June 1979
Background

Jonathan Hall, aged 8, was admitted for outpatient treatment at Warwick Regional Child Psychiatric Clinic after being reported missing for two days and subsequently picked up by police twenty-five miles from his home. He appeared to be suffering from acute paranoid schizophrenia, coupled with severe and recurrent *grand mal* epileptic seizures.

Diagnosis and treatment

Medication was immediately administered to counteract the convulsive condition. Initially dipropyl acetate (Epilion) was given orally but this caused abreaction and nausea. A mix of anti-convulsants was prepared, primarily phenobarbitone (Luminal), in conjunction with nicotinamide for the schizophrenic condition. However, dosage was subsequently reduced when he started showing symptoms of mania and confusional illness, together with skin rashes. At the same time he was put on a high-fat, ketogenic diet, based on medium-chain triglyceride oil. Social Services, however, report that this treatment is meeting resistance at home and suggest that the medication is not being regularly given.

General behavior

Jonathan rates in the upper quartile of IQ for his age group and there has been no apparent impairment of intellectual performance at school. However, his behavior continues erratic and disturbed (see Social Services minute).

Psychological tests have not yet been fully completed and results are not yet available.

At present the diagnosis of the disorder cannot be fully confirmed due to the masking effect of the anti-convulsants. Nevertheless, in view of the fact that the decrease in fit frequency has been accompanied by a parallel increase in the onset of the psychotic condition, this supports the initial diagnosis of schizophrenia. If symptoms persist, consideration should be given to hospitalizing the boy for a 10-day course of penicillamine—and a compulsory order obtained if the boy's mother continues to withhold permission.

"Penicillamine? Balls!" Lawrence sat back abruptly. "I know a schizo when I see one, and this boy isn't one. Let's have another look at the neurologist's report."

Blood and urine samples appeared normal and there was nothing untoward in the cardiograms. EEGs had yielded sporadic abnormalities but they had not managed to pinpoint the epileptic *focus*. Normally, the next step would be to induce artificial fits in the boy by such means as photic stimulation—that is, flashing bright lights in his eyes—and examine the results. But Jonathan had been withdrawn from the tests before they could be run.

All throughout, the evidence was incomplete. Why hadn't he stayed to finish the course? Puzzled, Lawrence scanned the next report.

Subject: Jonathan Hall

Date: 27 June 1979

The meeting heard a report on Jonathan's family background from the social case-worker.

Jonathan is an only child, brought up alone by his mother. His father, Ronald Hall, a self-employed car dealer, left the family very shortly after Jonathan was born and his twin baby brother died. Since then the boy has lived alone with his mother, Sarah Hall. He goes to Warwick Lower School, where his mother also teaches. Her own parents live a good distance away and there is little, if any, contact. Visitors and friends rarely come to the home.

At school Jonathan's behavior causes concern. Most of the time he is alert, confident, well-behaved, but he is subject to sudden and unpredictable changes of mood. His language then becomes crude and shocking and his manner extremely callous and aggressive. Recently he attacked another boy, for reasons unknown, and he has had to be segregated from the playground. When he calms down he seems to recall little of what he's done.

In summary, Jonathan is an unstable child, the product of a broken home and a mother who compensates by being over-protective. In parallel with clinical psychiatric and medical treatment, it is recommended that mother and son attend family therapy sessions on a weekly basis.

The file ended there. Had there been family therapy? What had happened to end the treatment? Was it because they moved to Bedford, and if so was the boy being prescribed anti-epileptic pills by a GP? Who *was* his doctor? He could check, though it meant twisting arms again in Records. It wasn't worth it.

Here, he said to himself, we have a mother who's lost a baby —the twin brother—and is sublimating her guilt feelings by excessive protectiveness of the remaining child. She's alone: she's lost her husband, she hasn't remarried, she has no apparent family of her own. Jonathan is all she has left.

And as for him, how would he be affected by losing a womb-mate? By becoming, from his earliest conscious moment, the focus of a double love and thus of a double obligation?

It would be fascinating to know.

It was a frustratingly incomplete file that lay before him here. He sighed and tossed it into the OUT tray. It was good enough for its present purpose, relieving Frank's anxiety. He reached for the phone, remembering this was Frank's morning at home with his paperwork.

"Frank? Set your mind at rest. Whatever else you've done, you haven't made that Hall boy an epileptic. He's had a long history of it, from way back in Warwick. So relax."

But Frank didn't sound relaxed. "Did he . . . go in for treatment?" he asked at once.

"No, they just stuck him on an MCT-fat diet and a cocktail of drugs that seems to have done the trick and reduced the fits. Epilion, Tegretol, the usual stuff. Plus nicotinamide, I gather. That's the stuff they give you for schizophrenia. That's what they thought he had. I'm not so sure it's that, though."

Frank went silent at his end.

"Frank, you still there? Look, just be grateful you haven't done any extra damage and don't worry yourself."

Frank spoke slowly. "So the boy is off his head."

"No, no. He's just a little disturbed, that's all. He's an only child from a broken home with a strong, doting mother. What do you want?"

"But if he's disturbed, shouldn't he be getting treatment? You said he wasn't."

"Frank, don't give me a hard time. I've had enough trouble finding out this much for you. The file's only half there. I'm not a child specialist, anyway. He's probably being looked after quite happily by an ordinary GP, so for Christ's sake stop worrying. I'm ringing off now: I'm late for a case conference. See you."

As he put the phone down, Lawrence thought of his friend Frank. He was an earnest, intelligent chap, perhaps too emotionally vulnerable, but, all the same, loyal, decent and caring. And here was Sarah Hall, also alone, an attractive yet stand-offish woman. They could do a lot for each other. The psychiatrist swept up the files for the meeting and hurried to the door. There were more urgent things to deal with.

7

The window of the potting shed at the bottom of the garden looked out towards the back lawn. Claiming Puck needed the dark to recover, Jonathan had pinned an old sack over it so that he would not be seen from the house. A bright autumnal afternoon sun filtered in through the gaps, catching the air's dust in its shafts. The shed smelled of lawnmower oil and dusty twine, and a brackish odor came from the rabbit's cage on the shelf. It was convalescing. Jonathan hadn't meant to hurt it, but then he hadn't been Jonathan at the time.

Standing on the duckboards, with the garden rakes and bundles of canes stacked neatly to one side, he took the rabbit gently out of its cage. He stroked its ears and pressed its soft gray fur against his cheek. Then he set it at one end of the shelf and took out the heart of a lettuce he'd brought. It nosed the air uncertainly.

"Come along, exercise time," he coaxed. "It's the only way it'll heal."

Holding the lettuce just out of reach, he lured the rabbit forward step by step. It hopped along, lopsided; the back leg was still stiff and dragging. He coaxed it back and forth down the shelf several times, then took it in his arms, cradled it close to his shirt and fed it the lettuce.

"Poor Puck," he whispered in its ear. "I didn't mean to hurt you. Only you and I know. Even Mum doesn't. She thinks you got into the next door garden and the dog bit you."

He pressed his face into its fur and breathed in the comforting odor. He wanted to escape from himself. Things were getting worse; the spells used to come once a week, or even less, but now it was sometimes once a day. How could he go on like that, living in fear of the attacks? He knew his mother was aware they were getting worse, but she didn't seem to pay much attention; she was always too busy to listen. Or if she did, she'd say it was because he was growing up and he needed a stronger dose of the pills.

"If things don't get better," she'd said just the day before, "we'll have to put you on an extra one at lunchtime."

He didn't want more pills; they made him feel low and soggy. And they weren't working. As part of the pact with his mother he'd promised not to tell their regular GP about his fits. For the Luminal they went to another doctor, the far side of town, having given a false address to get on his books. There must be some alternative to the pills, but who could he ask? He mistrusted the one who knew his case and he couldn't confide in the one who didn't. Perhaps he was incurable and condemned to a lifetime of madness. They'd wait until he was older and, if it didn't get better, they'd come and take him away. They had special places for the insane.

The rabbit sniffed the air and stretched out a paw. He bent

forward and brushed his mouth over its head. The rabbit-smell was warm and familiar.

When his attacks came on they always started with the funny taste of bitter almonds in his mouth. Sometimes it came like a small wave that stopped just at his toes; if he tried hard enough he could push these ones back. Humming worked sometimes, and so did reciting poems or rhymes. Singing was best, but you couldn't sing aloud in class. When he did the singing trick at home his mother was happy; she thought he was being cheerful. She didn't realize it was all that stood between him and his other self.

They sometimes came and went so quickly that people didn't even notice. And when he'd return he'd find the world had taken just a small step on—the teacher would have finished the equation she was writing up on the blackboard, or his mother would be putting her coffee cup down when he hadn't seen her pick it up. Once he'd been waiting on his bike at traffic lights and they turned green and back to red before he returned.

There was always a sudden, short moment while he still had the chance to fight his way out. Here he felt a strange tugging sensation inside his head, a feeling of having his brain squeezed and drawn out in a particular direction. Sometimes he could manage to arrest it there.

But very often the almond taste turned sweet and took on a purplish flavor, and then he'd know there was nothing he could do. He was invaded. Underneath his skull the alien creature would thrash its tentacles into the deepest corners of his mind, blotting out his own self and substituting it with another. All his sensations would take on a different feel—not his own, but yet not exactly unfamiliar. He might feel his stomach was very heavy and he'd half-understand he'd eaten too much suet pudding; or if his foot ached badly he'd be dimly aware of dropping a tire-wrench on it. Sometimes he'd remember things he couldn't really know and equally forget things he should, such as how to work the Spectrum. And he'd find himself doing cruel, violent things which seemed natural at the time but which later surprised, even shocked him. He could hate himself for these things.

"Like what I did to you, Puck."

He put the rabbit back on the shelf and gave it a small carrot from his pocket. The animal took it in its front paws but its back leg gave way and it almost tottered over. It looked up at Jonathan and blinked its large moist eyes, then took the carrot off down to the end of the shelf. It wanted to be back in its cage.

Indoors, he was standing in his stocking feet in the kitchen, having taken off his wellingtons, when he heard his mother's raised voice. She was speaking on the telephone upstairs in her bedroom.

"I don't feel it right to discuss Jonathan with you," she was saying in the distinctive voice she used when her temper was rising. "I'm sorry to put it like that. You may mean well, but you're a stranger."

He hesitated. He could picture her there, sitting at the folding mirror on her dressing-table, playing with the ends of her hair or cradling the receiver under her chin while she painted her nails with clear varnish. On impulse he crept quietly into the living-room where he picked up the extension phone on his mother's desk. He held his breath to see if she noticed the *ping*.

"But it's true," a man's voice was protesting at the other end. "I know for a fact he's having treatment. Or at least he was. At Warwick."

His mother interrupted. "Look, whoever told you that was in breach of confidence. In any case you have no right to pry into our lives, Mr. Fuller. It's invading our privacy, can't you see that?"

So it was Frank she was talking to.

"I don't mean to pry, believe me," replied Frank, sounding confused and distraught. "It's just that I feel responsible."

"We've been through all this before . . ."

"Now hold on. Put yourself in my shoes for a moment. I'm driving home through the countryside, it's dark and late, then this boy suddenly comes out at me from nowhere and I knock him down. When I get to him he has a seizure. Then everybody says there's nothing wrong with him when there obviously is. I may be to blame. If so, surely I have a right to know."

"Oh, for heaven's sake stop this nonsense about *rights*!" A new tone had entered her voice. She was no longer angry; rather, incredulous and almost amused. "You sound like a magistrate. So you think that running someone over entitles you to intrude into their private life?"

There was a pause from Frank's end.

"Lawrence Miller thinks they made a wrong diagnosis at Warwick," he went on in a more defeated tone. "If that's true, Jonathan should be getting treatment now. Different treatment."

"What makes you think he isn't?"

"Well, Lawrence said there weren't any files at the hospital."

"Did your friend Lawrence try the local child units?"

"He didn't say."

"Or the private clinics?"

"I don't know."

"Or the normal GPs' registers? Honestly, I'm glad you make your living selling books, not writing them. You'd make a pretty terrible Simenon, you know. I suggest you do your homework first."

"I'm trying to help. That's all."

Her manner snapped. "Then help by leaving us alone," she said with sudden asperity. "We're quite able to look after ourselves. We've done perfectly well until now, without help, yours or anyone's. Please let that be understood!"

"Mrs. Hall."

Now she checked herself. She'd gone further than she'd meant. And for the first time she called him by his first name. "I . . . I'm sorry, Frank. I got a bit worked up. Please understand. I appreciate your concern. . . ."

Jonathan gently returned the phone to its cradle and stood for a moment in thought. Was it possible that Frank Fuller understood? And cared? And wanted to *do* something about it?

Quite suddenly he knew what he had to do. He went quickly over to the back door and slammed it loudly so that it sounded as if he'd just come in.

"Mum?" he called up.

"I'm on the phone, darling."

"I'm just going out for a bike ride, OK? Won't be long. Need anything from the shops?"

It wasn't exactly a fib. He was going out for a ride, only it wasn't to the shops.

Twenty minutes' hard pedalling brought Jonathan to the village of Oakley. He took a fork that led downhill, deducing that a mill-house would lie on low ground. He found it readily; it was a timber-clad building on three floors, surrounded on three sides by pine trees, and lay at the end of a small, steep *cul de sac*. A station wagon was parked in the narrow drive and from a chimney rose a small coil of smoke into the crisp late October air. But as he caught sight of the house his resolve faded. He dismounted and hid behind the hedge at the gate; then, thinking he might be spotted from the house, he retraced his steps up the slope on foot. His heart was beating fast. Should he be doing this?

He wasn't ready; he hadn't prepared what to do. Frank's first question would be, "Why have you come?" Why *had* he? What was he going to say? He needed time to think. Perhaps he should reconnoiter the place first.

Swinging back onto his bicycle he coasted down to the river where he chained it to a lamp-post beside the old stone bridge. From there he slipped along the towpath until he was at the back of Frank's house with only a meadow and a rough, unkempt garden between them. Standing close against a bent and pollarded willow he surveyed the house. The only sign of life was a desk lamp shining from the rectangular attic window. From time to time, by squinting, Jonathan could see Frank's figure moving around. He seemed preoccupied with his own affairs. He wouldn't welcome disturbance.

Jonathan turned away and looked out across the brownish river and the fields and woodland stretching far into the distance. This was a perfect spot for fishing. Maybe he'd come out there during the week. Yes, that's what he'd do, and he'd take a rod along with him.

8

Sarah was taking on extra work at Brickhill Lower
School and that meant working longer hours. The deputy head
was leaving at the end of the academic year and she was in line
for the job. It would mean a great deal to her, more than just
status and salary. She'd be able to believe the past was buried
once and for all and the roots they'd put down in Bedford had
finally taken.

She'd moved too often in her life. During her childhood
her father had had a succession of Army postings from Malta
to Malaya and she and her mother followed. When he
finally retired to the country near Aldershot, father and daugh-
ter, thrown together properly for the first time, fought constantly. Against his will and as a means of escaping home she
took up with Ronald, a small-time car dealer, followed him to
Buckingham and married him. It was a disaster. Unsuccessful

and highly politicized, Ronald worked out his resentment violently on his middle-class wife. They lasted long enough together for there to be children. Then came the tragedy, the horror: and the death of one of the twins, Philip. Ronald, by then drinking heavily, walked out on her. Her father wouldn't have her back home; he even refused Jonathan his blessing, saying the boy had "bad blood." Her mother, sympathetic but weak, was ineffective against her father's anger.

The tragedy left Sarah alone in the world, with Jonathan an infant in arms. One day she took a suitcase and the folding pram and caught a bus to Warwick. It was the only place she could think of; a girlfriend from school had an apartment there. Ronald drifted south and was last heard of in London by the solicitors handling her divorce. He never sent a penny or made any attempt to enquire after his surviving son. Sarah managed to get a council house, where she set up a small nursery school in the front room. She continued with this until Jonathan was of an age to go to school, then procured a teaching job at the same school. Already his problem had begun to assert itself, and she felt the need to keep an eye on him.

Then came the next blow. She was working her way up the teaching hierarchy at the school when Jonathan's condition suddenly came to a crisis. After one particularly violent and public outburst they admitted him as a psychiatric outpatient to Warwick General Hospital, where his epilepsy was confirmed and a form of schizophrenia diagnosed. As the treatment progressed the doctors, not satisfied with the results, proposed a series of tests, tests which horrified Sarah. At the same time the education authority was cutting back on staff throughout the schools in the area. They never said as much, but she knew in her heart that it was because of Jonathan that her name was on the list for redundancy. She waited for neither the tests nor the sack; she took her beloved boy, the only thing in her life she could call her own, and ran.

This time it was Bedford. And now, three years later, as she watched his fits and his spells returning with increasing frequency, she asked herself anxiously: where will we go next time? Must there *be* a next time?

No: she was determined there should not be. They couldn't go on running away forever. In Bedford they had the ideal set-up; they lived five minutes from Jonathan's school and she herself taught just next door to it. He was doing well, he liked his work and he'd made friends; she liked her colleagues and she badly wanted the deputy's job. Here they'd dig in and fight it out.

And this time they'd win. If only Jonathan's problem could be contained.

Jonathan rode over to Oakley again in the middle of the week, but Frank's car was not in the drive. It hadn't occurred to the boy that he might be out at work. Jonathan cycled home in a drizzle of rain. His head hurt.

Friday afternoon, however, was fine and mellow. He cycled past Frank's house—he didn't know why—and went straight to his spot under the weeping willow. The river was swollen and brown. He unpacked his rod and tackle, made a cast, and sat watching the bobbing float, letting it drift downstream, then reeling it in, the hook empty, and casting again.

A black dog, a Labrador of sorts, sniffed around the basket and nosed his hand in a friendly way. It was a fine animal with an alert expression and moist, toffee-colored eyes. He patted its head and gave it a digestive biscuit. Someone in the field behind whistled and the dog pricked up its ears and bounded off.

What could he say to Frank anyway?

Late that night he'd finished his weekend's homework and was working on the idea of a backgammon program when he got the bitter almond taste in his mouth. Steady, he told himself. Hold on. It may not last. It *is* lasting. Fight it off. Hum. "Onward Christian Soldiers." "While Shepherds Washed Their Socks By Night." Fight hard, *harder*.

It didn't work. With a smack the inside of his head seemed to contract violently in the grip of the tentacles as they squeezed into every crevice of the cortex. For a moment the room lurched in and out of focus and he felt dizzy and slightly sick. His face felt thicker, his hands clumsier. He heard himself humming, couldn't work out why, so stopped. The pad before him with its coded letters and digits puzzled him; he knew they had a meaning, but what was it? His left hand, his writing hand, was locked rigid into a claw and wouldn't open. It hurt as if he was clenching something hard in it, a key or a coin, but when finally he pried it open with the other he saw it was empty. By now it was too late to resist the invasion. He had been taken over. And the measure of it was that none of this more than mildly surprised him, for in a way it was his natural alternative state. His Tommy state.

There was a tap at the door. A woman he knew as his mother (which mother?) came in, saying, "Darling, it's time your light was out." Then her expression hardened. "Jonathan?" she said sharply.

She's got the wrong *me* again. Why is she pretending not to recognize me?

"Jonathan!"

Can't she *see* which me it is?

"*Jonathan!*" This time she shook him by the shoulder.

Abruptly he felt a new focus slipping into place. The room began to look right and he felt his body belonged again. He knew he was returning. Blinking hard, he looked down to find one of his hands massaging the other as if it was in pain, but it wasn't. In his mother's blue eyes, as she brought her face closer to his, he could read something close to impatience.

"That's better," she said.

He wanted to cry. Instead he looked away and said, "Sorry, Mum."

"Now take off your dressing-gown and let's put you to bed. You'll feel better in the morning."

"I don't feel bad."

"You know what I mean." There was a trace of exasperation in her voice. "Now, come along. I've had a hectic day and I'm very tired."

She tucked him into the bed and kissed his forehead before turning off the light. She stood for a moment silhouetted in the doorway.

"Mum?" he said quietly.

"Ssh. Go to sleep."

"Mum? Am I really loony? Won't it ever go away?"

"Don't think those thoughts, darling. Tomorrow's Saturday and we can go and see *Superman*."

Jonathan said nothing. There was nothing to say. She didn't seem to *hear* him any more.

"I'm going fishing with Willie again," he'd told her as they finished lunch the next day. "I'll be back in time for the film."

That *was* a fib, he told himself as he pedalled hard through the countryside to Oakley. William, he knew, was helping his dad creosote the garden fence. As he turned the last corner the bicycle skidded and he lost control and came off, lacerating his palms and knees on the sharp gravel. He clambered to his feet and brushed himself down, wincing with pain. The bike looked all right, but the fishing rod was bent. Suddenly he felt very young. He turned down the lane to Frank's house, but faltered at the entrance of the drive, agitatedly stirring his toecap into the gravel and biting a fingernail.

Then he saw, in the middle of the drive, the black Labrador, his friend of the previous day. It barked loudly and bounded over, wagging its tail. Frank must have heard inside, for a moment later the front door flew open and his deep voice called out, "Jonathan!"

It was too late to withdraw. He had to go through with it now.

Frank came out into the drive. At the sight of the boy's cuts he exclaimed, "God almighty! Have you been arguing with cars again? You'd better come in and get cleaned up."

"It's nothing. I just fell, that's all."

Frank took his shoulder and steered him indoors. "I should think you did! There's first aid stuff in the kitchen. Then we'll phone your mother."

Jonathan held back. "No. Don't do that."

Frank stopped. "Oh?"

"I said I was going out fishing with William."

"I didn't see him."

"I'm on my own."

"I see." Frank sounded thoughtful. He led the way to the kitchen, Dog following. "So, tell me. What brings you here?"

He didn't meet the man's eyes. "Thought I'd see what the fishing's like down here."

"Not running away again, then?" he asked with a smile, then added quickly, "Come on, that was meant as a joke."

"Oh."

Frank gave him a can of Coke and a glass, then took out an old tube of first aid cream, gauze and bandages. "I'd better give you a good going-over with antiseptic."

Jonathan didn't want to be touched. He looked at the clock on the wall. Sometimes he got his spells around tea-time; he didn't want to have one cycling back. Or, worse, there, in Frank's house.

"Sit still," ordered Frank and began carefully washing out the gravel imbedded under the skin and dabbing the cuts with weak antiseptic. Jonathan winced but didn't complain. He went on, "So, you came over this way to do a spot of fishing. The river's very high at the moment."

"I know."

"You know?"

Jonathan felt himself blushing. "I mean, it's high everywhere. Round my way, too."

Frank looked hard at him. Could he see through him? Could he see his madness, did it show like that?

"Well," he went on, "I'm very happy to see you anyway. You know, I've been a bit worried about you. I tried to call and find out how you were."

"Did you?"

"Hey, are you all right?" He was peering hard into the boy's face. Maybe he already knew. He knew about the treatment in Warwick; perhaps he knew everything. If he did, why should he ask a question like that? The man went on, "Let's have a spot of tea. Are you hungry?"

"Got any biscuits?"

"Well, no, but I'm sure there's some cake somewhere. I never get through them by myself. Dog finishes them off as a rule."

"Dog? Is that her name?"

Frank nodded. "Original, isn't it?"

The boy grinned briefly.

They took a tray into the living-room and set it down on a low table. Through the French windows the weak sunlight cast gentle shadows from the oak beams crisscrossing the ceiling. Frank turned on a table lamp and put a match to the kindling in the grate. Jonathan sat among the dog hairs on the hearth rug and looked about him. Newspapers and magazines lay strewn over the soft, worn sofa and armchairs. Every surface carried some kind of ornament; there were candlesticks and vases, statuettes, pictures and postcards, and on one bookshelf an entire army of Victorian tin soldiers. It was like a lived-in junk shop, more comfortable than his own home where everything had to be tidied away at the end of each day.

But he felt uneasy too. Was Frank staring at him? He got up to examine the stereo in the corner. "You ought to get ELS-sixty-threes," he said. "And change the amp. This one's not much good."

"I'm sure you're right. I don't play it a lot. How's your computer? Taught it any new tricks?"

"I'm doing a backgammon program."

"But surely that's far too complicated!"

"Ready-made ones are too expensive. Mum might get me one for Christmas but I'd rather have a dot-matrix printer instead."

Frank shook his head as he handed him the cake tin. "I was brought up in the days of steam radios. Computers are double Dutch to me."

"You sound like Mum. She's stuffy."

Frank smiled. "Then I'm stuffy, too."

Jonathan sat on the edge of his chair, waiting. Wouldn't Frank say something, whatever it took to open the floodgates so that he could unburden his mind? The hall clock struck five. Night was falling and he was scared of having a spell on the way home in the dark. He saw his hands were shaking and sat firmly on them.

"You sure you're OK?" repeated Frank.

Go on, tell the man. Tell him you need his help. Say: Please, Frank, help me. Explain it all to me. Tell me I'm not really mad, tell me that the person who invades me doesn't exist, tell me how I can get better.

"No, I'm fine. Just in the wars, as Mum says."

He rubbed his cuts to make the point and smiled bravely. He'd missed the moment. It was too late.

"Cheer up, son. Look, why don't I drop you back home? You can put your bike and tackle in the trunk."

Try again. One last time.

"I was wondering," he began.

"Tell me."

He bit his lip and heard himself saying something quite different. "I was thinking maybe you should drop me round the corner, instead of right outside home."

Frank laughed. "I was going to suggest that anyway."

The moment vanished, unused.

They drove off, with Dog sitting on the floor between Jonathan's knees. After a while he looked across at Frank's profile. The man looked strong, fatherly. Maybe it wasn't necessary to tell him because he knew anyway.

9

Arriving home earlier than usual from his day's work the next Thursday, Frank saw a note tucked into the front door: Jonathan was down at the river, fishing. He put on a coat and boots and strode through his garden to the broad meadow beyond, throwing a stick for Dog, who bolted after it, retrieved it and dropped it back at his feet. Against the light reflecting off the surface of the river, he recognized the outline of the boy: the halo of fair hair. He called his name as he raised the stick high above his head again, to throw for Dog. Jonathan turned.

The stick. Outlined against the light. Raised, ready to strike. The punishment stick. The stick for beatings. Dad's stick.

It happened so quickly that Jonathan had no time to fight, no time to hum or recite or sing. The suckers whipped around his brain, squeezing and wrenching until the foreigner was in control. Dread burned like acid in his stomach. He'd broken the rules, done the forbidden, and now he knew what was coming.

He yelled out a foul curse. He felt wild, untameable, feral. He rose to a crouch. A black dog (whose dog? Not one of Dad's Patterdales) was growling at him, its ears flattened, the hair on its spine erect, its teeth bared and ready to snap. He knew what you did with dogs: you went for the muzzle with your metal toecap. Then the man rushed forward and tried to grab him. He fought back, hammering his boot into the man's calf and slashing up at his face with clawlike hands. In this mood he would kill.

"Jonathan!"

He was gripped in a fierce bear-hug and his arms immobilized against the man's body. He struggled but his strength ebbed out; already he could feel the unclenching in his head and the first sensations of loosening muscles. Then suddenly, smartly, his face was slapped and his name called again. He gradually sank into the man's gentler embrace and stood in his arms, yielding up all the weight and strain. They stood like that for what seemed minutes. A hand caressed his cheek and hair, a fatherly, manly hand. He felt tears coming to his eyes. He buried his face in the man's chest.

Quietly, carefully, Frank was saying, "There now, there now. I must have given you a terrible start. You're all right now, Jonathan."

Jonathan drew away slightly. On the ground he could see the spilled cans of bait. He shook his head.

"It wasn't that," he said.

Frank said nothing, waiting for more.

Jonathan snapped, "You *know* it wasn't. Don't pretend."

"OK, then. It wasn't because I startled you."

He wasn't satisfied yet. "I know you know. I heard you on the phone with Mum the other day. I was listening. You know all about what happened when we lived in Warwick. I'll hate you if you pretend you don't."

Dog had returned and was gingerly sniffing the boy's clothes. Frank bent down and picked up a reel that had rolled away. He handed it to him and held his eye.

"I won't ever pretend to you, Jonathan. You can count on that. But you've got to be straight with me, too."

"OK."

"Something's wrong, we both know that. You're scared. You have small fits from time to time, but you're really worried it might be psychological."

The boy dropped his gaze to the ground and nodded. To his own surprise, he felt suddenly calmer, more in control, more objective about his own condition than he'd imagined he could.

"Yes," he said seriously. "The trouble is, nobody will tell me what's really wrong. I don't think they even know. I once over-heard someone in the clinic calling me a schizo, and I know that's not good. The pills are supposed to stop my spells, but they don't. And nobody's given me anything for being a schizo." He looked at the man squarely. "Please won't some-body *explain*?"

"Let's sit down."

Frank laid his raincoat on the bank and reeled in the rod, carefully took off the bait and undid the hook. Jonathan sat staring at the ground and Frank joined him on the coat, looking out across the river and saying nothing.

"Who is your doctor?" he asked.

Jonathan kept his eyes down. "We have our usual GP but Mum has never told him. She gets my pills from another one. He knows, but he's miles away and I never see him."

"Do you know what kind of pills they are?"

"All I know is they make me feel rotten."

"They're probably a phenobarbitone, like Luminal."

Jonathan lifted his face. "That's them! How did you know?"

"Guesswork and a little bit of experience. I'm not a believer in drugs, but I had a time once when I thought I was going off my rocker. No, I'm being serious. I had a kind of mental break-down. Quite normal people get them." Frank toyed thought-fully with a wiry blade of grass. "You see, you can be a bit disturbed without being a real nutter."

In a small voice the boy said, "That's the difference. I'm not normal. I *am* a real nutter."

Frank smiled. "You wouldn't say that if you'd seen the inside of a mental home. I have. You may be slightly disturbed. It may even be a mild form of schizophrenia, I don't know. I'm not an expert." He stopped. "I've no business to be talking to you like this. It's your mother's job."

Jonathan looked out towards the late afternoon sun. "She doesn't understand. Well, she understands but she thinks I should be able to cope with it myself. She thinks that's the way to cure it. I can't always. Like just then."

"Tell me what it's like. How does it come on, what does it feel like?"

Dog came up and laid her muzzle in Jonathan's lap. Stroking her head he quietly described it all: the little moments that he could easily fight off and the bigger spells, the massive invasions that swept him overboard and that at times, led to seizures.

"It's horrid," he said at last, shaking his fair head. "It's like having another person living inside your head. He's asleep most of the time but when he wakes up he does vile, hideous things."

"And there's nothing you can do about it?"

"Not much. I try and fight it back, but it's hopeless. He's inside, he's *in there*." He tapped his head. "I'm mostly me, but sometimes . . . it's frightening . . ."

"And you think that's what being mad is like."

"Yes." He appealed to the man. "And nobody can help me."

Frank paused. "Maybe I can. I have an idea but I need to think about it. Come round Saturday, OK?"

"OK. You're very decent."

"Nonsense!"

"There's no one else who listens."

"What are friends for?"

Sarah had no lessons on Friday afternoon. Leaning against the wind, wrapped up in her tartan windbreaker, her scarf flapping around her ears, watching Jonathan ride erratic circles on his bicycle on the wasteland behind the house, watching him perform foolish antics—cycling with no hands, whooping with delight as he circled her, flying over the grass tussocks—she thought for a moment she had no worries either. Jonathan's sheer animality: the small perfections of his body, his well-formed head, those blue blue eyes, the pleasure of his being; there he was, compact, whole, the joy of existence in his eyes. And he was hers; she had made him. He had come out of her body.

There was nothing wrong with him.

Nothing much wrong with her, either, to have made him.

Liar, she told herself in a moment of revelation. Well, not exactly. It was just that if you didn't believe in the bad things, they stopped existing. If you didn't give them room in your mind, there was no air for them to breathe. They died. *That* was how you coped. And *that* was how Jonathan was going to cope —with this bloody thing, she thought quickly and viciously, that gives him nightmares in the middle of the day.

10

Lawrence wasn't at all happy with Frank's idea. He left Jonathan talking to his two eldest, Ben and Matthew, and took him into his study. Between the bookshelves the walls were crowded with his children's paintings. Old copies of the *Lancet* and the proceedings of various institutes lay stacked against the chipped radiators, and as the two men talked a cat was at work tearing the stuffing out of an armchair. Lawrence had taken up a formal stance behind his desk. Two spots of color glowed high on his smooth cheeks and his eyebrows jutted out more fiercely than ever.

"You've no right to do this, Frank," he said. "It's taking a bloody liberty."

"Look," replied Frank, trying to contain his exasperation, "Jonathan needs help. He *wants* help. I've told you what he told me about his odd times: don't you think he needs help, too? Christ almighty, where's your Hippocratic oath?"

Lawrence punctured the air with his finger. "*One*, I'm not a child psychiatrist. *Two*, the boy's not my patient. He's probably having private treatment at this very moment."

"He's got a GP he gets his anti-epilepsy pills from. He told me that. But he never sees him."

"*Three*," he went on, ignoring the interruption, "if you've got a problem, you don't roll up on the doorstep of your friendly neighborhood shrink, you make an appointment through your GP in the regular way. And if you never see him, you bloody well *go* and see him for once."

"Come off it, Lawrence . . ."

"And *four*, you're expecting me to treat a minor without his mother's permission. Do you know what that is? It's assault. Does his mother even *know* he's here, in this house? No, I thought not. You want me to lose my license?"

Frank fought to control his voice. "It's not a question of treating him, just of having a look. He's scared; wouldn't you be, at that age? He merely needs reassuring that he isn't the lunatic he thinks he is. Surely that's not assault!"

"Without the proper authority it is," said Lawrence with finality. "You'd need a letter from the mother, and even then I'm not the person he should see."

Silence fell between the men. Finally Lawrence came around to the other side of the desk and, putting a hand on Frank's shoulder, steered him towards the door.

"Look, I can tell you've swallowed the lad's story. I'm not saying it isn't true, but people constantly invent symptoms and color their story; it's standard attention-seeking behavior. I'd put it out of your mind, Frank. Be glad you aren't responsible and leave it there."

Frank pulled away and glared. "Listen, I came here because you say you care about people. People, not bloody red tape. So this is the real Lawrence: underneath all the unorthodox crap you're as hidebound and conventional as the rest. All you want is to protect your backside."

"Now look here, Frank . . ."

"Some friend I call you!"

In reply Lawrence swung the door open with a brisk movement. From the kitchen came the sounds of children at play, Jonathan's voice clear among the rest. "There's your answer. The boy may be a minor epileptic, lots of them are, but that doesn't mean he's bloody brain-diseased."

"If that's what you really think, then tell him so. Imagine Ben or Mattie had those scary times, wouldn't you give *them* an honest answer? You're always going on about the damage taboos and secrets cause. Just tell him what you've told me. That's all I'm asking."

"Oh, Christ, let's go and have a cup of tea, then."

They went into the kitchen. Fiona was out and the four children were having high tea. Olivia, the nine-year-old, was toying shyly with her spoon and casting Jonathan sideways glances. He was talking to Ben, the eldest at thirteen, who went to a rival school and had just come back from a soccer match with Jonathan's school. Matthew and Simon were squabbling over a comic book.

"Tea's cold." Their father had to raise his voice to be heard. "Whose turn today?"

"Mattie's," cried Simon and snatched the comic book.

"Get cracking, then." He went over to Jonathan. "Don't let Ben show off. I saw him miss a doddle of a goal."

"But we still lost," said Jonathan dolefully.

Lawrence and Frank sat at opposite ends of the long refectory table, avoiding each other's eye. Lawrence was observing Jonathan closely but discreetly; Frank thought he saw a frown flit over his face from time to time.

When it was time for Jonathan to go home Lawrence led the

way to the front door. Jonathan held out his hand and smiled brightly. "Thanks for the tea." He added after a moment, "You're going to help me, then?"

Lawrence put his arm around him and steered him out into the drive. "Now listen. You're a fine, healthy young chap. There's nothing wrong with you, apart from the fits and those should clear up in time if you keep on with your medication. Otherwise, you're A-one OK."

Jonathan looked down, then out into the open street. A sigh caught in his chest. He turned to the psychiatrist with a look of utter despondency on his face, a look of hopelessness and disillusionment.

"I'm not, you know," he said quietly.

On Sunday morning Sarah, waking late after a deep dreamless sleep, threw the bedcovers back and then lay for a moment on the bed in mock-innocent abandon, one knee raised, an arm flung back. It was a fine, bright day; the sun streamed in and touched her where she would not touch herself, for fear of real abandonment.

She rose, put on a dressing-gown and went to the bathroom. On bare feet and thick carpet she was silent, and the bathroom door opened with no noise. She was half-awake. The full shock didn't come immediately.

Jonathan was standing in front of the mirror, his face cast in the parody of a lunatic. One eyebrow was raised, the other aslant; his nostrils were flared and his mouth grotesquely turned down at one corner. The pupils of his eyes were small enough to make the blue in the sea of white seem black. His whole head was thrown back, and somehow his features seemed to be composed in the leer of an old man.

It was a moment before he saw her and in another moment his face had re-composed itself, but there was nothing he could say. He brushed past her before she could blink. Her tears came like a flood as she heard the door of his bedroom slam.

Late that afternoon, Frank, followed by an unwilling Dog, strayed far along the embankment by the river. He trudged half a mile through the swirling leaves, the dampness of autumn heavy in the air. On top of a narrow suspension bridge he stopped and looked down into the swollen brown water below.

What had they given Jonathan for his schizophrenia? Nicotinamide, wasn't it?

Drugs, he thought with disgust. Drugs *create* illness.

He strolled back down the embankment, unaware of the world about him. The sky was darkening and the wind carried the smell of rain. Let's start at the beginning, he told himself. Let's get the whole thing in proportion. *What are we dealing with here?*

Start with first principles.

No one had ever properly defined the human mind. Trying to define disorders of the mind, therefore, only led to confusion. Yet you could at least categorize the forms they took; Lawrence broke them down into four main types.

First there were the organic diseases, such as dementia and toxic confusion. Jonathan was obviously not one of these.

Then there were those with personality disorders, such as psychopaths.

Third, you had all the neurotic disorders: those with anxiety states, conversion and dissociation reactions, obsessions and compulsions. Again, on the face of it, Jonathan didn't seem to belong to this group.

Last of all, the psychotic disorders. Psychosis was a disease, not a personality disorder. Apart from manic-depressives and hypomanics, by far the largest group here were what Lawrence termed the "catch-all": schizophrenics. These were basically people whose reactions to the world could be described as "inappropriate."

Frank kicked a stone into the water. These are all words, he told himself; words, words, *words*. Jonathan is a living human being. A boy. Maybe even the son he might have had. Then he frowned to himself; you're cheating, he muttered, you're being a sentimental fool. It's not impossible to be small and mad. Or have a crazy mother.

OK, then. If he's small and mad, what could it be? There were many kinds of schizos. People who were deafened by whispers, whose skin felt as if it was crawling with worms, who believed time had stopped altogether. People who saw the world about them as two-dimensional or gray like a television with the color turned down. People who felt flat or depressed for no obvious reason. People who saw visions or heard voices and commands. There were those who lurched between withdrawal and excitement; these were hebephrenics. Catatonics were slightly different; they oscillated between deep stupor and violent arousal and their speech was full of odd neologisms. But those who cleverly wove their delusions into a consistent logical system, and especially those who felt that their thoughts weren't their own but came in from outside, these were the paranoid schizophrenics.

What had Jonathan said? *It's like having another person inside your head. . . . I'm mostly me, but sometimes. . .*

. . . Sometimes I'm not? Was that paranoid schizophrenia? But, wait, was the boy *really* a schizo? Lawrence had made a remark doubting it. It sounded to Frank more like a neurotic state.

Suddenly he felt very cold. What was he doing? He wasn't an expert. He was just guessing, jumping to wild, uninformed conclusions. His little knowledge was a dangerous thing.

.   .   .

As he opened the back door the phone was ringing. Dog slouched in behind him as he went to pick it up. It was Lawrence.

"I've been thinking," began the psychiatrist. "Maybe young Jonathan does deserve a little more attention."

"I thought you said . . ."

"The poor blighter's only got that tyrant of a mother to turn to. I'm not suggesting taking him on, mind—don't get me wrong. I just thought a small chat wouldn't do any harm. We'd have to make it at your place, though. Off the premises, so to speak."

"I don't know when he'll come by again. We left it open. I can hardly call him at home."

"You can catch him as he comes out of school. He goes to Brickhill Middle. Why not try tomorrow?"

So: Lawrence had gone to the trouble of finding that out—presumably through his son Ben.

"I'll try." Don't, he said to himself, ask him what changed his mind.

"Let's aim for next Sunday afternoon, around three, at Oakley. I'll be there unless you tell me otherwise."

"OK."

"And Frank, I'm not there as a shrink. Just as a friend of yours, right?"

Frank laughed. "I'm sorry I got so wound up; I didn't mean what I said. You're all right, Lawrence. See you Sunday."

And that was how the Sunday afternoon sessions began.

11

A blustery late November wind rattled the leaded panes during the silences that fell between Jonathan and the psychiatrist. They sat either side of the fire in an informal manner, while Frank sat at his desk, slightly apart. Jonathan felt uncertain how much he dared reveal to Lawrence and from time to time cast Frank a quick glance for support. Lawrence kept passing a hand over his forehead; the fire was hot, too hot, but he kept his jacket on. He spoke in a hypnotic, gentle tone, rather in the bedside manner of a priest, and Jonathan wasn't sure how to react to the subtle, probing questions.

"Ben tells me you're good at games, Jonathan," the psychiatrist was saying.

"Not specially."

"But you played soccer for the under-elevens last year, didn't you? Don't you like playing any more?"

"They thought I shouldn't."

"Who's they?"

"Well, Mum. She knew a bloke who got kicked in the knee and was crippled for the rest of his life."

"That's not the real reason, is it, Jonathan?"

He shot a glance towards Frank. Of course it wasn't. He'd been having spells on the games field recently and been sent off for fouling. The silence stretched between them. In her basket, Dog snored.

Lawrence suggested gently, "Perhaps it's to do with your . . . odd moments?"

Jonathan found he'd been unpicking a thread from the arm of his chair. A wave of panic lapped over him. Discussing his spells openly was forbidden territory; that was part of his pact with Mum. He shrugged, buying time.

"Those funny times you've told Frank about," continued the psychiatrist. "When you feel there are two people inside you."

Jonathan felt suddenly trapped. "Oh. He's told you."

"Yes. But I'd like to hear it from you."

"Well, it's nothing much. Mum says lots of people have them."

"But you don't believe her, do you? That's why you're afraid, isn't it?"

Jonathan looked up sharply. A tiny drop of sweat was trickling down Lawrence's cheek, but his face was sympathetic, open. The man knew everything. He'd probably read all the files. Could he trust him? He had to take the chance: that's why he'd come in the first place.

"Yes."

"Afraid of being mad."

"Yes."

Lawrence wiped a hand over his forehead and examined it with a detached expression. His small, bright eyes were rich and warm. He smiled and sat back in his chair.

"Then you're not," he said conclusively. "You can't both be mad and be afraid of being mad. It's a paradox which the brain won't allow."

Jonathan didn't understand. Frank was frowning, but smiled when he caught Jonathan's eye. The atmosphere in the room grew tense.

"But sometimes I *am* mad. Not all the time, just sometimes," said the boy, looking down at the carpet.

"Nonsense! You can't be."

"You don't live inside me! You can't tell."

"I can't tell what? Exactly *what?*"

Jonathan saw he'd been trapped. By the time he'd finished describing his spells, their onset and their development and the terrible, uncontrolled things he did while under their influence, he saw he'd picked a hole right through the fabric of the chair. Lawrence looked as if it was what he had expected to hear all along.

"So you'll give me some new pills that will make me all right?" ended Jonathan. "That's all I need."

Lawrence cleared his throat. "It's not quite as easy as that, old son. A doctor can't prescribe pills until he knows what's really wrong."

"But you do. I've just told you."

"You've described symptoms. I've got to find the cause before I treat it."

"Oh. I thought . . ."

"Look, Jonathan, don't misunderstand me. We're dealing with the human personality here, not with a sprain or a twisted ankle. It's a very subtle and complex thing. Don't expect an instant, overnight cure."

Jonathan felt he'd been betrayed: tricked into speaking the forbidden truth, then denied hope.

"But . . . you *can* cure me? You can, can't you?"

Lawrence smiled, got up and put a hand on his shoulder.

"You know what I'd like to do?" he said easily. "I'd like to see you again next week and ask you to do some simple tests. Visual tests, perception cards, maybe an IQ test or two. Easy and fun."

"Next *week*?" echoed the boy.

"Yes. Same time next Sunday, then?"

Jonathan looked across at Frank.

"All right, then," he replied.

Lawrence knew he was already plotting his moves. A different motive lay behind the idea of bringing along a bag of perception and personality tests; of course the boy had no visual defects and Lawrence wasn't concerned with the results of Gesell, Kostick or other personality profile systems in this case. No, this was to be the magician's hand that distracted the audience's attention while the other was doing the real work.

He drove to Frank's house the following week with an eerie, uncomfortable feeling in his stomach. The moment he'd looked properly into Jonathan's eyes he'd been struck by the dilation of the pupils. That, by itself, was the first give-away. There was the constant fidgeting, too. Then there was the way he wanted to lift the veil on his problem and, at the same time, keep it drawn down; he hid but wanted to be caught too. Among the patients on his wards this flirtatious routine was perfectly normal. Normal behavior for the abnormal.

The boy had been on his mind off and on all week. He'd re-read the Warwick file and was dissatisfied with its diagnosis. Was that why he, a busy man, was now driving out to Oakley on the first Sunday in December when he should be talking children's Christmas presents with Fiona? Frank had put his finger on the question. Why had he changed his tune so suddenly?

"Christ, Frank, what a dumb question," he'd retorted irritably. "I'm a pro, not an amateur. Maybe you can't tell the difference in the publishing business."

He was irritable because the spot was sensitive. Where were all those reasons *against*, which he'd earlier reeled off to Frank? A simple chat: that was all he'd offered. He sensed now it wouldn't end there. He'd brought with him a small tape-recorder, concealed in his jacket pocket. Should he stop it all now while there was still time? A professional psychiatrist couldn't investigate a case and avoid becoming involved. Hold on, he said to himself: you're already calling the boy a case.

Jonathan arrived early at the second session, his face flushed from cycling. Lawrence met him coming in through the gates.

This time they sat on the floor, an array of cards and objects scattered over the carpet. He knew the boy would be disappointed the meeting wasn't going to end with a simple prescription of drugs, and so he had to fight hard to win his confidence. He thought it best to do this by coming across as an uncontestable expert and, from time to time, he dropped names and scientific facts into the conversation. Generally he addressed these to Frank, for he quickly realized that Frank was the key; Jonathan trusted him.

"Well," he summarized to Frank after half an hour, "your young friend is a bright lad. Without putting him through the Stanford-Binet I don't know, but I'd put his IQ in the upper quartile. In attention-span and concentration he knocks spots off Ben, who's a couple of years older. You saw how he did on the Thematic Apperception Test, though it's interesting how quickly he picked out the angry, hostile faces from all the others." He turned to the boy. "You're a lad who needs his security, aren't you?"

Jonathan looked back without expression.

"We went through some visual illusion cards and he's perfectly OK. He had no trouble either with the McKay figures and all those zig-zaggy rays." Lawrence paused for a moment. That had been a slight shame; it would have been interesting if they'd provoked a minor seizure. It often happened with epileptics. Still, it would be too much to hope for that so soon. One day, maybe, he'd try photic stimulation; flashing lights usually did the trick. The result would be useful to observe. He carried on with the résumé. "I'm intrigued by the fact he's left-handed. That suggests dominance of the right hemisphere in the brain."

He was about to expand the idea when he stopped. Maybe Jonathan didn't know about the circumstances of his birth. In all probability his mother hadn't told him; there was already a lot of evidence of family taboos, family secrets.

"How do you feel, ready for more? Have another slice of that terrible cake."

"Thanks."

"We haven't talked much about your mother, Jonathan," said Lawrence, settling back in the armchair. "She teaches, doesn't she? Has she ever taught you in the same school?"

"She did in Warwick for a bit."

"What was that like?"

"Awful. She was specially hard on me to show there wasn't any favoritism. She took me to school and back with her, and sometimes I had to wait hours till she'd come out. She made me sit next to her when she was on lunch duty. The others used to laugh."

"She sounds very protective of you. Do you think a person can be too protective sometimes?"

Jonathan looked down at the dog so that Lawrence could only see his tousled fair hair. "I love her."

"You're an only child, of course," the psychiatrist went on, half to himself. "So you don't know what it's like to have a sibling."

"What's that?"

"Oh, a brother or a sister."

"No."

"I mean, you've never had a brother or a sister."

"No."

Jonathan's gaze faltered and he looked quickly across at Frank for guidance. He was about to say something, then stopped.

"Tell me," encouraged Lawrence, watching closely.

Jonathan hesitated. "Well, I think there were two of us when I was born. The other one died, though."

"Oh? Died of what?"

"It never came out of hospital. Mum never talks about it."

The psychiatrist leaned forward slightly. "But she must have talked about it at least once, or else how do you know?"

"I came across a birth certificate in her desk drawer. There was me and another name on it. That's when she told me."

"Did she tell you anything else?"

"She said we looked like two peas in a pod."

"You were identical twins, you mean?"

Jonathan looked up quickly.

"I suppose so."

The odds of having twins were about eighty-to-one against, reflected Lawrence. It was about three times that for having identical ones.

And another thing. He reverted to the original thought which had puzzled him. It was well known that left-handedness was more common in twins than in the singleton population—about twenty percent more—and that was thought to be the result of brain damage caused by intrauterine crowding during fetal development. And that might very well be the cause of the epilepsy. Now, left-handers generally had speech and language in their right brain hemispheres. But he remembered the curious change in vocalization during the "absence" he'd witnessed in the hospital—and Frank had confirmed just the same the other day when he came upon the boy by the river. If this meant a brain malfunction in Wernicke's area, a major speech center located in the temporal lobe, this could well be the site of the *focus*. The temporal lobe was in the *left* hemisphere. So, here we'd have a brain-damaged left-hander with left-hemisphere speech. Very unusual indeed. It would be interesting to do a sodium amytal test to check.

Lawrence shook himself out of his train of thought. This was going *too* far. He was already imagining sticking needles in carotid arteries and freezing the brain hemispheres separately to find out which side controlled language. He wasn't in the hospital here! Jonathan was looking at him oddly, his face very pale. He needed to change the subject.

"Tell you what, let's do a Rorschach, shall we?"

"What's that?" The boy sounded suspicious now.

"I show you some blots of ink on a page and you tell me what they make you think of. Say the first thing that comes into your head. OK?"

"All right."

The first ink-blots became exploding beetles, galaxies with the sun turned off, fish-eye views of anglers. "You're very form-labile," said Lawrence, pleased. He was thinking: this kid's no schizo, I've always said that. Schizos are very form-bonded in responding to this test. But what the hell *is* he?

The next diagram gave him his first solid clue.

"It's a face," said Jonathan quickly.

"Whose face is it?"

Then the boy clammed up. "I don't know. I don't recognize him."

"So it's a man's face?"

"Can we do something else? I don't like this one any more."

"You're afraid of the man. Who do you see there?"

"I dunno."

"You do. You were about to tell me. Think." Behind him Lawrence was aware of Frank stirring; he'd be thinking the boy was being pushed too hard. It was disturbing to have him in the room. "I'm going to count to three. One."

Jonathan fidgeted but stayed mesmerized by the blot on the page.

"Two."

The boy mumbled indistinctly. He was trembling.

"Three. *Who? Tell me NOW!*"

"Dad."

As Jonathan blurted out the word his hand flew to his mouth.

"Dad?" said Lawrence in a half-whisper.

"Dad thinks I'm a dumdum."

"Tell me about your dad, Jonathan."

But the boy's face suddenly flushed and his eyes filled with fear. "I . . . I don't have a dad. You know I don't. You're trying to catch me out."

Lawrence let the atmosphere gradually cool down; the critical moment had passed. In a quiet voice he said, "I'm only trying to help. Believe me."

The boy pushed the book away. "I don't see what you're trying to do. What's the point of these tests and things? Can't you just give me something to take?"

"I think that's enough for today anyway."

Lawrence went over to the far end of the room and looked out across the untidy garden to the dull, bleak sky. He was puzzled. What had the boy's Warwick file said? *Ronald Hall, a self-employed car dealer, left the family very shortly after Jonathan was born and his twin baby brother died* . . . There was no way an infant could recall his father's face. This was a clear case of projection. But why the fear and the anguish? At a subconscious level he might believe he was responsible for his father leaving the family; indeed, at the Oedipal stage he'd have believed he'd actually killed him. Was this a subconscious fear that the father would return and exact revenge? Revenge perhaps, too, for an unnaturally close bond with his mother? Were the angry, aggressive faces he'd picked on so quickly in the T.A.T. projections of *his father's?* What a pity he couldn't examine the mother. The crux lay there, he was sure.

Psychoanalysis was the first line of attack. It could, of course, be a purely organic condition. If asked to diagnose his condition during the "spells," he'd say that Jonathan was a case of MBD, minimal brain dysfunction. That tied up with the fact he was a twin. The incidence of perinatal morbidity was well known to be higher in the case of twins, possibly due to crowding in the womb or difficulties at the point of birth. Lawrence was one of those who took the view that, ultimately, every psychotic condition was organic at root—although the cure might be therapy rather than drugs or surgery—and thus finally he might have to consider Jonathan as a case of brain damage.

But for the present he had to re-establish links with him. Jonathan was now petting Dog in an effusion of transference behavior. He went over and joined in. It was some time, however, before the boy would meet his eye and he was left with the uncomfortable feeling he wouldn't return for another session. But he *had* to.

12

"Frank, is it going to be all right? Why's it taking so long? Does Lawrence really know what's wrong? If so, why can't he fix it? When's he going to make me better? *When?*"

For the whole of the next week the boy's questions on the drive home that Sunday, and his desperate, frightened face, haunted Frank as he went about his work. He was extremely busy with the pre-Christmas rush; his working days were long and seemed still longer as the days drew in towards the solstice. He'd pack the Cortina wagon with car-stock from the garage in the chill and dark of the early morning, spend the day on a hectic round-robin of the bookshops in his area and return home in the dark. He seemed to live in the car; he wondered what had happened to the mythical carefree life on the open road. But the long cross-country drives gave him time to think about Jonathan. How could he answer the boy's questions?

Lawrence could only offer a half-picture. He spoke of guilt. Guilt! muttered Frank angrily to himself one night on the way home as he deliberately overtook a car on the crest of a hill. That's all they think about. The infant Jonathan guilty of parricide and murdering its twin, the mother guilty of a broken home and rearing her child fatherless. And what about Frank's motives, too? Was it his own sense of guilt that drove him towards this young boy? Guilt at running him over and possibly of causing him brain damage? Or was he just a frustrated father playing family with someone else's?

He was tired. That evening he had no will to cook himself a meal. He wasn't looking forward to another winter alone, the third since Cathy died. He had a girlfriend, a bookshop assistant, but she lived an hour's drive away. Shouldn't he find some Bedford girl and hole up with her for the winter? Piss off, he told himself smartly, pouring a large whisky; you're not some bloody hibernating hedgehog. But everyone else had their people. Lawrence went home every night to a raucous, unruly, warm-hearted family. The sales manager had his fine Scots wife and two beanstalk girls. Even Sarah had Jonathan. He didn't even have a mother; she'd passed into glory, as she had liked to say she would, five years before. His only sister had emigrated to marry a doctor in Australia. He no longer saw Cathy's relations. He always had Dog, of course. So, it was to be Christmas As Usual, with Dog. Christmas, climbing in the Welsh mountains.

"Come on, old girl," he said wearily and took the leash off its hook. "You'd better keep in trim if you're going to look after me in my old age. Race you to the wellingtons."

Always after a whisky and a walk he felt better. But he was tired in his soul. And as his exhausted head hit the pillow he found himself thinking about Jonathan Hall and asking himself questions to which he could find no answers.

. . .

It was Friday and Jonathan was still undecided whether to go along on the Sunday again. After school he went down to the garden shed to think. Puck's leg was mending very slowly; if the weather turned any colder he'd bring the rabbit indoors. He was scared. What had he let himself in for? There was still time to stop. The psychiatrist frightened him with his clever logic. Why did he have to ask all those stupid questions? If he was so good, why couldn't he just say what was wrong? It was scary, too, the way he looked at him sometimes: those bushy eyebrows, that tiny baby mouth and all that bluster and commotion with his arms. Frank meant well but maybe he was just wrong.

Besides, he felt bad about Mum. Each time he saw Frank or Lawrence he was betraying their pact. He'd have done anything to have her approval, but he knew she would be furious if she knew. That day was her birthday and she was cooking them a special supper. To bring it up then would only spoil the evening. He'd have to stay quiet and work it out, just as he always had to: by himself.

Sarah smiled to herself as her son came downstairs to supper. She told herself how fast he was growing up; soon he'd be bigger and taller than her. Bigger and taller, and *better?* She loved him for his bravery, too. Perhaps it was partly because he'd known no other condition, that he'd grown up with this fanciful idea that there was someone else inhabiting his mind from time to time. Would adolescence and the onrush of adult hormones do the trick where the present drugs were patently failing? They'd simply have to hang on and see.

He was struggling to open a bottle of wine and refused her help, though he broke the cork. "Mouthwash," he pronounced.

"Have some, fifty-fifty with water," she suggested. As he poured the wine out she added, "You hold a bottle by the neck but a woman by the waist. That's what they say."

"There's a girl I could hold by the *throat*," he said with

warmth. "The Barns girl. She's always cribbing off me."

"Ask the teacher to move you, darling."

"It would only make a scene."

That silenced her. Don't make a scene, avoid fuss, keep out of trouble: that was the deal. He took out a present for her from behind the bookshelf and she opened it with ceremony, carefully preserving the paper for re-use. It was a small brass dish he'd made in metalwork classes.

"It's lovely," she exclaimed. The thought flashed through her mind: metalwork classes are safe, he can't do much damage there if there's trouble, maybe he should be encouraged to go more often. She went on, "I'll put it on my dressing-table with potpourri in it. Come here, my sweet." She drew him to her and kissed him.

Frank's name came up over supper. Jonathan was boasting about a new way of playing backgammon which he'd shown him. She felt her face setting into a frown, but her pulse was quickening too. She was torn between wanting his help and being unable to accept it.

"You haven't been . . . seeing him?" she asked.

"Of course not. He told me the other time, when he came round."

Sarah knew he hadn't. She'd overheard every word of their conversation. But it was not the time to press the point. Instead she said, in a sharp tone she regretted at once, "I don't want you involved with that man."

"But . . ."

"Darling," she went on more mildly, "we don't need him or anyone else. People just want to interfere. We know what's best for us, don't we?"

"Yes, Mum."

That night, in the bathroom mirror, Jonathan craned his neck to examine a small tan-colored blotch the size of a postage stamp high on his right shoulder blade. His birthmark.

His mother came in. "Hurry up, sweet," she said. "It's getting late."

"Did Philip have one too?" he asked.

He saw she had her back to him and was rearranging the towels on the rail. "Philip who?" she asked without turning around.

"You know, *Philip*."

"You mean Mrs. Richardson's Philip. Darling, how should I know? I don't expect so."

"I mean our Philip."

She turned sharply.

"You know, Mum."

She gripped his shoulder. "What made you suddenly think of that? It's past and forgotten. It doesn't need to be brought up."

"You said we were identical," he persisted. "That means he must have had one too."

"Jonathan, what is this nonsense?" Suddenly her grip softened and she turned him gently round to face her. "Of course you have a right to ask questions. If it's important to you, I'll tell you. No, I don't think he had a mark. Not there."

Jonathan started. "Where did he have one, then?"

He could see her faltering. "Well, I'm not sure, maybe he did have a little something on the other side now I come to think of it. Now does that satisfy you?"

Jonathan weighed it up, but something didn't fit.

"But how could you *tell*?" he went on. "I mean, if he was in hospital all the time?"

Her tone sharpened again. "Just what *are* you getting at?"

"Oh, nothing. Just seemed odd, that's all."

"What's on your mind?"

"No, nothing, I promise."

She straightened the towels. "Well, it's not healthy to dwell on these things. We've had a lovely evening and let's not spoil it. Anyway, you're tired and it's past your bedtime. You're getting bags under your eyes."

He said nothing.

"Give Mummy a kiss."

When he embraced her this time he could feel his own body tight and resisting. He went off to his room without meeting her eye. "Night, Mum," he called and shut the door.

He lay in bed awake, puzzled and sad. So that was how it had to be. He was still on his own. Nothing had changed. After a while he heard her footsteps and shut his eyes, feigning sleep. When he heard her going away he saw she'd left the door open an inch or two. She often did that.

On the Sunday, when Jonathan cycled over to Frank's house, he arrived late. He'd stopped twice on the way and almost turned back. He wasn't worried about deceiving his mother so much now; he hated being a burden to her, especially at school where he felt he was getting in the way of her career. If only he could be cured, that would make everything easier. But was this the right way? He wasn't sure about Lawrence. Even at Warwick they hadn't gone about it in such a longwinded way. He'd give it one more try, then pack it in. Then he'd spare Mum and run away and live somewhere where no one knew anything about him.

When he finally arrived Lawrence was clearly annoyed he'd been kept waiting. It wasn't a good start to the session.

13

"What are you planning to do with him this time?" Frank was arranging the furniture in the living-room in the manner Lawrence had prescribed. "Go gently. Last time you really frightened him. Is it really necessary to go in so hard?"

"The boy's late," said Lawrence briskly, ignoring the question. "And can we please have the dog out of the room. It's distracting."

"But you know how fond he is of her . . ."

The psychiatrist stared for a while out into the wintry garden, deep in his own thoughts, his hands folded behind his back. Then abruptly he turned, drew a small tape-recorder out of his pocket and placed it on a low table near the leather stool. He arranged a newspaper casually on top.

"Come here, Frank, will you? When we get going I want you

to start this thing. I've put it on Pause. You've only got to release this button here."

"You can't do that!"

"Don't be a prig, Frank. You know I've been recording him right from the start. Look, it's about time we got one thing straight. You talked me into these sessions, quite against my will. Now I'm involved I'm going to do things my way. OK?"

"I think you're making a mistake."

"I'd rather you kept your thoughts to yourself. Do you want me to help the boy or don't you?"

Frank looked away, distressed. This was all going too far. How many more "sessions" would it take to answer the simple question?

"I know what you're thinking," said Lawrence more gently. "But you can't rush these things. The human brain is more complex and powerful than the world's largest computers linked together. The system's malfunctioning. Don't expect ready-made answers in ten minutes flat."

"Sure, but . . ."

"Look, let's worry about the boy instead. Where has he got to? Do you suppose he's giving it a miss? Or maybe it's raining in his part of town: look at the sky."

Frank shook his head. Calling Dog, he went into the kitchen; he would put a kettle on and keep out of the way until things cooled down. As he let the dog out there came a ring at the front door.

Frank brought the tray in and put it on the small table, covering up the tape-recorder. The psychiatrist glared at him but went on talking to Jonathan. He was asking him where he went for his holidays.

"Cornwall usually," replied the boy, once again fidgeting with the chair cover. "This year it was Polruan."

"Staying with friends?"

"No. We usually take a chalet. Right on the sea front. Mum says people don't get enough ozone."

"There's ozone outside Cornwall. There are some nice resorts in other places. Wales, for instance."

"Oh, yes, Wales too."

Frank looked up sharply from his chair beside the desk where he was pretending to read a book. He spent most of his holidays climbing in Wales; once he'd talked to Jonathan about the country and the boy had said he'd never been there. Frank remembered because he'd thought how good it would be to take him climbing one day. Jonathan caught the look on his face and faltered. From under his bushy eyebrows Lawrence was watching.

"Oh. I mean no."

"Was it a long time ago you went?"

"I said I didn't."

"Or did you go to the mountains instead?"

"I didn't . . ."

"You did. You just said so."

Jonathan reddened and began to pick at his skin. "I don't remember."

"Yes, you do."

His hands were trembling. "I . . . I'm not too sure. Maybe it was a camping holiday. From school." He looked up at Frank again. "Any more orange juice going?"

At Lawrence's small hand gesture Frank stayed in his seat. The psychiatrist went on in the same easy tone.

"Was this Brickhill?"

"Brickhill?" A puzzled, far-away look glazed the boy's eyes. "Oh, no."

"You mean Warwick, then? But surely you were too young for camping holidays then? You can't have been more than eight when you left."

Jonathan's empty plastic beaker shook in his hand. "It must have been somewhere else. Another school."

"But you told me Warwick was the only other place you'd been to."

"Well, it was."

"But there was another?"

"I don't know. I can't remember. I suppose there may have been."

"What was its name?"

"I don't know."

"Of course you know."

"I don't, I don't. It's gone all . . . fuzzy."

"I bet it was fun in Wales. Tell me about it."

"Bet it was fun," echoed the boy. Then a light shudder rippled through his stocky frame and he snorted, "Fun?"

Lawrence remained quiet as the silence lengthened.

Frank watched, horrified, as Jonathan's color heightened. The veins of his temples stood out with the effort of an internal struggle. His eyeballs fluttered upwards and his head began shaking. From between his thickening, contorting lips came the sound of a tune, perhaps a hymn. One hand flew to his head and tore at his hair. The other tightened in a distorted fist around the thin beaker, until suddenly, with a sharp crack, the plastic glass split. His strength seemed unnatural. Frank recognized the state and was on his feet at once, but Lawrence impatiently flagged him back. The boy regarded the splintered beaker in his hand with a strange look of disbelief, then he looked about the room as if seeing it for the first time.

"It broke." His voice was thick, slow, accented.

"It's okay," said Frank gently from the wings. "No harm's done."

"You broke it," corrected Lawrence, drawing the boy's attention. "Let me look at your hand."

"Get away!"

"Do as I say. Give me that hand."

Cautiously, slyly, he stretched out his hand to Lawrence, who examined it briefly.

"No cuts. No blood."

Jonathan's voice lowered to a growl.

"Blood. There's blood."

"Nonsense. It's fine."

"Blood in the barn. Coming oozing out of the sack. The badger got 'im. Poor Rocky. 'E's a gonner now."

Frank felt the hair on his neck prickle. Lawrence didn't move a muscle. He merely said, "Rocky?"

"The Patterdale what Dad works the setts with."

Lawrence managed to keep his voice even. "Dad?"

"Fuck 'im."

Frank involuntarily drew in his breath, but the psychiatrist didn't take his eyes off Jonathan for a second.

"Tell me about Dad," he asked carefully.

Jonathan flinched, then started scuffing up the carpet hard with his shoe. He grunted and pressed a shard of broken plastic into the palm of his hand. He didn't seem to feel the pain. Avoiding the eye of either man, he kept his mouth tightly shut.

Lawrence was trying another angle. "Tell me about the school. What was that like?"

The boy shrugged. "Got expelled, didn't I."

"Why?"

"'Cause of what happened camping, what else?"

"In Wales, that time?"

Jonathan nodded. "Go on, laugh."

"I'm not laughing."

"Then you're angry I got the boot."

"I'm not angry. I care about you."

The boy grunted, disbelieving.

"I care a lot about you. Do you hear me, Jonathan? *Jonathan?*"

Once again, at the repetition of his name the gradual change came over him that Frank had witnessed some weeks before beside the river. He blinked, his face muscles relaxed and his hands untwisted. It was as though he'd awakened from a dream. He looked at the splintered beaker on the carpet.

"That's me," he said. "I did that, didn't I? I'm sorry. I'll buy another out of my pocket-money."

Lawrence rose to his feet and stood in front of him. "That's not important. What *is* important is what you've just been through. Let's talk about that, shall we?"

Jonathan's voice was weary. "Talk? What's there to talk about?"

"You don't remember breaking the glass, do you?"

"Not really. It's all blurry."

"Or remember anything you said either, eh?"

"No."

Lawrence stood with his back to the fire and rubbed his eyes. He let out a long, slow breath. "Well, in a way that's to be expected." He nodded thoughtfully.

Jonathan turned his blue eyes on him in appeal. "What *was* it, then? Tell me!"

"I'll tell you. For a moment you were in another state of consciousness, my lad. We call it a fugue—a flight, if you like—and one of its characteristics is amnesia. It's as if you're running away from your immediate environment because you can't cope with it." He paused again. "What we have to find out is *why*."

"I like it here, at Frank's. Why should I run away?" Jonathan laughed uncertainly.

Lawrence smiled briefly. "You're an intelligent boy. You know what I mean."

"OK, then. Why?"

Lawrence hesitated. "I can't answer that."

"You don't *know*? But you're supposed to know everything!"

"I'm sorry, Jonathan, but it isn't as easy as that. These things take time to find out."

The look of utter disappointment on Jonathan's face reminded Frank of the time he'd driven him away from Lawrence's house. The boy sat in stony silence, coming to terms with the let-down by himself.

The psychiatrist laid a hand on his shoulder and said carefully, "We'll have to keep on going, that's all. Take heart. We're almost there."

"Are we? I don't see it."

Frank shot the man a glance. Give the boy the lifeline he's crying for, he pleaded quietly. You'll lose the boy's trust. You'll lose the boy.

"Lawrence's right," intervened Frank lamely. "You're almost there. I'm sure it won't be long now."

As he looked at the cynical, perceptive look in Jonathan's eyes he felt a traitor to the boy.

Before eight the following morning Frank received a call from Lawrence saying that it was imperative that they meet. With great effort he rearranged his calls to spare half an hour at lunchtime. They met in the canteen of Bedford General. The room was hot and noisy and though it was still a fortnight to Christmas the paper-chains and decorations already looked tired and wilting. Condensation from boiled cabbage clouded the windows.

"Right. I want you to nail this Hall boy down," Lawrence was saying. "We're just getting somewhere. I don't want him running out on me half-cocked, like he did at Warwick. It's your job to pull him in."

Frank was feeling slightly ill. "Is that all you dragged me here to say? I'm up to my eyes in it. I don't know what's rush-hour in the nuthouse but it's a bloody scramble in my business right now."

"I know, I know." Lawrence was cramming steamed pudding into his small, delicate mouth, but his eyes were hard on Frank's face. "But think of the boy."

"Think of the boy," echoed Frank sarcastically. "Are *you*? I asked you to go easy on him yesterday but you pretty near steamrollered him into a fit. As it was you pushed him into one of his fugues or whatever you call them."

"Sometimes when you're running with the flood you've got to force things."

A trolley came past to collect the plates; scraping off the last of his custard Lawrence handed his up. Frank loosened his tie. "Anyway, you're alienating the lad. Is that some novel kind of treatment? Alienation therapy? Or is it a version of the primal scream?"

"What's eating you, Frank? Anyway, just hold on. No one's talking of treatment, let's keep that clear. Just diagnosis."

"OK, you tell me: what's the diagnosis, then?"

Lawrence smothered a belch. "Come off it, Frank. You know better than to put a hack shrink on the line." There was a snide irony in his tone.

"No, I mean it. You're on the line."

"OK. I'll tell you what I think. From what I've seen so far, I'd call it a pretty severe case of conversion hysteria."

"The boy's a hysteric?"

"Yes. A neurotic hysterical state, in the Freudian sense. He's trying to escape from the consequences of his personality, so he invents another *persona*. One that can cope with what he can't. Only, what's specially curious is that this other personality has all the markings of subnormality. MBD, I'd call it."

"What's that?"

"Minimal brain dysfunction. But that's not my point. What you saw yesterday was not an epileptic absence but a fugue. The epilepsy has masked the psychological state all along. That's why they got it wrong at Warwick; they assumed that the epilepsy was linked to schizophrenia. It's an easy assumption to make, in fact."

"But you don't deny he does get fits?"

"Indeed he does. What you saw at the accident was a *grand mal*, sure enough. But my betting is they're *brought* on psychologically. I'd even go so far as to bet the anti-convulsants he's taking don't do anything except perhaps dampen down the effects of the more violent attacks. I wouldn't mind trying to switch them for a placebo, just to see. But we'd need the mother's co-operation for that."

"Come off it. You're talking treatment now."

Lawrence ignored the interruption. "Which brings me to my next point. I want you to try and get through to that woman. But carefully, mind. Sound her out. Use your fabled charm."

"Take your mind off sex," said Frank. "You spend too much time on your couch."

"But think of poor Jonathan having to lie to his mother and all the guilt and distress that must be causing him. Surely you don't like the idea of that?"

Frank knew he was cornered. "All right, I'll see what can be done. But last time she sent me away with a flea in my ear. Look at the time!" He rose to his feet and winced with the first pangs of indigestion. "No wonder people die in hospital, with food like that."

His friend walked him to the door. As they parted he added amicably, "Oh, and one last thing, Frank. Next time it might be better if you weren't around when I'm with Jonathan. Maybe you could be upstairs in the study or something."

His tone raised Frank's suspicions. "What are you going to do, then?" he asked, immediately defensive.

"Do? Nothing different. Just more chat. He's clamming up at crucial moments and I need to break through the barriers."

"And I'm in the way?"

"It's better to keep it one-to-one, right?"

Frank puzzled about that later; he was sure he shouldn't have agreed to it. The psychiatrist's manner had become altogether more secretive, calculating. The whole point of their meeting was probably incorporated in those last few casual remarks. Lawrence certainly had something in mind. Whose side was he on?

14

"Mrs. Hall? It's Frank Fuller here. How are you? Look, I'm having some people round for a Christmas drink on Wednesday week. I wonder if you might be able to come."

Frank felt a slight rush of adrenalin as he phoned her one evening that week, and he recognized that it wasn't just on Jonathan's account. The woman was attractive, there was no doubt about that. After he put the phone down he was surprised how readily she'd accepted. Perhaps he'd caught her without an excuse. Then he realized that, of course, she had no idea of what was going on in the sessions. Sooner or later it would have to come out into the open, and that would surely destroy the possibility of any friendship they might have in the future. Anyway, the deceit was unfair to Jonathan: Lawrence had been right there.

Not sure if she'd accept, he hadn't yet invited anyone else except Lawrence and Fiona and, fearing she'd suspect a trap being confronted with the psychiatrist again, he now set about diluting the gathering heavily. He opened his address book; who the hell could he get along to make up numbers? He ended with the neighbors on either side, the major from the manor, some former work friends of Cathy's, the local bookseller and the Strang and Longley accountant who commuted from Bedford. It was a curious bunch to throw together. He'd better make the first drinks very strong.

While he chased around the countryside during that hectic week, replenishing shelf stock and delivering final orders, he was struck by a pure example of synchronicity: everywhere he looked he was reminded of twins. Wednesday's *Daily Mail* carried a center-spread account of an emotional reunion between two long-separated twins, now grandmothers; quite independently, each had married a Peter and named their two daughters Eleanor and Atlanta. That month's *Nature* had an article raising the old question of nature versus nurture, bringing up to date the idea begun by Sir Francis Galton a century before of studying identical twins reared apart.

And, later in the week, he crossed paths with the area rep of another publishing house and invited him to his drinks party, too. Over a lunchtime pint of beer the man told him about a book they'd just brought out on the comprehensive study of identical twins undertaken by the world-famous team under Professor Bouchard at the University of Minnesota. Frank bought a copy from his car-stock and read it that evening. One conclusion in particular struck him: human intelligence was sixty percent inherited, forty percent due to environment, while the influence of each on personality was about fifty-fifty. No doubt, he said cynically to Dog, opponents of the integrated society would use that to argue for keeping the gene-pool undiluted, while liberals and educationalists would use just the same figures to argue the importance of upbringing and the welfare society. But what did it have to teach him about Jonathan's particular case?

Lawrence's words about Jonathan kept recurring in his mind: "He invents another *persona*, one that can cope with what he can't." Where did this other *persona* come from? His first idea was crazy and he dismissed it almost at once. Might the other personality be some bizarre mental recreation of the brother who'd died soon after birth? It seemed hard to believe that, eleven years on, he could have such a clear memory, but maybe one didn't need a memory to invent a fantasy. Maybe the twin was just a convenient figure to latch onto. It would be interesting to know whether the fugues and fits originated before or after Jonathan found the birth certificate in his mother's drawer and learned the story of his dead brother.

But what kind of experience might it have been that the boy couldn't cope with? Unless worse traumas had befallen him since, it seemed reasonable to suppose it was connected with the death of his twin. So, was it the guilt of fratricide, as Lawrence seemed to suggest? Or had the shock and grief felt by Sarah been somehow transferred to him? He'd need to know far more about the circumstances of Jonathan's very first days. And here at least he could do some basic investigation of his own.

In cases of multiple births in England the babies' names were recorded on the same birth certificate, along with the precise time of delivery. Given Jonathan's birthday, which he could find out easily, he could track down the original birth certificate at St. Catherine's House, the country's repository of birth, marriage and death certificates. With the full name of the other twin he could trace its death certificate and thereby learn how it had died. Or could he? He simply didn't know what actually happened when a person died. Lawrence would, though.

"The doctor writes out a bloody death certificate, what do

you think?" replied his friend when he called him with the query.

"In every case?"

"Well, if it's death from natural causes he gives the relatives a copy of the certificate and they file it with the registrar of deaths. If the cause of death is anything else—say, an old lady died of hypothermia or a fall—the registrar automatically refers it to the coroner's office. A post-mortem is conducted. The family can only stop that being done by taking out a warrant at a divisional court."

"Suppose it was a child. A crib death, say?"

"Frank, what's all this in aid of? Ah, it's Jonathan and his dead brother, isn't it? That's what you're really on about."

"Well, yes."

"Forget it. There was no question of foul play."

"How do you know?"

"Remember Jonathan said the baby never left hospital? That I *do* have on tape," he added with a sour emphasis that was not lost on Frank.

"I see."

"Mind you, the real damage caused then would be the trauma to the mother. She'd blame herself, of course, whether it was her fault or not."

"Maybe she thinks it *was* her fault, supposing it died of something terrible, something inherited from her or its dad."

"Look, don't rush things. We'll find out in the proper way. There's no point playing the guessing game." Lawrence paused, in thought. "All the same, I might try and have a discreet word with her at your party."

"None of your rough handling, please. She hasn't volunteered to go through all that."

"Give over. You just want to get your hands on her and you're using the kid to get you there. Don't think I don't see through you." He laughed. "Mind you, I don't blame you, with a shape like that."

"Talking of shapes, how's Fiona keeping?"

"Bugger off. I'm late for a meeting. See you Sunday. The boy *is* coming, isn't he?"

That Sunday the weather changed and a Siberian wind carried the bitter cold without interruption to Bedford. As they'd agreed, Frank met Jonathan by car around the corner from his home. He chained his bicycle to a lamp-post, already red-faced and numb in the fingers, and climbed into the car. He told Frank his mother had tried to dissuade him from going fishing with William on a day like that. Frank promised they wouldn't be out too long, adding that this time he'd be leaving him alone with the psychiatrist. This made the boy extremely anxious and it took Frank all the drive to Oakley to reassure him it would be all right.

Lawrence had been delayed. "A manic depressive I discharged a few months ago had a freak-out," he explained. "They always choose Sunday lunchtime to attempt suicide, I don't know why." Then he smiled broadly, reassuringly, to Jonathan. "Welcome again, young man. How's the week been? Did you keep a diary of your spells, like I asked?"

Jonathan went on shaking his head in reply rather too long, it seemed to Frank, and his eyes darted around the house as if to line up an escape route. "I couldn't," he replied. "Anyway, I didn't have any."

Lawrence frowned, unbelieving, and turned to Frank. "We'll get started, then. I'll give you a shout later."

Frank turned to the boy. "Don't worry," he said with a smile that felt like the kiss on Judas's lips. His heart was heavy and anxious. He piled coal and logs on the sitting-room fire and closed the door gently. He went upstairs to his study.

He waited almost three quarters of an hour before going

down for a cup of tea. He knew by the way he crept silently down the stairs that this was really a pretext. As he passed the closed door of the living-room he stopped and listened. The boy was talking, but not in the voice of the Jonathan he knew.

At four o'clock Sarah looked up from her desk and out towards the darkening sky. Rain, half turned to sleet, drove pitilessly against the window panes. She frowned. This was no weather for fishing; she should have put her foot down.

She reached for the phone that lay beside the homework she was correcting and dialled. William's mother answered after a moment.

"Jonathan? No, Jonathan's not been round. Haven't seen him in ages. Willie's here, though. Would you like to talk to him?"

There was no need. She put the phone down with a polite, calm word of thanks. She sat there for a good ten minutes, scarcely moving, and was surprised later to look down and see she'd wound the phone cord so tightly around her finger that it was numb and bloodless.

"Mum's ill."

What's the bloke asking dumb questions for? he asked himself. He's a doctor, ain't he? He should know, or else ask his pal that comes round to the farm every day. Dad makes me stay in my room then. I'm not to be seen. Tommy the Invisible.

"Oh? What's wrong with her?"

Ooh, we do have a posh voice, don't we. C'mon, Tommy, answer the man.

"I dunno. She's proper bad, though. We can't drive tractors or trucks in the yard. She's going to die."

"How do you know that, Tommy?"

The boy bit his lip. He shouldn't have told the man his name. Now he'd been *got*.

"I can smell it. She's in bed in the small room, all wrinkled like old rubber gloves. That's where Gran died."

"How do you mean, smell it?"

Dumb question. Anyone with a nose can smell death. I can smell blood miles away. "When the piebald foal kicked it in the spring, she stank up the stables for a whole week before."

That foxed him, he thought. He doesn't know what to say next. I've got him on the run.

"What does your dad say?"

Don't answer. "Mum's nice, she's decent. But she's going. Then I'll be alone."

"But your dad, Tommy?"

Dad? I hate him. I *hate* him.

"I asked about your dad. Did you hear me, Tommy?"

The boy felt the rage rising like a tide. Uncontrollable, he sprang to his feet and kicked over the chair. He let out a wild howl and grabbed the first thing his hands found. A book. With all his force he hurled it towards the man sitting in the chair opposite. It glanced off his shoulder. He seized another object, a vase. This was heavier. It smashed into a thousand pieces against the wall. He laughed, he bared his teeth, he formed his hands into claws, he spat. No one could get him. He was Tommy the Invincible now.

The slaps on Jonathan's cheek stung and there was a searing pain in his stomach where he'd winded himself. Frank had burst into the room. Lawrence was shouting, "Stand back!" They circled him like an exhibit. He looked about him. The room was a complete mess. In his hand he still held a lump of coal, his next weapon. Oh God, he thought. Oh dear beloved God. I did it all.

He had to get out of there. In a small, dry voice, he said, "I want to go home now, please."

The psychiatrist advanced. "We're not quite finished, Jonathan. You're to stay here."

He got up and backed away. "I'm going! I can't bear this! You're making me madder than ever!"

Frank stepped between the two. "I'll take you home right away."

"Frank!" cried Lawrence in exasperation.

"Shut up!" snapped the other man. "Here, Jonathan, get your coat. We're leaving now. Lawrence, you can let yourself out."

Lawrence was scribbling on the back of a card. He handed it to the boy. "Here, this is my home number. I can't make next Sunday but we must, we *must* do it again the next one. It's vital we don't lose momentum. Frank'll be away then but we can use his house, right, Frank? Look, unless you call, I'll pick you up where he usually does. OK?"

Jonathan said nothing. He looked at the disarray he'd caused. "I'm sorry," he muttered to Frank as he led the way outside.

Lawrence followed, talking all the way. "That's nothing. It's easily fixed. But I promise you, lad, we're getting there. It's bound to hurt, but isn't that better than letting it fester inside? It's the only way of knowing what's *really* going on inside."

Jonathan stepped into the car. No, he thought to himself, the man's wrong. It's better to let it stay inside. Don't bring it out. Keep it in, clamp down the lid and no one will see. He's only using me for his own purposes; he's treating me like a freak he's newly discovered, not *me* myself. He hasn't even started curing me. I don't want to be analyzed; I want to be better!

Frank pulled away sharply, leaving the psychiatrist on the doorstep. Jonathan huddled into his duffle-coat and didn't say a word all the way home. He was going to play it differently now. Keep it to himself.

Sarah heard the back door closing and Jonathan's cheerful whistle. "Hi, Mum," he called. She came to the kitchen and stood in the doorway, her arms crossed.

"Catch anything, darling?" she asked mildly.

"A few tiddlers, but Willie threw them back."

"You're not very wet."

"Oh, we found a shed."

She felt her face hardening. She hated having to do this. "Jonathan, you've not been telling me the truth."

"I am, Mum. It didn't rain all that long."

"You weren't with William. I phoned his home."

"Oh? Why?"

"I'm asking the questions, my boy. Now, what were you doing? And those other times you said you were going fishing with William? Are you seeing somebody?"

Jonathan clenched his teeth and looked her straight in the face. She knew the trick from children at school; you stare at a point exactly between the person's eyes and after a while they become almost invisible.

"No."

"Well, then?"

"I go for bike rides on my own."

"But you don't need to cover up by fibbing."

"No."

"That's not what you've been doing anyway or you'd be soaked. Darling, I'm your mother. You can tell me. I'm only asking because I love you."

Jonathan looked at the floor. "I went over to Frank's place. The river's good there. He's got a nice dog too. Mum, I know you don't like him but he's very decent really. We don't *do* anything. I haven't let on about . . . things. It's just somewhere nice to go."

Frank! He'd been seeing the boy all along, behind her back.

He hadn't mentioned anything on the phone. See, she told herself: men are all the same. Treacherous, unreliable, two-faced. She rubbed her hand against her forehead where a low pain was throbbing.

"I don't dislike the man, darling, but he has his life and we have ours. We've been through all this before." She paused as another thought struck her. "What do you *do* with him? What do you get there that you don't here, in your own home?"

"Oh, Mum, it's not like that."

"What is it like, then? What happens if you have one of your spells there?" She drew in her breath. God, she thought, that's all we need. Frank Fuller's altogether too close to the family already. If he saw another of Jonathan's moments he wouldn't stop interfering. Everything would come out, the social workers would be around, Jonathan would be compulsorily admitted to a clinic, the news would get back to the school and, worst of all, they wouldn't even heal the boy. It would be a repeat of Warwick.

"I know when they come on," he said, his eyes averted.

"Darling, you can't be sure of that. That's why we have our pact. Now, promise me here and now you won't see the man again, at least until I've had a chance to speak to him."

Jonathan shrugged. "All right."

She kissed him on the head and said, "Well, that's better. Now let's have some tea and we won't say any more about it."

That evening he put on his duffle-coat and went down to the shed at the foot of the garden. He took along some lettuce leaves, which his mother saw, and a box of matches, which she didn't. Carefully, under the shelf, he struck a match and set fire to the card Lawrence had given him. He burned it down to the last piece. He wasn't going to the sessions any more.

15

The skies sat leaden over the countryside, pregnant with the threatened snow. In the town the shop lights burned all day, their windows glittering with the season's slogans in gold, red and green. Wednesday closed dark and heavy. Christmas makes fools of us all, Lawrence thought. And maniacs out of some.

Driving with Fiona towards Frank's, he began to feel a sense of focus again. They arrived at six-thirty precisely, well before anyone else. Frank was busy hanging up decorations he'd obviously dug up from Cathy's day. Either side of the fire was pinned a meager collection of Christmas cards, several of which bore the same design.

He helped Frank cover a table with bottles.

"Establish a *rapport*," he urged. "That's the target tonight. Don't go over the top."

"She'll see right through me," he replied, popping a bottle of sparkling wine and pouring it into glasses already half filled with brandy and sugar. "What's your angle?"

"Leave that to me." Lawrence turned to his wife, who seemed to be rearranging the decorations. "I'm telling Frank he's not to try for a hole in one tonight."

"Don't listen to him," she responded automatically.

Frank held her out a glass. "Fiona, you will, won't you?" He glanced at her stomach, which was now in the last stages of pregnancy. "Hadn't you better get a stocking ready for it?"

"Lawrence has already set up the manger." She smiled.

People began to arrive. First the major in tufted tweeds to match his complexion, and his wife in a shrill cocktail-dress to match her voice. Then the accountant in the uniform spectacles of his trade, with a dazzling Nordic blonde who could just get her tongue around the word "wife." The other publisher's rep brought his own Scotch and talked community welfare with Fiona. The neighbors stood in their pairs, an imaginary garden fence between them, discussing how much to give the garbage men on Boxing Day. Finally Sarah arrived. She looked more stunning than Lawrence had recalled; a tight turquoise dress made her eyes shimmer and her fine mid-brown hair moved in waves with each movement of her head. But he could not miss the purposefulness in her stance, and when she saw him across the room she held his eye in a positive, thoughtful stare before allowing him a slight smile. Then she turned away and sought out Frank.

He watched her, reading her body language. She was standing forthrightly on one side of the fire, looking firmly in Frank's eyes and asking him one question after another, some defiant, others almost flirtatious. Her fingers were shredding a swizzle stick while the attitude of her hips suggested allurement; he was amused to note the contradiction. He caught

Frank's eye and went over. Frank introduced them and excused himself. Her posture perceptibly altered to one of defense and suspicion.

"Of course I remember you," she said with attempted warmth. "You're the psychiatrist at the general hospital, aren't you?"

Of course: she knew he was a psychiatrist from hearing him paged that time in Casualty. But there was one thing, above all others, he wanted to investigate; but how could he, without arousing her suspicions? He caught Fiona's eye, beckoned her over and introduced the women.

"How's Jonathan?" he asked, to break the ice. "Not shocking people again with his tricks, I hope?"

Sarah managed a cool laugh.

"Jonathan's your only?" asked Fiona, unconsciously stroking her stomach. "My goodness, you must be glad at times like this. Our house is like Aladdin's cave."

"We have four of the little monsters, soon to be five," added Lawrence. "Since I'm Jewish and Fiona isn't, they think they can get the whole thing twice over in a year. Financially it's crippling."

"It must be quite a struggle," agreed Sarah politely.

"He seemed a bright lad, your Jonathan. He's what age—eleven? What *do* you give a bright eleven-year-old? Space-invader stuff, I suppose."

"Jonathan's very keen on computers," she volunteered.

"Ah, that's a doddle. You can keep him happy forever with all that hardware on the market these days. What did you get him, in fact?"

"I got him a dot-matrix printer."

Fiona said, "Sounds very advanced. I wouldn't understand all that."

"His dad probably wouldn't either," said Lawrence.

Sarah looked up sharply. "I'm sorry?"

"I just meant, kids are more technically minded than their parents these days. Unless your husband's in computers?"

"I'm divorced," she replied coldly.

Fiona pulled a regretful face. "I'm sorry."

"But, darling, fathers seem to see a lot of their kids nowadays," Lawrence said to his wife, "even if the wife has custody. Isn't that so, Mrs. Hall?"

"Not in my case."

"But surely," Lawrence persisted, now aware he had overstepped into the area of pure risk, "his dad sees him at Christmas-time, the season of goodwill and all that?"

Sarah raised an eyebrow at him but said nothing.

"Lawrence," Fiona intervened, "I'm sure Mrs. Hall doesn't want to talk about all that. Ah, look, there's that interesting chap I was talking to. Would you like to meet him?"

Lawrence said yes, but he didn't care. He'd got what he wanted. Not once had Sarah used the word "we." The car-dealer husband who'd walked out on her when Jonathan was an infant had never come back into her life. Jonathan could not have anyone in his life he called "Dad."

Then who *was* this Dad he shrank from talking about, even under mild hypnosis?

From that point on he lost interest in the company. Since it would have seemed rude to leave he concentrated on getting drunk—and the drinks were extremely strong. Quite suddenly he became aware they were the last people left. In her quietly competent way, Fiona had cleared up the glasses and ashtrays and was helping Frank put the furniture back in place.

As they said goodbye Frank shook his head. "The cat's half out of the bag," he said. "She knows Jonathan's been here; she gave me a piece of her mind about that. She found out he wasn't going to William's and she dragged it out of the lad. But not everything: she's got no idea what we do, or about your part in it. I tell you, though, I don't like it."

"What's the alternative?" asked Lawrence fervently. "We've got to carry on. Thank God she doesn't know I'm involved, all the same. I've got to be careful. There's always someone out there ready to get the knives out."

"Well, so much for the *rapport*. I tried, though."

Lawrence paused with his hand on the doorhandle, half sensing Fiona's impatience behind him. The cold outdoors air bit sharply into his nostrils and lungs, making him feel giddy.

"You've done me in, Frank. Listen, you're off on Friday, aren't you? Let's have a drink at the golf club tomorrow. I can be there at six."

"Fine." Frank kissed Fiona and saw his friend to his car. "See you tomorrow."

"Sorry it was all slap and no tickle. G'night, lad."

Frank drove slowly to the golf club the following evening. He didn't quite know how he was going to say it. Finally, braced by a large whisky, he decided on the direct approach.

"Lawrence, I'm feeling rather uncomfortable about you seeing Jonathan while I'm away. I'm asking you not to."

A roar from the far side of the bar at the punchline of a long joke forced a momentary silence between them. Then Lawrence said simply, "Sorry, it's on. You may have found him, but I'm the one he needs."

"I could always remove the door key."

"Don't be childish; that wouldn't do any good. I'm picking him up round the corner from his place. I could just as well take him to my house. In fact, it might be better," he added, looking into his drink thoughtfully. "The atmosphere, and so on."

Annoyed, Frank knocked back his drink and ordered another round. A light wind from the greens curled around the old building and moaned through the leaking casements.

"I'm not happy."

"We weren't born to be happy," responded Lawrence, lapsing into bogus Yiddish melancholy and letting the phrase linger among the listless coils of cigar smoke. Then he hardened. "Look, we're getting places with the boy. Can't you see how he's opening up at last?"

"Opening it up is only making it worse. You're stirring up things that should lie dormant."

"Exactly! That's the whole point!" Lawrence raised his glass in mock triumph. "Look, let me give you a small example. Remember you called me the other day to ask about the facts of death? That got me thinking about the boy's birth. I contacted the bloke at Warwick General and he called me back today. He'd checked, and there's no record of any Jonathan Hall being born there or in any of the other hospitals in the area."

"Maybe it was a home delivery," suggested Frank.

"A young car salesman and a girl who's left home under a cloud—you think they're likely to go private? Come off it."

"I don't see the point you're making."

"Think. It's another possible lead. If he was born somewhere else, maybe that's where the school was he spoke about. So, there *could* have been another school and maybe he *was* expelled after some terrible incident. That would explain a lot: he is suppressing the memory and transferring it onto another *persona*, while the mother is desperately trying to cover up the fact she's a respectable schoolteacher with a delinquent as a son. Doesn't that fit the evidence?"

"That's the Tommy person he answers to, then?"

Lawrence looked up sharply. How did Frank know that name?

Frank went on quickly, "So what does that make him? Is he still a case of conversion hysteria, or was that flavor of the week, last week?"

Lawrence turned to the barman and ordered a pack of cigarillos. He waited to light one before answering. Frank had to lean back to avoid the smoke. He spoke quietly and between the two words he paused to pick out a shred of tobacco caught on his tongue.

"Multiple personality."

Frank snorted. "Jekyll and Hyde?"

Lawrence answered him seriously. "No, he's not schizoid, but it's a hysterical state, as I said at first. As this Tommy *persona* comes forward we will learn what it is that he's repressing. What he's transferring onto it, if you like."

Frank had finished his glass and he signalled for another. His spine felt chilly and his stomach was tight. How could he go off and leave Jonathan at this crucial moment?

"I'm more worried than ever now. Look at this so-called Tommy person: he's a little maniac, a psychopathic nut-case. What'll happen if he comes *too far* forward? Maybe the wind will change and he'll be stuck in it forever. No, I'm not joking. You've opened up a valve of some kind and he flips over into the fugues when you're not around."

Lawrence swirled the remains of his drink around the glass before replying. "Well, of course the next step is to do some proper physiological tests. Analysis is all very well, but a good part of Jonathan's syndrome is physical. He gets epileptic fits. Somewhere, in that small head of his, is the *focus*. I don't know if I can go much further without doing EEG's and proper brain scans . . ."

"Are you saying he should be admitted?"

"What I'd like to see happen and what's legally permissible are two different things. At present, he can't be admitted. While his condition is stable and he's not causing a breach of the peace, there's nothing anyone from outside can do."

"I'm glad to hear it!" said Frank warmly. "But if things get out of hand . . ."

"The normal procedures would operate. He could go into

care, he could be admitted to a child clinic under an order, and so on. But that's hypothetical."

"Hypothetical," echoed Frank doubtfully and downed his glass. "I suppose I've got to leave him in your care. But, please, Lawrence . . ."

"Of course, of course. I understand your feelings."

"It's not my feelings, it's the boy's bloody sanity I mean."

"Look, you're reacting emotionally. Jonathan's in good hands here, believe me." Lawrence spread his hands as if to display their trustworthiness. "Remember what *you* went through. Compared to this kid you're as normal as . . ." he searched around to complete the simile, "those piss-artists boozing their heads off over there."

An acknowledging roar came at that moment from the group of golfers by the bar.

"Thanks a bunch," said Frank sourly.

Lawrence flagged the barman again. "One more, then it's time for the road. Christ, I'm busy, though. Suicides at least keep to Sunday lunchtimes; that shows manners. But everyone wants to have a go at Christmas. We'll soon be two to a bed. You should pay us a visit, if you can get through the paper-chains. The ward's like a battery chicken-shed. Cheers."

"Cheers," responded Frank, wishing he could be cheerful.

With just a handful of shopping days to Christmas, Frank had just about finished his year's work. He paid his last call on the Monday to the bookseller in Deanshanger; he bought from him an angling encyclopedia for Jonathan and delivered to him a copy of an autobiography ordered by the lady of the manor for a relative abroad. Discovering she'd long missed the last posting day for overseas mail, she'd just cancelled the order. Frank was annoyed; he'd gone to great lengths to get the book, even defying union rules and phoning the warehouse direct.

Partly guided by his common sense, the bookseller's business had taken an upturn and that evening it was sparkling wine instead of sherry. Over the second glass Frank made the mistake of adding up the direct cost of delivering this special order. He gave up when the variable costs, excluding overhead, came to more than double the cover price.

Still, the prospect of his climbing holiday in Wales lay ahead. He'd be spending ten days in a cottage in the Black Mountains where his old trainer lived. The man's name was Doug and, though now retired, he kept his hand in by inviting chosen former pupils to stay with him for a spell on the rock faces. Frank had been a good climber, audacious yet methodical, and in years gone by the two men had forged a close bond between the long pitches and overnight bivouacs on the Welsh carregs. Doug had lost his wife too, in a climbing accident many years before, and in a way Cathy's death had brought the men closer. Their friendship existed despite differences of age and background. Frank looked forward to stretching himself to the physical limit and pitting his wits against nature and the elements.

It took him almost an hour to drive home; the roads were dark and treacherous with black ice and, ever since the accident with Jonathan, he'd avoided that short-cut. Yet each time he made the return trip from Deanshanger he thought of that night. What had the boy really been running away from? Would it come out in the sessions?

At home the lights had come on automatically and around the door a group of carol singers clustered. They'd obviously been there for some time. He invited them in and made them tea and cocoa. One of the younger lads looked so like Jonathan that he gave Frank a start, and when they left he gave them far more money than they were expecting.

He took Dog for a walk and poured himself a large whisky. He didn't feel hungry. Instead of cooking anything he dug out his Brasher boots, the Karrimor knapsack, the chocks, the caribiners and the coils of rope he'd be needing; his waterproofs, breeches, sweaters and sleeping-bag could be sorted out later. Dog sniffed around, excited. But Frank was of two minds. It took him another whisky and a long, hot bath before he realized why. He didn't want to leave Jonathan behind, alone with Lawrence.

16

"Mum blames herself," whispered Jonathan to the rabbit, cuddling it close to his parka. It was cold in the shed and the naked lightbulb glared in his eyes. "She thinks a boy should really have a dad. . . ."

A dad. He had a dad. Or the Tommy him did.

The sickly bitter almond taste again and that trembling deep in the marrow of his bones. The blinking and head-nodding, the painful curling-over of the hands. The first threshing within his skull, tugging and sucking, nudging giddiness over him. No time to hum or chant. Quick, put Puck back in his cage! There. What's that on his hand? A drop of blood from the rabbit's leg. He looked at it. It seemed to draw him on.

Blood. The memory veered in and out of focus, like a slide getting too hot in a projector.

There was blood this morning. Squirtin' everywhere. They'd come to clear the chicken. Christ, it was freezing and dark outside, but sweaty hot in them sheds. Two of the little bastards flew up into the fan blades and got their heads chopped off. Went around spewin' blood. Then after, guess who had to pick up all the deaders? Over seventy there was.

Jonathan gripped the side of the shelf and fought with himself.

I'm Jonathan. I'm me. This is the garden shed, at home. This is my home. Where my mum and I live. Mum's indoors right now. She's doing the washing. It'll be supper time soon.

The creature within gave another violent convulsion. He clutched his head. He fought. Doubled up as if smacked in the stomach by a football, he fought on. He wouldn't give way this time. He'd see it through himself.

Mum was poorly today. It was all over Dad's face. He's watchin' me like a hawk. Has been for these past weeks. He blames me for Mum being ill. He snoops around at night, checkin' the medicine drawer. He's padlocked up the weedkiller, too. He's afraid. Dad's afraid of me. Good! He knows if I can do it to a horse I can do it to anyone. Maybe even Mum. Maybe I have and it's too late. That would show 'em.

"Jon-a-than! Sup-per!"
The call percolated through the blurry haze in the boy's mind and gradually returned it to focus. Supper? He'd had his tea. He looked at his watch.

His face ached and his forehead was damp with cold sweat. He took a deep breath and clenched his teeth. He had to fight, to go on fighting. He'd have to do without anyone's help. He was on his own. He opened the door and turned out the light. "Coming!" he called back down the garden.

· · ·

Two pills with supper. Sarah had laid them out on their special saucer beside his glass of milk. She smiled as she watched him take them and asked him routinely how he felt. They both knew what she was referring to.

"Oh, fine, Mum," he replied, avoiding her eye. "Puck's not healing properly. I'm going to bring him indoors tonight. It's freezing out there."

"But that's what rabbits have their coats for."

"It's not fair, even so."

She hesitated. Why not? She was always saying "No" to things. She even discouraged pets; most children had a cat or a dog around the home. A rabbit was harmless enough.

"Well, if you keep it by the back door."

She looked intently at her son as he concentrated on his food. It was Christmas Eve. Perhaps, if he couldn't sleep, she'd take him along to the midnight carol service in the church at the end of the road. It was holiday time, after all. The thought of kneeling in prayer was curiously appealing to her. She'd never before had much time for religion. But perhaps there *was* someone out there who could help, someone who could see into your heart so clearly that there was no point in hiding anything. Things had grown worse in recent weeks and her own confidence had been shaken. She badly wanted Christmas to go well.

Oh, please, not again.

Twice in one day: that was frightening. Jonathan sat against the bedstead, fully dressed, gritting his teeth and praying that this would be a mild one. His radio was over on the table, but he didn't dare get up to turn it on. He sat there, waiting, his hands tightly clutching his head. Go away, Tommy. Please, God, make it into a dream.

He'd done something bad again and Dad had sent him to his room. He was in for it tonight.

It weren't his fault. They were lorrying up the steers for the knacker's yard. Frampton, the bastard, was prodding away with the electric stick but the ramp was muddy and a big 'un slipped and fell. It went crazy. It burst through the railings and charged straight past him, through the paddock fence and into the fields. Frampton got the others on board, yelling blue murder. The big bugger had stopped right down by the ash spinney, but when it saw them it broke away. It ran for miles, through the winter barley, over the sheep fields, giving them the slip every time they cornered it. It jumped the stream by the old fir wood but then it got tangled up in the brambles the other side. Frampton leaped in and gave it the prod right up the bum. Christ, it bellowed! They got a rope around its neck but it broke free and crashed back across the stream. Then suddenly it stopped, just like that, and keeled over on its side. It lay kicking the air with bright bubbly yellow stuff coming out of its mouth. Frampton booted it in the crotch but it was no good. The froth grew red and it began choking. It had bust its spleen.

Dad arrived on the scene, and saw. Tonight he'd be coming up to see him. He knew what that meant. The belt.

At eleven-thirty that night Sarah was in the kitchen downstairs making cocoa for Jonathan. She'd take it up and if he felt up to it they'd go along to the carol service. She cupped her hand against the window and peered out into the dark. It was a wild, windy night but dry and less cold than before. She was just waiting for the milk to rise in the saucepan when she heard the crash upstairs and the first gruff cry of pain. Oh God in your mercy, she muttered. Taking the pan off the ring she walked steadily, without hurry or panic, towards the stairs. She knew what to expect.

What she did not expect was what she saw the following day. It shook her to the roots of her being.

In the morning she took Jonathan his breakfast on a tray as a Christmas treat. He woke up slowly, from a deep sleep. As he moved he winced in pain. She thought nothing more until that evening when it was time for his bath. She came into the bathroom to rub him dry. As she turned him to dry his back she let out a small gasp. Crisscrossed across the flesh of his back and bottom, like a faint ghost image, was a pattern of long, faint, pink stripes.

17

Dead Man's Fall was the morning's climb and it was Doug's turn to lead. This was a classic on which he'd brought up a generation of climbers. He'd given his name to a line of ascent that zig-zagged up the sheer rock face and ended on a wide overhanging ledge with views that commanded a good part of Wales. The wind had fallen, and though there was ice in the rock crevices the conditions were just passable. Doug belayed at the top of the first pitch and called down.

"Frank?"

"That's me."

"Climb when you're ready."

"Climbing."

The retired trainer was one of the old school who obeyed the drill meticulously. Discipline was, for him, the first rule in climbing. Frank took a deep breath and started up behind.

Coming to the first runner he took out a chock and fixed the caribiner to his belt. He leaned away from the rock so as to give his boots a better purchase and continued on up. This was his fourth day and only now did the tendons in his legs and hands feel properly loosened up. He hoisted himself onto the small ledge where Doug sat in a crouch, belayed, and the men exchanged a brief smile. Behind and below them gorse and scrub stretched for miles, dotted with sheep and streaked white where snow still lay in the hollow ground. In the distance layered mountain ranges merged gently into the leaden sky. The morning air was sharp and the rock cold and slippery. As he looked up the sheer smooth face above him, he promised himself a cigarette at the next pitch.

"Right."

Doug straightened and set his eyes upon the rock above. His hair was white and wiry and the skin of his face and neck had grown to match the granite upon which his life had been spent. He set off at a slow, steady rate. Hand, toe, hand, toe, without using chocks and yet finding a purchase on the smallest feature of the rock's surface. For several minutes he ascended the face, then called down again, "Frank?"

Frank had studied his route and began on up. He was nearly at the top when he was hit by the freeze—that terrifying feeling of insecurity that all climbers dreaded. Quite suddenly, without reason or warning, he had the sensation that the whole mountain was falling away from him, that it was turning to void and he'd be left hanging there with nothing but empty air beneath him.

Breathe, he told himself.

He concentrated on filling his lungs deeply and expelling the breath with a rhythmic hiss through his throat. At the same time he stared straight ahead at the surface of the rock, just inches from his face. He forced himself to examine the colors of the crystals and imagine he was wandering among a giant landscape of lichen. Very gradually he felt the terror receding and he knew he'd mastered it, but it left a sick, tarry residue burning in his throat.

When finally he perched on the ledge beneath the overhang and reached for a cigarette, his hands were trembling. Doug had seen and understood. He smiled.

"It never leaves you," he said with a knowing chuckle, "however much you climb, however experienced you are. I still get it myself. It creeps up on you, just like that, then *wham*." He took two puffs of an herbal cigarette of his own and rubbed it out between finger and thumb.

Frank nodded. Doug had seen it all. The man had once managed to keep clinging to the rock while the woman he loved, his wife, fell crashing to her death in the sea a hundred feet below.

"Can't you conquer it somehow, for good?" he asked.

Doug shook his head. "Fear can't be conquered, only controlled. Everybody has their threshold, not just climbers. Remember that Scots Grand Prix driver a few years back? Thunder and lightning petrified him and he wouldn't race without an anesthetist standing by. That's some kind of fear, but look how he conquered it on the track."

"Maybe he relied on it to help him push the car through a faster line."

"Exactly. First control it. Then you can use it."

Frank looked up at the sheer overhang above them. "I could use a little less of it right now," he said.

Doug gave his former pupil a careful look, then smiled.

"Right, boyo," he said. "You lead now."

Frank gritted his teeth. It was typical of the man to give him the most testing task now; but he was right. He ground out his cigarette, took the rope and began to examine the rock face for the best line of ascent.

· · ·

Jonathan spent much of the afternoons that week out in the field behind the housing estate. He felt driven to go outside whenever he could. He was afraid to stay indoors in case . . . in case he did things he didn't mean to. Already he'd broken the new printer and had had to cover up to his mother. Around the house most of the time he wore a pair of stereo headphones, listening to pop tapes. He kept them beside his bed at night, too, for he could sense things were coming to a head and he didn't know how he'd cope.

The Sunday after Christmas was a clear day with a brisk wind and he spent the morning pottering in the field behind the house where a colony of bungalows was being built. He prowled among the freshly dug foundation trenches and peered in the windows of the empty workmen's huts. He felt restless and uneasy. After lunch he returned to the field, this time roaming over the strip of woodland at the far side that divided it from the river where he usually fished. He didn't feel like William's company today and his mother was going out to tea at the headmaster's. He was glad to be alone. He had enough company within himself.

He waited until he was sure she'd have left the house and returned by the garden gate. He felt furtive, excited, disturbed. He had the house to himself. He could go through her things, help himself to the sherry, get into her bed, let the rabbit loose in the living-room. Though he knew it was empty he went through the place on tiptoe. He felt jumpy. One moment the boiler in the kitchen burst into life and startled him and then an open window in his room upstairs brought a photo frame down with a crash. He began to tremble. His mouth grew dry and as he swallowed he tasted bitter almonds.

That morning, in the cold early hours, he'd heard a fearful cry. A kind of gargling, choking noise. He'd listened, terrified. An owl echoed from the woods. Then it had come again, this time more like a long, sad sigh. The sound seemed to coil up through the house, through his bedroom floor and the ceiling above, and release itself into the starry night air.

He knew she'd died.

In the morning he was banned from the house. From the outsheds he watched the doctor arrive. Then, a long while after, an ambulance drove down the potholed drive: slowly, without its light flashing, taking its time. The driver and his mate stopped for a cup of tea. They carried out the stretcher as if it had nothing but a bundle of sheets to weigh it down. They drove away and stopped around the corner while the driver took a leak.

The house became as silent as the death it had harbored. Even the mantlepiece clock had stopped and when he looked in through the kitchen window at lunchtime there was nobody there; not even the radio was on. He crept quietly in and was helping himself to cheese from the fridge when he heard hobnailed boots on the flagstones in the yard. There was nowhere to hide. Large and menacing, his dad stood in the doorway, his weathered face flushed with anger. He'd caught the boy in the act. His mouth full of cheese, Tommy ran upstairs to his room.

Jonathan ran upstairs to his room and shut himself in. He wheeled the chest of drawers against the door and looked at the window. He'd escape down onto the kitchen roof, as he had done last time. He'd run away for good.

Why was he thinking of running away? This was home. His home with Mum.

But Mum's dead, he remembered. They took her away this very morning. Mum's dead and you're alone.

Mum was dead and he was alone. He'd better pack. Money: he cracked open the china pig. Food: no time for that. He grabbed his carryall and crammed into it a sweater, socks, his clasp-knife, his air pistol and a can of pellets. Fishing-line to catch rabbits with. And matches to light fires with.

Matches to light fires with. Fire meant goodbye to the house. Death to the farm. Death by fire.

Death by fire. Matches in hand, Jonathan landed lightly on the kitchen extension roof and listened. Not a sound was to be heard. He lowered himself down onto the outside window sill, carrying the carryall like a knapsack with his arms through the handles. Noiselessly he dropped into the back yard and crouched close to the door, alert to every sound.

He turned the handle carefully and inched the door open. The kitchen was empty. On the shelf he saw what he wanted. Firelighters.

Firelighters. They would do the trick. Dad's study was the place to start. He listened. He heard the tractor starting up in the field behind the house; that was his dad driving. Quick! Lock the back door to stop them coming in too soon. He'd leave by the front door and slip the latch.

He ripped open the packet and dropped a trail of the white naphtha bricks all across the study, connecting them with lines of newspaper like fuses. With all the oil in the wood, the gun cabinet would go up nicely. Then the curtains, the bookshelves, the door, and the rest of the house, room by room. He struck a match.

Jonathan struck a match. He waited long enough to make sure the first firelighter had caught. The flame gathered momentum, winding its way in a line from the curtains by the back windows along the baseboards to the kitchen. He watched for a moment, fascinated, then ran for the door.

It opened and he tripped and fell among brooms and dusters. But there was no time to stop and think. He burrowed among them, deep into the smell of polish and dust, seeking to find his escape.

Escape. Run, dodge, vault the gate, don't turn round, doesn't matter about the barbed wire slashing and ripping. Stop only when there's a good mile gone. Spit out the saliva. Turn and you'll see. There's no mistaking the long, thin spiral of blue smoke.

He knew where to go, he knew every inch of the farm, this was his life's home. He made for the sheep fields where the going would be easier. He'd go on until darkness fell, then he'd be safe. He mustn't let up till then.

He heard dogs! Dad had got the dogs out.

Panic seized him. A stitch tore through his stomach. His hands bled and tears blurred his eyes. Water was the only way to escape the dogs. The stream at the bottom of the hill. The wind carried the sound of yelping to his ears. It carried the man's voice, too.

The stream: upstream or down? Down!

He stumbled on blindly, whipped and slashed by briars, slipping and skidding on the mossy stones, tripping and tumbling over submerged rocks. The cries were close upon him now. Frantically he lashed out, kicked and scrabbled. But suddenly the dogs were all around, all teeth and claws, snapping and jabbing, yelping and snarling. He fell face-down into the water and saw it stain red. His head went under and he gulped in water. He was choking, drowning. And there, on the bank above, stood his dad, with a bugle to his lips. But he wasn't blowing the bugle, just waiting, waiting. And under his arm, in a casual fashion, the shotgun.

Lawrence looked at the clock on his dashboard, then at the street around. Had he got the right spot? Mentally he checked the instructions again; he was sure this was the place. But if the boy had decided not to come, surely he'd have phoned? Unless Sarah had dragged the whole story out of him. The thought chilled him. He'd wait another ten minutes.

He got out of the car to stretch his legs and clapped his arms around his back. He'd had a hard time over Christmas, with staff on holiday and the extra crop of cases to deal with. He really didn't have time for this sideline. He should leave it to Frank.

The minutes passed. Lawrence returned to his car, partly

relieved. As a last chance he thought he'd drive back past the boy's house just in case he met him on the way. He started up the engine. The house numbers were badly marked and he had to go slowly to find the right one. He pulled into the curb opposite. It was in darkness and looked empty. On the spur of the moment he reached into his briefcase and took out a plain envelope; in it he slipped another of his cards, with a message to Jonathan to call him any time he wanted to. That satisfied his honor. Cautiously he walked up the path, watching to see no one was at home. He had no notion of what he'd say if confronted by Sarah.

As he opened the letterbox he was aware of a faint, acrid burning smell. He frowned, then knelt and peered in through it. The living-room was thick with smoke. At the far end he could see small orange flames. He leaned hard on the bell, then thought twice, stood back and, bracing himself, rammed at the door with his shoulder.

It took three punishing blows to break the lock. Smoke billowed out at him as the door flew open. He burst inside, shouting, "Mrs. Hall! Jonathan!"

He spotted a phone on a desk under the stairs. Holding his sleeve to his face, he snatched it up and dialled the fire brigade. The flames were already taking hold of the room and he backed away towards the door.

As he was leaving he heard a muffled threshing sound above the crackle of the flames. It seemed to come from a closet beside the front door. He listened for a second, then wrenched the door open.

There lay Jonathan, huddled on the floor, his head thrown back, his eyes uprolled and his tongue protruding purple and the whole of his body from head to feet twitching in the final spasms of a seizure.

18

Sarah had good cause to feel pleased as she drove away from tea with the headmaster. He'd taken her to one side and asked if she would understudy the deputy head next term, "to get the feel of things." This would be the step up in her career she badly wanted. Once in the job she could relax a bit and devote more time to Jonathan. Everything would work out well.

Rounding the corner of her street she saw the fire engine, its lights flashing, and wondered which of her neighbors' houses was on fire. Then she saw. Ramming the car to a halt against the curb, she tore past the firemen in the street, past the neighbors clustering around the gate, up the path alongside the hoses and in through the smashed front door. At the end of the living-room, through the acrid pall of smoke and steam, she saw firemen shattering the glass in the back windows and around them black scarred walls and hulks of burnt-out furniture.

"Jonathan!" she screamed.

A figure to her side straightened up. Lawrence. Beyond him, under the blanket on the floor beside the window, lay her son. With a cry she flung herself down beside him.

"He's out." Lawrence's voice was tight, harsh. "I've given him an injection. He'll be all right, though."

Crouching protectively over his head Sarah looked about her. Hoses snaked across the living-room carpet and from the blackened kitchen came the sour smell of doused plastic. The psychiatrist stood over her.

"What in God's name has happened?" she demanded. "And what are you doing here?"

"Leave him there and don't move him," Lawrence ordered her curtly. He turned to the foreman. "This is Mrs. Hall."

"You're a very lucky lady, Mrs. Hall," said the man. "If the doctor here hadn't been passing we'd have had a tragedy on our hands."

"But what *happened?*" she insisted.

"Your young lad got playing with firelighters, that's my guess."

"Jonathan did?"

"It'll have to be reported."

"But . . . I don't understand."

The foreman, long-faced and lugubrious, took off his helmet and wiped his forehead. He called out to the men in the street to start reeling in the hoses and beckoned Sarah over to inspect the damage. "Fire's all out now, but you won't be making a cup of tea in a hurry. That window there: I could get one of the lads to block it up for you, if you like. And I wouldn't be happy with your front door like that. You haven't a snowball in hell's chance of finding a carpenter now, not with the holiday season on. As it happens, the driver's mate's a handyman."

"Yes, do anything, please," said Sarah. Anything at all, so

long as all these strangers would leave her house and she could see to her son.

The man produced a clipboard and wiped the surface of the kitchen table clean of soot and water. "Paperwork," he explained and licked the point of his pencil. "Shall we begin?"

At the far end of the room, beside the front window, she could see the psychiatrist, his hands in his car-coat pockets, staring down at Jonathan. She took a deep breath. She'd take it step by step. First, get rid of the firemen.

Finally they departed and Sarah was left alone with Lawrence. He carried the boy upstairs to his room, now almost clear of smoke, and helped her put him to bed. She went around the house opening all the windows and she turned the central heating on full. The electric cables at the back had burned through and looked unsafe, so she set up lamps on an extension cord from upstairs. There was no possibility of boiling a kettle. Instead, in silence, she took a bottle of brandy from the charred kitchen cabinet and poured herself a drink. As an afterthought she poured one for Lawrence and left it on the mantelpiece, avoiding direct contact with him. The smoke had cleared in the draft but the pungent smell remained. Coughing and shivering, she surveyed the fire-stained wreckage of her home.

Lawrence broke the silence. "It's time we had a talk, Mrs. Hall."

"I want you to drink that and go."

"I think you owe me a word of thanks. I saved your boy's life."

"Explain what you mean," she responded coldly.

He described how he'd found Jonathan in the closet and the state he was in. In another few minutes he'd have been asphyxiated.

But she wasn't satisfied. "Perhaps you'd tell me what you were doing here. Did Frank Fuller send you? You could have phoned me first. Ah, no: I get the picture. You came to see Jonathan, not me. My God, what conspiracy is going on between you two men?"

"I think it's time you learned a thing or two," said Lawrence. "Put a towel or something over that chair and sit down."

Mesmerized, she obeyed and sat toying with her glass in bloodless hands. The aftermath of the shock was just beginning to hit her. She felt nauseous; panic rose in her like heartburn. But as she listened to what Lawrence had been doing with Jonathan those past Sundays, a violent wave of fury seized her.

"My God, this is utterly outrageous! I'll have your license! How *dare* you!"

On impulse she rose, strode across the room and slapped Lawrence on the face as hard as she could. He grabbed her wrist and bent her arm down hard, almost bringing her to her knees. Unrelenting, he forced her back to her chair and threw her back down into it. His tone was so controlled that it frightened her.

"Now, just listen to me, woman. Let's talk about Jonathan. He needs psychiatric help, and you are going to admit him to hospital. If you refuse, I'll have him committed. Compulsorily."

Jonathan *committed*? Taken away from her, put in a home, locked up with a lot of loonies? She laughed aloud. He was bluffing.

"You'll do nothing of the sort! Jonathan's mine. He belongs here with me."

"He belongs where he'll get the treatment he needs. And that is not in this house."

"Now just look here . . ."

"Be quiet and listen. Your boy has committed arson. He's shown himself to be a danger to himself and others. He has a record of mental disturbance—in fact, he was having psychiatric treatment until you chose to take him off it in mid-stream. Either you admit him to hospital or else I'll have it done myself. I can have him taken in under Section Twenty-five. It only takes two signatures. Mine, as a psychiatric practitioner, and your GP's."

He *was* bluffing. "Our GP knows nothing whatever about it."

Lawrence's tone was deadly even, as if dealing an ace.

"I'm referring to the other GP, the one other side of town, the one you get his Luminal from. You're dealing with a small community here, Mrs. Hall. We doctors know one another. Even if he knows *you* by some other name."

Sarah could feel the blood draining from her face. This man was evil. He'd been spying. Why? What possible motive could he have had to destroy the harmony of a family?

He went on, spreading his large hands in a sarcastic gesture of generosity, "You can always appeal to the tribunal, of course. Any time in the first six months you can put your case before them. But now the local authority is involved things may be different. I imagine the social services department will opt straight for a care order . . ."

Sarah drew in her breath sharply. A care order? The state take over as guardian of her boy?

". . . and they'll lock Jonathan up in the local assessment center until they can get him up before the juvenile court. Then, I'm afraid, it may be a case of a regional secure unit. Don't look so shocked. They're not nearly as Victorian as they used to be. He'll probably go to Brentwood. He'll have a nice room of his own and a special warder to take an interest in him. I think there's even a small gym on the campus. Of course, he'd be up against the older delinquents, but they aren't all psychopaths . . ."

"What are you telling me this for?" Sarah clenched her teeth.

"Now, getting a child *out* of care," he continued, as if he hadn't heard her, "is a great deal harder than getting him in. After all, the state will be legally responsible for Jonathan. Then it'll be very much up to the social worker on the case in discussion with the senior management of the social services department."

"Now, wait a minute, this is out of all proportion! Jonathan's only been a bit careless with some matches."

Lawrence stood squarely in front of her, triumph glinting in his small bright eyes.

"Wrong, Mrs. Hall. You know it as well as I do. Don't let's beat about the bush. Jonathan has a severe neurotic disorder. He adopts another personality to protect himself from traumatic memories he can't cope with."

"Are you trying to tell me Jonathan's schizoid?"

"Not exactly—in his case it's not dissociation but a severe form of conversion reaction. The epilepsy is partly psychosomatic, of course, but it's the neurosis that's at the root of it."

"My God, you're a monster!"

The color of his cheeks heightened momentarily and he stepped back. The gleam in his eyes hardened. He enunciated every syllable clearly as he spoke.

"Now, try and think what you're saying. You're blaming me for telling you what you know is the truth. That's understandable, but rather immature for an intelligent woman. You'd do better to consider how *you* are to blame."

Sarah rose to her feet again and faced the psychiatrist. "Me to blame? I've given up everything for Jonathan. I've sacrificed my life to bring him up the best way a mother can. I've had no help from anyone. It hasn't been easy, especially with his . . . in the circumstances. How dare you stand there in judgment!"

"You've been too afraid for yourself to take him in for proper treatment," responded the psychiatrist at once. "He's been brought up in an atmosphere of taboos and secrets. Take his twin who died, for example. How did he find out about that?

By accident. Because he happened to stumble across the birth certificate. You weren't going to tell him."

She froze. He knew about the twin! But how much? She'd have to step very carefully. Pretend. Laugh it off.

"Oh, for goodness' sake," she exclaimed, "what would have been the point in telling Jonathan he had a brother in the womb, when it died a few days later?"

She watched him carefully as he replied. He'd swallowed it. A seamless passage.

"But hasn't it ever occurred to you," he went on, wiping his forehead with a handkerchief, "that the Tommy side might be a *projection* of his dead twin brother? He's got the *persona* there ready-made: a twin, his other half, his *alter ego*. The evil to his good, the black to his white."

My God, she thought, he even knows about Tommy! Perspiration started out on the back of her hands. There was no point in trying to deny or back-track. Better give him a half-truth and hope it would be mistaken for the whole.

"That's utter nonsense! For one thing, we christened the baby Philip, not Thomas, and Jonathan knows that perfectly well. And besides . . ."

"Yes?"

"Jonathan invented the Tommy character long before he came across the birth certificate."

A puzzled look flashed briefly across the man's face. She bit her lip. Had she gone too far? Had he tricked her into letting too much out of the bag by threatening to have Jonathan taken away and locked up? But it would never come to that. If need be, she'd take him and run, as she'd done last time. They'd up stakes and put roots down in another town, until the day would come when time and love had healed him.

She moved towards the front door, now roughly repaired with battens screwed across the splits.

"I think it's time you left, Dr. Miller."

"Yes, I've said all there is to say. You have the choice to make." He picked up his Gladstone bag and took out a bottle of pills. "Give him a half-tablet of these when he wakes up, then the same every four hours. They're just a mild tranquilizer. I'll be speaking to the department tomorrow. I'm sorry it has come to this. He's a brave boy and I'll be sad to see him go." He shrugged briefly, then snapped the bag shut. "I'll call you tonight and expect to have your answer."

"Get out of here."

"Till tonight, then."

She shut the door and sank back against the wall. Bitterly she surveyed the blackened wasteland to which the rear of the house had been reduced. It was a sign. The sooner she started packing up the better.

Run, but where to? Could her mother find something in the village? Weren't there some second cousins in Scotland? Yes. Cut and run. Anywhere.

Sarah hauled out suitcases onto her bed and began opening drawers. Then she stopped. How could she fit a life's acquired possessions into two suitcases and the trunk of one car? Jonathan's stuff alone would fill a van. How much time did they have? Presumably the psychiatrist would have to put it all in writing. And Monday was New Year's Eve; surely the system ground to a halt around then. Or did it? She knew from experience at school that in cases involving children the lumbering local authorities suddenly became very nimble.

A surge of anger flooded her. By whose grace did Lawrence appoint himsef judge over her? What had given him the right to take Jonathan on in the first place, without her permission? It was intolerable.

To take Jonathan on. An idea occurred to her.

The boy had gone to see the psychiatrist voluntarily, trusting his own judgment. Why shouldn't these sessions be allowed to carry on? Meting out the treatment himself, surely Lawrence would be satisfied? And then it might not have to become public knowledge. It could all be kept quiet. The school needn't be told; the local GP needn't be involved; the social services department needn't be called in. There'd be no question of having Jonathan compulsorily admitted, of his being locked away in a mental institution. He could go to the therapy sessions each week and everything could remain as it had been. And this way, just as she did at school, she could keep a close watch on his progress. She'd even attend the sessions herself.

And there'd be no question of uprooting, either. No question of going on the run again. If Lawrence had so easily found out about Warwick, the doctors in the next town would just as easily find out about Bedford. Running away was no real solution.

It was a possibility. Would Lawrence agree to it? She'd preempt his call and tentatively sound him out. As she picked up the phone on her dressing-table she heard a whimpering from Jonathan's room next door. Wasn't he supposed to be drugged to sleep? She listened for a moment to the low, agonized moaning and made up her mind.

It had been the worst one ever. His brain still hurt from the clawing and lashing. What had he done? Dimly he had a memory of striking matches, then suddenly of being inside a closet, catapulted into a far-away, black world where he was running, always running. After that everything had grown darker towards a total eclipse. Now, as he surfaced drowsily, he could smell scorched paintwork and singed fabric and he knew in the depths of his being that he was to blame for it.

He veered in and out of consciousness, never sure which state he was in and terrified of them all. He'd never lost control quite like that before. What had sparked it off? Was it the sessions with Lawrence? He should never have given in to Frank.

Then another blurry gray wave of nauseous terror swept over him and, moaning aloud, he huddled into a tight ball under the bedclothes. Maybe if he made himself very, very small the black angel would somehow pass him by.

When he arrived home Lawrence went straight to his study and shut himself in. From his jacket pocket he took out the tape-recorder, but found that during the activity the microphone had become dislodged and his conversation with Sarah was too indistinct to be of any use. He sat at his desk, his hands folded, and reflected on the meeting.

Her body language had been a give-away: the jabbing of one nail into the quick of another, the aggressive forward-sitting posture on the chair which signalled defensiveness, the widening of the pupils whenever he touched a nerve. But had he pushed her too far? Or not far enough? He'd had to extemporize, but he'd come away with the feeling that the chances were better than even that she'd agree to take the boy in. He'd been slightly dishonest: there were other options he hadn't mentioned, and he wasn't sure if he could really make a Section 25 stick long enough to be of any use. But, with luck, she wouldn't see beyond the choice he'd presented her with.

An hour before he'd planned to make his call, he received one from her. He carried the receiver over to the fireplace where he could see himself in the mirror over the mantelpiece. He found it helped him think. Her first words sent an unaccustomed thrill through him and instinctively he frowned; he was getting emotionally involved in this case, and that had to be watched.

Sarah made her suggestion about continuing the sessions in Frank's house, under her own supervision.

"It's not quite as easy as that, Mrs. Hall," he responded, carefully choosing his words. "You see, Jonathan and I met just so that I could form an opinion of what the trouble was. What he needs now is treatment, therapy. A private house isn't suitable for that."

"But does it matter where the analysis takes place?" He could sense the desperation in her voice. If her own alternative was rejected, she'd be forced into accepting his. "One place is surely as good as another. Especially if Jonathan's used to it."

He watched his mouth forming the words neatly and elegantly and he paused between phrases to let them sink in.

"We're talking more than just analysis. Let me explain. Alongside psychotherapy we'll have to run a small program of tests. That's to make sure the problem's not organic. We need to rule out any actual physical causes, causes within the brain structure itself. Most cases of epilepsy are organic in origin."

Sarah's tone grew cautious. "What kind of tests would you be talking of?"

"Oh, the usual routine ones. Some scans and, of course, EEGs."

"Electric shock treatment? You will absolutely *not* do that on my son! I forbid it!"

He noted she'd dropped the conditional tense; he was gaining ground. "Good heavens, no! I'm talking of electroencephalograms: just tiny electrodes taped to the head. There's no electricity used at all. It's absolutely painless, entirely harmless and quite routine, merely a convenient and accurate way of reading brain-wave patterns. We do them all day long here."

"You mean he'll have to go into hospital for these . . . tests?"

"Yes, but only as an outpatient. Maybe we'd need him in for a day or so to begin with. Then I imagine a check-up session with therapy once a week would do. It's an attractive alternative to putting him in care and maybe committing him to an institution."

Sarah said nothing.

"I know what you're thinking," he went on sympathetically.

"You're worried that if he's put into the child psychiatric ward he'll be among a lot of screaming nut-cases and that'll upset him. Still, there may be a way around that."

A murmur from the other end told him she was receptive to suggestions.

"It's rather . . . irregular, but I might be able to wangle it so that he is put on the regular pediatric ward. I'm on close terms with the consultant there. That way I'll be able to keep an eye on things personally. And there at least he'll be with kids with broken bones and appendicitis and so on."

"I'm not sure what to say."

"In my honest opinion this is the best possible thing you could do for Jonathan. But I need to know your decision now."

"Right now?"

"Yes."

He held his breath during the long pause that ensued and made no attempt to interrupt it. The pressure of the silence built up. Finally she replied. Her voice was tight, grudging.

"Very well."

"Good. Bring him in in the morning."

"*Tomorrow* morning?"

"There's no saying how he'll react to the shock once he wakes up. I want him safely in hospital as soon as possible." There was a silence at the other end. "Mrs. Hall?"

"All right. After lunch tomorrow."

19

The following morning the doorbell never stopped ringing. Every few minutes one or another of her neighbors came by with a kettle of boiling water or a thermos of hot soup. One, an electrician by trade, spent the morning putting the power back on. In the three years she'd lived there she'd kept very much to herself and hardly ever invited them in. In the garden she'd had tall trellis-work set up on the walls and covered it with ivy. But now her home, her soul, everything she'd worked for and all that she could call her own, was laid bare to their prying eyes and fingers. She felt almost physically ravaged.

She'd cleaned out the kitchen using a dust-pan and thrown out the shattered television with the other charred furniture. From floor to ceiling the rear half of the house was wrecked. The carpet was ruined; she'd taken it up and stretched it out over stools and boxes with fan heaters blowing underneath. It filled the house with a stench of steamy, sodden flax. As she was washing down the walls that morning a uniformed fire officer came by and went through the whole paperwork procedure again. She wondered if the damage was covered by insurance and, if not, how she'd manage to pay for the repairs. Later on, a sharp-eyed reporter from the *Gazette* paid her a visit and, on being refused entry beyond the doorstep, stood in the front garden taking photographs through the window.

Jonathan slept through most of this. Around eleven he came downstairs in his dressing-gown and looked around, his face white with shock and distress. She held him tightly to her and stroked his fair hair. When should she tell him? How should she tell him?

Without saying anything, he drew away and went out into the garden in his slippers. She watched at the kitchen window as he took a spade from the shed and dug a hole beside the fence. Then he went back to the blackened rabbit's cage which Sarah had put out by the dustbins and reached in for his pet. It had suffocated and lay stiff in death. Cradling it to his cheek he carried it down the garden and, whispering a few words in its ear, lowered it into the small grave. He then returned to his room and refused to talk, but merely lay under the bedclothes, staring up at the ceiling.

All the while she was scrubbing walls and sponging floors, Sarah had been turning over her decision in her mind. Was she doing the right thing? Was there no real alternative? And was it fair to Jonathan, in his present state, to land this extra worry on him? But next time he might burn the house down and himself with it. Already she was fearful for his safety: she'd tried to stop him going on cycle rides or fishing on his own without William. Sooner or later he'd have an accident. Something had to be done.

But it was Jonathan's life, Jonathan's mind, and it was only fair to let him decide. He'd already demonstrated he was capable of forming his own judgments about his condition. She'd lay the cards squarely on the table, without influencing him either way. It would be *his* decision.

However many blankets he piled on, he still shivered. From time to time he lost the idea of where he was and who he was. He dreamed fitfully. Sometimes he grew afraid to move a single muscle and lay in a pool of terror, as if his head were a bomb and the slightest movement would trigger something off inside. His mother came up every quarter of an hour, her apron wet and her hands smelling of scouring powder, and gave him hot milk and chocolate to drink. She brought him lunch on a tray, but his hands trembled so much she had to spoon-feed him the soup, and his stomach was too tight to accept anything more solid. The whole world took on a fearful, hostile aspect. The sunlight hurt his eyes and the voices on the radio seemed to be talking about him.

This was how mad people went. It was no use fighting any more. He had to give up. Give up and just be mad.

When his mum went downstairs, he let himself cry a little.

By the time she returned with pudding he'd dried his eyes. Make an effort, he told himself. Poor Mum; look what I've done to our home.

"I'll put it all right, Mum, I promise," he said. "There's three weeks of holidays left. I'll strip the paper and redo the plaster. William's dad's got one of those special folding tables and we can easily hang some more."

"Darling, there's something more important." His mother laid a hand on his shoulder. He felt agitated.

"The carpet? I'll do a paper route and save up for another. What color shall we have it? You choose."

"That's a lovely thing to say and we can talk about it later. There's something else I need to discuss with you first. I want you to listen very carefully. It's not going to be easy for you."

She sat on the bed and took his hand in hers. He listened in silence as she told him everything Lawrence had said to her. The choice had to be made: accept his offer of help or take a chance on the authorities. There was one alternative, though. They could try and start again somewhere else; she thought the second cousins in Scotland might take them in until they found a place of their own.

He felt bemused. Suddenly this wasn't him they were talking about, but another person, another boy altogether.

"So what do we do about him, Mum?" he asked.

She looked puzzled for a moment. "I want you to decide for yourself."

"He needs help."

He looked around the room. The objects had taken on the appearance of cardboard: familiar, but changed. He felt a moment's giddiness. He had to keep hold of the real things. Don't move anything or it'll change and melt into different ones. He looked up at his mother. What had she been saying?

"Stay put. That's the thing. Here's home."

"And the hospital tests?"

The hospital tests, he echoed to himself. Yes, the tests. "Will they make him better? Not mad any more?"

"Darling . . ."

"*Will they?*"

She squeezed his hand. Her eyes were gray with love and worry. "Probably," she said.

Probably. Was that good enough?

He found himself nodding slowly. "All right, then."

Lawrence returned from the hospital that evening and rubbed his hands at the sight of the steak Fiona had cooked him. The house was in uproar; the television was struggling for dominance with Olivia's discordant piano-practice and Mattie had acquired a police car with wailing siren. But none of this marred his delight at having Jonathan now under his eye, in his control. He'd stay in until he'd recovered from the shock and the first basic tests could be done.

Using Dr. Cameron, the pediatric consultant, had been a stroke of genius. It was New Year's Eve and a case of whisky had secured a bed in his ward. Lawrence tucked into his meal with relish. Half-way through, the phone rang. He answered it with his mouth full.

It was Frank, from Wales. The line was terrible; he must have been in a pub, for there was singing in the background and he kept having to feed coins in. He wanted to know how the session the previous day had gone.

"No show," replied the psychiatrist. "The lad didn't turn up."

"Maybe it's as well," said Frank, adding something too indistinct to catch.

"How's the weather?" shouted Lawrence. "When are you back?"

"Weather's lousy. Rain, rain, rain. Growing grass on my head. Be back Friday night."

"Call me when you arrive. Don't fall off a mountain first."

"You what?"

The line became too bad and Lawrence rang off. He'd been right not to alarm Frank; knowing the man, he'd probably come rushing back if he knew. Friday was still four days away; by then he'd have found a way of breaking the news to him. He wasn't going to like it. Lawrence rubbed his face. "He's not the boy's bloody *father*," he said aloud. "Though you wouldn't think so, the way he acts."

He poured himself another glass of red wine and sat back in his chair to study Fiona's rump at the sink. A moment's anxiety came over him at the thought of another child on the way. Was he putting his career on the line over Jonathan's case? Certainly he was calling in a lot of favors. He'd have to be careful. Sarah would have to be watched. And Frank too: he was bound to meddle unless he was contained. But it might all pay off.

20

In accordance with the rules of the state system, Sarah had to go to the pediatrician living on the far side of town and collect a letter referring Jonathan to Lawrence. This caused her embarrassment, for the letter had to be made out in her real name and delivering it by her own hands to the hospital made her an accomplice in an act of betrayal. Time and again she found herself going over the apparently inescapable logic of the decision.

Under the referral system, Lawrence was now the consultant in overall charge of Jonathan's case. Of course she was glad he was being admitted as an epileptic rather than as mentally disturbed, but here was the hospital's adult psychiatric consultant apparently taking on a child with a nonpsychiatric problem. How long would that go unnoticed? True, Dr. Cameron, the general pediatric consultant, was prepared to play along. But what would actually happen in the ward when Jonathan had one of his spells? Wouldn't the officials and nurses query why the child psychiatrist wasn't on the case? She remembered that Lawrence had, by his own admission, called it "irregular" and she'd had, at the back of her mind, the idea that in the final analysis she could use this as a lever over him. But she knew that no one in a hospital was higher in status than a consultant. Who could she threaten to complain to if it came to that?

When she arrived at the hospital to deliver Jonathan, Lawrence took them at once to meet Dr. Cameron. He was a middle-aged Scot with the mild manner of a scoutmaster and gray-streaked hair like heather thatching. Jonathan was shown around the ward by a nurse while the adults talked—or, rather, Lawrence talked; it was immediately clear to her that Jonathan would be strictly his patient and the pediatrician was only brought in to offer the resources of a children's ward. Dr. Cameron wasn't going to be any use if she had to put pressure on Lawrence. Meanwhile she observed with suspicion the kind, concerned image Lawrence was projecting towards her and she compared it with the ruthless man she'd last confronted. He enquired about her home and suggested people to help with the repairs. He mentioned nothing of the recriminations of their last meeting but instead conveyed an air of calm, unbiased professionalism.

She was increasingly on edge as the time came to leave her son behind. As he led her to the bed they'd prepared for the boy, Lawrence was saying, "Of course, if the tests show up no obvious *organic* defect, then we'll have to look at the psychological side again. And there I'll need your help."

"My help?"

"Yes. To get a proper grip on the etiology I'd need to know a great deal more about Jonathan's background. His home life, his upbringing, the circumstances of his birth, and so on."

She felt a chill pass through her. Holding his eye squarely, she replied softly, "Let's wait and see the results. But whatever you do to my son, just don't you dare mess him up. That's all I'm going to say."

"Trust is the first step to cure, Mrs. Hall."

"And trust has to be won first."

She felt herself trembling as she shook hands with the doctors and watched them depart. They were going to start with Jonathan first thing in the morning and until then they'd made sure he got a good night's sleep. She sat for half an hour on his bed, reading to him, until visiting hours were over. And as she turned to wave to him from the far end of the ward she felt a tear falling down her cheek. In the corridor she doubled up and fought for breath, leaning against the wall for support. They'd wrenched out her womb and left her bleeding.

Jonathan woke the following morning more lucid than he could remember for days. Whatever they'd given him had made him feel awake and renewed. Perhaps he was beginning to get better already.

He sat upright on the high couch, his legs swinging over the edge, and watched intently as Lawrence in person supervised the senior resident and the nurse preparing the electroencephalogram equipment. He'd been shown to a small room on the second floor off the radiology department that looked out across a light-well onto a staff canteen and, below it, the hospital laundry. Besides the couch there was a metal-frame chair and table with an assortment of toys and crossword books, but otherwise only banks of electronic instruments that gave off a sweaty electronic smell like his Spectrum when he left it on all night. They looked very impressive. One day he'd like to be a doctor, or an air traffic controller, he wasn't sure which.

"What are those for?" he asked, pointing to a row of screens in a green metallic housing.

"VDUs: visual display units," replied the psychiatrist. "But we keep a permanent record with a pen recorder. Come over here. I'll show you. You won't have seen a U/V pen before. It uses ultra-violet light to make the mark, not ink." He tapped a finger on the boy's head. "You've got two pinky gray dumplings in there with billions of cells firing away—just like your home computer, only a bit different. The computer works by electrical impulses only, but the brain works chemically too. What I'm telling you now is being stored electrically at the moment, but soon it'll get converted into a chemical code for long-term storage. So much of the immediate activity of the brain is electrical that it's important to check the circuits are working properly. That's what we're going to do now."

The nurse wheeled forward a trolley on which was a tangle of small round sensors, each imbedded in a clear plastic aureole and linked to a box on the trolley by fine wires.

"These are electrodes," he went on. "They don't transmit anything, they merely listen and pick up the cells as they fire. We're looking for places where too many cells suddenly start firing simultaneously. That shows up on the chart as wild squiggles, not normal, even waves."

"So if I have a brainwave you can tell?"

Lawrence smiled and patted a hand on his shoulder. "I can see it's going to be a pleasure working with a bright lad like you," he said. "Now, what we're going to do is stick thirty-six electrodes on your head—quite literally, stick them with glue. Ready? Come back to the couch so we can start."

Helped by the nurse, the registrar systematically glued the electrodes in a regular formation over Jonathan's head, then wrapped cotton bandages over them. It didn't hurt at all but it itched terribly. He wasn't to scratch or he'd dislodge them.

"Now shut your eyes and relax. Think of something really nice. Think of your holiday last summer. The place you stayed in. Imagine the sea, the waves, the gentle breeze. I'm going to leave you now for a while, Jonathan. You can move around a bit later if you want, but be careful not to pull the wires out. We'll leave you on for a few hours. OK?"

Jonathan nodded and shut his eyes. The summer holiday in Cornwall had been a good one. Warm sea. Ice creams. Mum had let him watch TV late and given him extra pocket-money. And he'd scarcely had any spells: just a few, but very faint. As if he'd left them too far away to get through properly. In the end he'd almost forgotten he had them at all. It had been wonderful. Holidays always were. Maybe Mum was right: it must be the ozone.

"Six hours isn't enough," said Lawrence to the registrar later that afternoon as he examined the long coil of paper on which thirty-six perfectly regular wave-patterns were inscribed. He turned to the nurse. "No signs of any epileptic behavior, of course?"

"Not exactly."

"Oh?" he said sharply.

"I brought him tea and a bun after lunch. He could have been daydreaming, but I thought it might be a minor *absence*. I can't be sure. He soon snapped out of it, though."

"When would this be?"

"About three or quarter-past."

Lawrence ran the coil of paper through his hands again until the time indicator showed three o'clock. The alpha-rhythms weren't down, there was no surge of muscle tension, no tell-tale rise in arousal potentials. An *absence* or a fit of any degree would show up as violent squiggles on one or more of the lines. "No spike discharges," he muttered. "It can't have been anything." He tugged at his ear in thought. "All the same, I want him back on the EEG. Give him a good twenty-four hours. If we're lucky we'll get a *grand mal* then. Otherwise we'll have to stimulate one out of him."

He left to pay a brief visit to Jonathan, now back in the

145·

children's ward but sitting apart from the other children with a chess book which he clearly wasn't concentrating on. His eyes roved restlessly from one object in the room to another and he'd begun his head-twitching again.

Sitting on the end of his bed, Lawrence began to describe the next stage of tests. On his head they were going to fit a unit rather like a cyclist's crash-helmet; it had no wires trailing out of it, so that he could move around freely, and instead it had an FM transmitter mounted on the top which sent the signals to the chart-recorder across the room. It meant staying in another day but he was sure they'd get some useful results then. Jonathan's concentration wandered; he seemed agitated about something else. There was no more Lawrence could do and he left for his own department. In the lift he reflected on what the nurse, an experienced woman, had told him earlier; she could surely tell an *absence* from a child's daydreaming. Was it possible Jonathan had had a minor seizure and it hadn't shown up on the EEG? Was the *focus* somewhere other than in one of the thirty-six areas conventionally charted on the brain atlas? The twenty-four-hour test would tell.

He knew the sounds hospitals made at night; he recalled them all from Warwick days. He lay in bed, trying to conquer his fear by identifying them one by one. A boiler firing in a distant basement. The central heating pipes tapping like prisoners with Morse code. The siren of an ambulance and the endless squelchy sound of crêpe soles passing down the corridor outside. Occasionally he fancied he heard a scream but it might have been the wind. Hospitals never grew dark either; the lights from the laundry below in the opposite wing lit up the floral patterns of the curtains and in the room itself, over by the electronics, burned a low blue safety-light. The air was hot and smelled of plastic. He'd tried to open the window wider but it had a stop screwed into the frame. Under the apparatus on his head his scalp itched furiously. An LED clock on the wall told him it was almost midnight. He lay on the bed, trying to sleep, but afraid to slip over the edge.

One was coming, a big one. All day it had been stalking him, circling the hospital grounds outside, biding its time, waiting for dark. A black panther, so black as to be invisible except as claws and fangs and the whites of eyes. No window open the meerest crack would bar its way; it could melt its glistening black body through the aperture and drop noiselessly onto the linoleum.

The curtain billowed slightly. He lay frozen with terror, waiting for the soft thud of the pads. The taste of bitter almonds rose in his throat. He didn't dare move, hum, sing, reach for the radio. He waited for the tentacles in his head to stir in response. There was no escape. He had to lie and let it take him.

Full moon. Bitter cold. Thick frost on the fields and outbuilding roofs. Clear, starry sky; nothing to stop the spirit rising to infinity. A perfect night for the sacrifice.

He crept downstairs, avoiding the creaking boards, past the light under the door of his mum's old room which was left on at night ever since she died, and out through the kitchen door, pausing only to put on his jacket. He patted his pocket to check the penknife was there and went out into the biting cold.

He knew exactly what he was going to do.

He slipped the peg off the door-catch on the small lean-to shed where he kept the rabbit. He raised the lid of its cage and fumbled around in the straw until he found its head. With a quick movement he swung it up and out by its ears.

"It's time, Puck," he said.

He noticed its back leg was still hanging at an odd angle, but that didn't matter any more. It wriggled and he had to hold it firmly to his chest as he took it out into the moonlit yard, behind the hay barn and over the fence to the spot. The large circular grinding stone lay imbedded in the frost-scarred earth, abandoned there from the days when the farm had milled its own corn. The rabbit put up no struggle. It allowed itself to be held between his knees as he knelt on the stone, opened the penknife, drew back its head, placed the blade to its throat, raised his eyes to the moon, and struck.

"Go to Mum," he whispered. "Tell her."

He held its head so that the blood squirted over the stone. The rivulets froze hard even before they could trickle over the edge into the earth. For half a minute the small, furry body twitched as it shed its spirit. Then he laid it on its back and neatly cut into the skin, making incisions the length of the belly and in circles just above the feet. The pelt came off like a glove. Bending its neck back he angled the knife between the upper vertebrae and severed the head in a single movement. Next he dismembered the body of its limbs and spread them out in a square at the edge of the stone, propping the head up at the top and setting the truncated torso in the center. He stood up and regarded his ritual altar; it made a pleasing sight. He rubbed the blood off the pelt and carried it back to the house. He'd cure it later.

As he put his hands under the warm tap of the kitchen sink to thaw them out he heard the lavatory flushing upstairs. Would Dad come down for a nightcap and catch him? He held his breath as footsteps began to descend the stairs.

The night nurse who came in at the sound of the crash found Jonathan in the corner, cowering behind the upturned table. She noted the time—half-past midnight—and reported it to the main nurse who returned to duty in the morning. In turn she informed Lawrence. Immediately he examined the EEG printouts. But he didn't find what he was expecting at the specified time. He searched the hours either side without finding any evidence other than increased brain activity consistent with a mild state of arousal; it didn't even look like a minor alarm seizure, let alone the decrease in consciousness coupled with massive spike discharges he'd have expected to accompany an epileptic attack.

"Bloody machine's up the spout," he muttered to the resident. But he knew better; he could see at once from the waveforms it had made that it was functioning perfectly well. "I don't understand it."

"I'll arrange another run-through," suggested the man. "I think his head will have to be shaved too. Maybe the scalp contact isn't good enough."

"No, I'd hold off on that just yet. I'd like to do a CAT scan first."

Lawrence went to tell Jonathan the results and found Sarah there, visiting. Her blue eyes registered relief. "That's great news, isn't it?" she said. "If nothing's showing up, then that must mean there's nothing there."

Lawrence shook his head and rubbed his balding forehead.

"I'm sorry, it's not as simple as that. Last night we had all the behavioral manifestations of a major seizure. That's incontrovertible. Just because we can't pinpoint the actual area doesn't mean it isn't happening *somewhere*. We've got to go on looking. Unless it's idiopathic, but those cases are very rare."

"Oh?"

"I mean, unless the outward physical signs of the fits don't have a source within the brain but come about for other reasons instead. Purely psychological factors, for instance."

"I see." She frowned.

He could tell she remembered his warning about what he'd do if the problem proved to be psychological, not organic. But why was she so reticent about those early days?

"We're going to cover everything systematically," he went on. "I'm afraid I'm going to ask Jonathan to stay in for another couple of days. We'll take a brain X-ray—quite routine. And

I'm sorry, Jonathan, but you'll have to put up with that contraption on your head for another day, too."

The boy nodded and looked down at the floor. "I know you don't believe me, but it did happen. It wasn't a dream. I wasn't inventing."

Lawrence studied the abject figure. The boy's conviction was surely right; his condition was not idiopathic but an organic malfunction of the brain itself.

21

Frank's regular routine in the evenings on holiday was to sit in front of the fire, a whisky in his hand, and go through the ritual of deciding to give it all up and scratch a living off the land. But this time it had been different; staring into the flickering embers he'd found his thoughts back in Bedford, with Jonathan. Why hadn't the boy turned up for the meeting? He was still uneasy about having left him in Lawrence's hands. Besides, after what the psychiatrist had said at the golf club, he wasn't so sure about his own theory. Fine, he could imagine Jonathan inventing a transference personality, but why a mentally subnormal one? What was this sinister disease Lawrence had spoken about, MBD?

Yet, as he neared the town, his climbing gear stowed in the trunk and an exhausted Dog in the back, he succumbed to routine holiday nostalgia. He wasn't looking forward to going back to work. What a waste of his new fitness to spend the days cooped up in stuffy cars and offices! It helped to pass life, but what *kind* of life? Who was it all for? The empty house was his answer: no one. Nobody *needed* him. What was the point of work if it wasn't *for* someone?

He recognized the post-vacation melancholy, and, besides, it wasn't entirely true: Jonathan needed him. He looked at the time; it was too late to call Lawrence. He ran through the accumulated mail, pushing the bills and circulars into a drawer, then went downstairs to find something to eat. A stench of rancid milk hit him as he opened the fridge door and he shut it quickly. The bread in the bin was mouldy, his stomach rebelled at the thought of sardines on toast and the water was too cold for a bath. He took a whisky to bed and, with the electric blanket on, settled down with some of his books on psychiatry.

Minimal brain dysfunction, he learned, was a made-up disease used to refer to children whose behavior adults found troublesome: untidiness, nail-biting, masturbation, not attending in class, being restless or impulsive. Hyperactivity, or what was known in his day as high jinks. The standard treatise on MBD listed ninety-nine such symptoms. It came down to one thing: the inability of parents and teachers to manage unruly children was no longer their fault, nor society's fault, nor even really the child's, but the chemistry of his brain. Two million schoolchildren in the States were on manageability drugs. In Britain it was maybe fifty thousand, and doubling every three years. The fact there was not one shred of hard scientific evidence to support the idea of an organic disease didn't seem to stop the mass feeding of Western youth with psychoactive drugs . . .

First thing in the morning Frank phoned Lawrence. He wanted to see him.

"Ah, I'm glad you've called, Frank," said the psychiatrist. "I wanted a word, too. We've had a slight set-back with Jonathan. Come over for a drink tonight and I'll tell you about it."

"Why, what's happened, what's the trouble?"

"I'll explain this evening. Sorry, I can't stop now: my turn to drop the kids off to school."

Alarmed, Frank dialled Sarah's number, but he put the receiver down before it could ring. What kind of a set-back? What was the trouble? All through the day he felt a thick knot of anxiety tightening in his stomach. When he went out to the supermarket he left the front door unlocked and twice in the afternoon he went down to check the river, but there was no sign of Jonathan.

Six o'clock came and he was punctually on Lawrence's doorstep. The man arrived late. He took him into his study, cleared a cat off the armchair and put a large whisky into his hand. Drawing up his own chair so that they were both sitting on the same side of the desk, he proceeded to tell him about the fire and Jonathan's admission to hospital. Frank listened, paralyzed. This was all his fault. He shouldn't have let Lawrence force the pace in the sessions; he shouldn't have gone away just at the moment they were turning critical.

"That's the sum of it," concluded the psychiatrist. "I wanted to tell you face to face so there'd be no misunderstandings."

Frank spoke slowly. "But I thought we'd decided it was a case of personality transference. Something strictly psychological."

"I'm not so sure now."

"But it's obvious! This Tommy business is to do with the twin he lost. We agreed that before."

"What you don't know is that it all started before Jonathan knew he'd had a twin at all."

Frank swallowed. "Then there's this business of MBD. I've been reading up on it, and . . ."

"Now, wait. First things first. Is it physiological or not? That's the first question. If it is, we're dealing with one personality, not two. At this stage, my presumptive diagnosis is temporal lobe epilepsy. That fits well enough with his odd speech during the fits, without going so far as talking of multiple personalities. You commonly get aphasia with minor seizures. When he says 'Dad,' for instance, it might just be a semantic substitution for some other word."

"Come on! When he's in the Tommy *persona* it's not gobbledygook. He talks like a complete and integrated personality. A bloody odd one, I grant, but what he's saying makes sense, internal sense. Anyway, you said the EEGs didn't show anything up, so how can you say what kind of epilepsy it is?"

Lawrence grew uncomfortable. "I called it my presumptive diagnosis," he stressed. "I'm running the EEGs again precisely to check. Something's going on in there. I mean to find what, and where."

"What in the meantime?"

"I'm reducing his medication . . ."

"The Luminal? That'll only provoke the seizures. Is that *right*?"

"And I'm having X-rays and scans taken . . ."

"Let's get back to the sessions. I'm not sure I approve of these tests. You're just poking around, not knowing what you're looking for."

Two red spots glowed high on Lawrence's smooth cheeks and he seemed to find it hard to control his breathing.

"Look, Frank," he said tartly, "you'd do as well to understand this. Things have changed. Jonathan is in hospital, he's part of a system, he's my patient. By rights I shouldn't even be discussing his case with you."

"Piss off. I brought him to you in the first place."

"That's no longer relevant."

"Not *relevant*?"

"I'm not prepared to argue over it, Frank. Just leave the medical side to me, OK?"

"But I have a right to know what's going on."

Lawrence rose to his feet. "What right? You have no right whatsoever. You're not the boy's father. You only came into the picture by running him over, if you remember."

"Christ, Lawrence, what's come over you?"

"Wake up, Frank. It's a whole different ball game now. Jonathan's had a history of mental disturbance and he's just had a major crisis. He tried to burn down his home, and whatever name you want to use that makes him a delinquent. He's now been referred to me officially and, as my patient, he's my responsibility and mine only. You wouldn't expect to be involved in my other cases, so why should I make an exception here just because you happen to know the boy? Go and visit him if you must, but don't start putting ideas into his head. I'm gaining his confidence and I don't want you stirring things up. Do you read me?"

Frank knocked back his drink and stood up too. "Loud and clear," he said testily. "I think you're mishandling the whole thing. I only hope to God the wretched kid doesn't suffer because of it."

Lawrence's manner suddenly eased. "Look, I understand how you feel. Fine, be his friend, screw his mum, anything you fancy. Only leave doctor's work to the doctor. Hey, come along, let's see what Fiona's got for grub. You'll stay to supper, won't you?"

They'd said he'd be an out-patient and that meant living at home. But every time they did a test they seemed to want to do it over again. The days were passing and no one was telling him when he could go home. Each visiting-time his mum brought some more of his things over—clothes, books, games. What had he let himself in for?

Jonathan didn't like the nurses; they made him uneasy. He could see through their false cheerfulness and sometimes he thought they resented the time Lawrence spent on his case—or "Dr. Miller," as they tried to get him to call him. Worse, whenever the shift changed there'd be a lot of low talk in the office at the entrance to the ward and he'd see them staring at him above the glazed partition. When they came to take his temperature or make his bed, they looked at him oddly, in the way visitors at home sometimes did, and he'd wonder if he'd had a tiny spell without realizing it. He took to trying to keep his face as expressionless as possible; perhaps, that way, no one would notice that he was mad.

The morning of the CAT scan he was taken along to Radiology, where Lawrence joined them. He tried to behave normally and show an interest in the machine—a large cylindrical unit with a hole in the center that lay at the end of a narrow bed.

"The idea is to X-ray the soft tissue of the brain," Lawrence was explaining. "We're going to take eight scans, rather like slices of bread. You stick your head in the hole, but it doesn't hurt in the least. No injections or anything. Only, you mustn't wriggle."

"What does it show?"

"Well, if you'd had a stroke, the areas where the brain cells had died would fill up with fluid, and they'd show up as dark patches on the film. I'm not expecting anything like that, though; strokes can cause seizures, but I'm sure this isn't your case. We're only doing the scan to eliminate one possibility. Ready?"

"Ready."

Nervously, Jonathan lay down and placed his head in the cylinder. The machine clicked and whirred. He formulated on the tip of his mind the rhyme he'd recite if he felt the first stirrings in his head. Somehow he didn't want to be caught having a spell, though he knew Lawrence was waiting for it to happen again. He felt sticky with fear, but the scan didn't take more than a few minutes. Lawrence helped him up and put a fatherly arm around his shoulder.

"We're going to put that contraption on your head again for another twenty-four hours, Jonathan. The last time we didn't get any positive readings." He paused. "You have a watch? Good. When you get back to the EEG room I want you to get a pen and paper ready and note down the exact time you get any of your . . . spells. Try and write it down the moment you feel it coming on. It's important. Will you do that for me?"

Jonathan looked at the man and nodded. "When will I be going back home?"

"Oh, just in a day or so. It rather depends."

Depends on what? He couldn't ask. Besides, there was something else he wanted to ask. "Frank will be back home by now," he began. "I'd like to see him. Will you ask him to look in?"

"I'm sure he'll be very busy catching up on his work. You'll be out of here before he has time to come, I expect." Lawrence waited for him to meet his eye before continuing. "By the way, I'd rather you didn't go telling Frank about everything we're doing together here. Outsiders often get wrong ideas. It's often best to keep mum."

Jonathan was startled. He tried to see behind the sympathetic smile on Lawrence's face. Why shouldn't he tell Frank? But he'd decided to behave, to co-operate, to act normal.

"All right," he said in a small voice.

"Good lad. I knew you'd get the point. See you later, old chap."

Jonathan followed the nurse back to the EEG room. She chatted all the way but he wasn't listening. What was going wrong? He didn't feel any better. These tests weren't curing him. Was Lawrence afraid Frank would see that and make a fuss?

When alone, the headset strapped over his skull, he took a pen and paper and wrote a letter to Frank. He folded it carefully, Scotch-taped a makeshift envelope around it and addressed it. He waited for one of the cleaners, a fat black lady whom he liked, and entrusted it to her to post. Hurry, hurry, he prayed.

That Sunday morning Frank phoned the hospital to enquire about visiting times but was told that Jonathan was having an EEG and couldn't be seen for twenty-four hours. He badly wanted to make contact of some kind and scoured the house for a small gift, eventually finding the old bone-handled penknife he'd had as a boy, complete with spike for digging stones out of horses' hooves. It was a perfectly useless present for a child in hospital but it held a sentimental value for him and, besides, it gave him a reason for visiting Sarah. He drove over to her house without phoning first.

Sarah drew up in her car as he arrived, obviously just from church. She wore an old cashmere wrap-around coat and a headscarf, and her strong face was set firm and purposeful. But she hesitated when she saw Frank. He felt like a trespasser. They met at the gate.

"I'm so sorry to hear about Jonathan," he began, searching her blue eyes for signs of empathy. "How is he?"

She hardly thawed. With gloved hands she fumbled in her bag for her latch-key. It fell onto the frosty pavement; their hands met briefly and awkwardly.

"I suppose your friend Dr. Miller has told you what you've started with those . . . sessions of yours," she said coldly. "I'm sure you don't need to ask me how Jonathan is, either. He'll have told you himself."

She went up the path, leaving Frank trailing uncomfortably behind. A sudden gust of wind filled the air with small flurries of frost from the trees. She turned on the doorstep and they faced one another, in deadlock.

"It really wasn't like that at all," he began. "We can't stand here and discuss it. Let me come in."

"Very well."

Indoors, she took her coat off to reveal a woollen dress that hugged her figure. Frank was momentarily distracted. But she started in at once.

"Frank, I'm not stupid. And I don't, frankly, want to discuss it, after all I've been through recently." She cast a glance across the room; decorators' sheets still covered the furniture and in the air hung the residual stench of burned plastic.

"But you've got it wrong, Sarah. I know what you're thinking . . ."

"It's obvious!" Her eyes blazed suddenly. "You decided to have a go at what you thought was the problem. You wangled your way into his confidence and started giving him these bogus therapy sessions behind my back. Well, you can see how successful you've been. That's why he's where he is now."

"I did it out of the best motives, believe me. I . . . love the boy."

"Love? Don't use that word! Anyway, look where it's landed him, this love of yours."

"Christ, you're an unreasonable bitch!"

She froze him with a look of cold pity. Her voice quavered. "Please go."

He nodded and went over to the door, but stood with his hand on the handle. "I can't leave you like this," he said. "I'm very sorry for what I said. And I'm sorry if anything I've done has made things worse for Jonathan." There was no more to say. He wanted to add he was sorry because he was fond of her, too, and her anger at him upset him. He shrugged helplessly. "I'm sorry," he repeated once again.

"I accept your apology," she replied formally. "I think you should go home, now."

He went down the path, full of self-anger. He revved the car harshly. Well, he'd tried his best. If that wasn't enough, then stuff the lot of them. He wasn't going to do any more.

He put his foot down hard, spinning the back tires on the frosty road, and pulled out in front of an oncoming car. He drove petulantly and badly all the way home and then took Dog for a long walk to calm himself. He was acting like a willful child who couldn't get his way; he should be ashamed. Anyway, his work began again in earnest the following day; at least there he was wanted, and his efforts recognized.

22

"Dear Frank," the letter read. "I'm in hospital. Something terrible happened, but it's OK now. I've got to see you. They're letting me out tomorrow (?). I'll come Friday afternoon. The river, like usual. OK? Best not to tell Lawrence, he's being funny. Must see you. Please be there. Yours, Jonathan"

That short note threw Frank into a mixture of delight and anxiety. Troubled, desperate for the days to pass, he launched himself into his work. He accomplished long feats of driving, taking back the Christmas returns from one customer and selling in the spring list to another. He spent a full evening helping the Deanshanger bookseller with his year-end stocktake and, once back home, he drew up plans to redecorate his study in bright, cheerful colors. He worried endlessly about Jonathan. Lawrence was surely on the wrong track, expecting to find the answer in some malfunctioning of brain cells. Bloody, blink-

ered scientists, he cursed; they take no account of the im-
material, the soul. We are surrounded by life, yet what scientist
armed with scalpel, laser or microscope has ever defined life,
ever put a finger on it?

One of Lawrence's remarks kept recurring in his thoughts:
Jonathan had invented Tommy *before* he knew about Philip.
Far from suggesting an organic condition, surely this was the
proof it was psychological! It was obvious. Something critical
had occurred around the moment of birth to make Jonathan
adopt a twin personality.

He waited impatiently for the appointed afternoon. The day
was cold, crisp and clear. He found Jonathan sitting by himself,
crouching over his rod and huddled deep in his parka, his fair
hair poking out of a fur-trapper's hat. Dog rushed up, overturn-
ing a can of bait. Jonathan got up. He looked paler, more
drawn and his eyes had that hollow, distant, darting quality he
associated with pain, Cathy's pain. He drew the boy close and
hugged him.

"Christ, lad, it's good to see you. I missed you."

"And me you."

"Here, what's all this nonsense about hospital?"

He listened to Jonathan's story of the crisis, the fire and
why he'd opted to go into hospital for tests. He bent down to
help pick up the redworms. "What exactly are they doing to
you?" he asked.

The boy shrugged. "Oh, just tests," he replied. There was a
pause.

"Tell you what, pack up your gear and we'll go for a walk.
Then we can have tea. I cleaned the whole of Bedford out of
ginger cake."

They deposited the basket and rod by his bicycle and walked
along the towpath alongside the pollarded willows. Frank described his climbing holiday and Jonathan agreed to find a way
of getting his mother's permission to go with him next time.

Finally he broached the subject on his mind. "Tell me honestly," he said. "What's it *really* like when you get the spells?"

The boy kicked his feet through the leaves before replying. In a quiet voice he said, "It's terrifying."

Frank said nothing.

"It's like being taken over," he went on. "I can't help it, it just comes over me. I try and fight it off, but mostly it's no use. It hurts, inside. It's like he's asleep there, in my head, all the time, and sometimes he wakes up. Then he just smothers me, takes me over."

"Go on."

"It's stupid. I know Tommy doesn't exist, he can't exist. But he does, in my head. I haven't invented him, he's there. I can't kill him, I can't do anything. That's why I know I'm mad."

"But, Jonathan, you're not mad . . ."

"I am!" he replied with sudden vehemence. "I know what madness is."

Frank let them walk on in silence for a while. They passed a solitary angler and, to divert the boy's attention, he remarked on the man's up-to-date tackle.

"Terrific gear," agreed Jonathan, "but hasn't a clue. Imagine sticking reds onto a hook that way! And his swivel and bead's hopeless for a leger stop." He went on to deplore foul-hooking fish and to praise the new carbon reels.

"Maybe you should have a new reel for your birthday," said Frank, disingenuously spotting his opportunity. "Is it soon?"

"I'll be twelve on March the ninth."

"That's not so very long." He went on easily, "I suppose you were—what?—eight when you left Warwick."

Jonathan nodded.

Frank remembered Lawrence telling him there was no record of the boy being born in the Warwick area. He was careful to put his question casually. "Where were you before then?"

"Well, I was actually born in Buckingham, but I don't remember the place. We moved when I was tiny."

Frank's heart gave a small leap. He'd landed his fish, even if he'd foul-hooked it.

Twilight was creeping up over the river and they turned around and headed for home. The solitary angler had caught something. "Bream," confided Jonathan under his breath. "A whopper. He's a lucky bloke. They mainly go for paste or corn."

"Maybe you'd have got it if you'd kept on."

The boy smiled. "There's always other times."

"Yes. Plenty of them."

"Birth, copulation and death," mused Frank to himself, "and all under one roof."

He'd reshuffled his itinerary so that early the following week he found himself in Buckingham with an hour to spare. He went to the modern registry building. Standing in the lobby he surveyed the list of offices. Births were registered on the ground floor, marriages were conducted on the floor above and the registry of deaths was housed on the top floor. There was even a marriage guidance council quartered in between. Human life was simply an ascent through this building.

He began on the ground floor and readily established the first fact he was after. Knowing the year and date, he quickly turned up the file copy of Jonathan's birth certificate. It was pasted into a large bound book and, as he'd expected, registered the twin birth on the same slip: Philip Andrew Hall.

Ascending to the top floor, he had less luck. Deaths were filed in date order and there was no cross-referencing by name. He went through the crop of dead for the days following the twins' birth. An epidemic must have smitten Buckinghamshire that month, for it took him almost half an hour to cover two weeks. But by the end he'd established one thing: Philip Andrew Hall hadn't died in the first fortnight of his life.

The registrar, a frail but kindly man, was perturbed to see a customer leaving unsatisfied. He took down the baby's name and date of birth in a careful copperplate hand and promised to do a search himself. Frank was to come back in ten days' time. With a warm word of thanks he left, praying the old man wouldn't have become an addition to his own lists by the time he returned.

Some time later, with school in full swing, Jonathan was called into hospital again for a further series of EEGs. His mother had obtained a sick note from the GP the other side of town, saying he had suspected glandular fever. That was the story she was going to tell at school.

This time they shaved his head. They did it behind a curtain at one end of the children's ward. The nurse with the bristly legs took charge. First she used large scissors, then finished with an electric razor. At the end of four minutes the floor around the chair was carpeted with his fair hair. When the curtain was drawn back his head felt cold in the draft. Some of the boys sniggered when they saw.

He followed the nurse in his dressing-gown down the corridor to the EEG room where the senior resident was once again waiting with the equipment. On the way he caught sight of his reflection in a glass door and started. He tried to cover his head up with his hands, but the nurse laughed and told him not to be so silly.

In the early evening of the same day, when the taste of bitter almonds again rose in his mouth, he felt too nervous and insecure to try and fight it back. He knew he'd given in. Helplessly he witnessed his whole being submit gradually to the alien grasp until it was overwhelmed entirely.

Sarah used the sick note to keep him at home, off school. It was inconceivable to go like that. Heads were shaved for ringworm or lice, not for glandular fever. Hair in winter grew slowly and it would be weeks before it would even pass as a crew-cut. She bought him a knitted balaclava; that would do for outdoors, but not for the classroom. What should be done? He couldn't stay away from school indefinitely. She was furious with Lawrence for not warning her; at least she'd have had time to plan. And she was haunted by her first sight of him when she'd gone to collect him from hospital, the image of a retardate or a victim of the concentration camps. It had made her almost physically sick, and at church that Sunday she prayed God for guidance with a fervency she'd seldom felt before. What could she do but pray?

But early the following week Lawrence rang again; still unsatisfied with the results, he wanted to run more tests. This time Sarah wasn't taking chances and made an appointment to see him herself. She met him in his office, through the small high windows of which she caught frightening glimpses of the heads of patients moving past: slack-jawed, drooling, squinting, glazedly staring, cross-eyed, fidgeting.

"We haven't exhausted all the physiological tests yet," said Lawrence, stroking his smooth cheek, "I've booked him on the PET scanner in London next week. It shows the metabolic turnover rate of the brain. We use it mostly for detecting tumors, but we might get something interesting on your lad."

"All this trial and error worries me," said Sarah in exasperation. "He's in and out, in and out, the whole time. Why can't you find out what's wrong? Are you competent with children?"

Lawrence held her eye calmly. "Dr. Cameron is closely involved."

"But he's a pediatrician. I mean a properly qualified child psychiatrist."

"My dear, we're dealing with a human brain here. At Jonathan's age his brain is essentially the same as an adult's. If we were talking psychoanalysis, I might agree. But it's a matter of brain chemistry at the moment."

"I see." Sarah frowned. Had she miscalculated? She'd assumed the man was taking a professional risk in taking on the case himself without involving a child specialist. She returned to the offensive. "I thought you said it was electrical, anyway. A short-circuit or something."

Lawrence perched on the side of his desk. "You know we've run EEGs endlessly. We tried to stimulate seizures photically, but that didn't work. His fits come from a different source. I can't see it's electrical; that's the puzzling thing. The other night he had a massive attack. We had him wired up. All we got were readings consistent with a high state of arousal. Nothing like an epileptic fit."

"What about the X-rays you took?"

"The CAT scan? Well, I did have hopes there. We know schizophrenics can literally have malformations in the structure of the mid-brain. We didn't find anything of that kind with Jonathan, so it's hardly a gross structural problem."

"Then what's this thing in London supposed to show?"

"It should reveal which parts of the brain are unusually active, neurochemically speaking." He paused. "That's pretty much all there's left in the arsenal before we go to something more intrusive."

"Intrusive?"

"Well, we'd be talking next of taking a CSF sample—cerebrospinal fluid, the stuff the brain floats in. One usually reserves a spinal tap if one suspects the brain is hemorrhaging, but it could throw up the presence of abnormal chemicals in the fluid."

Sarah felt her mouth go dry. She said nothing.

"After that there are the more radical solutions. One might well consider doing a muscle biopsy as a next step, though only if we'd pinpointed the *focus* would we really know how to treat it. Finally there's either drugs or fullscale surgery. Don't be alarmed! Surgery is always the very last resort. It would take a massive deterioration in Jonathan's intellectual performance before one took that drastic step. If the condition is stable, medication is usually sufficient."

"Drugs? But they've done nothing so far except maybe dampen down the attacks. All this poking around is, frankly, terrifying. I wonder if we've really progressed since the dark ages."

"We can only prescribe drugs when we know what the cause is," replied Lawrence in a rehearsed tone. "You wouldn't want me to take him through the whole pharmacopeia on the off-chance one drug might work, would you?"

Sarah felt weary. She'd exhausted all the alternatives. In a resigned tone she said, "Well, what do you want me to do, then?"

"See he gets up to London for his appointment. Here's a card; it's at the Hammersmith. Reassure him there won't be any pain. Just a touch of radiation sickness afterwards, but that'll pass."

"Radiation sickness?" Sarah sat upright.

"Oh, nothing dangerous. There's a minute radioactive dose in the gas he'll breathe, just as a marker. He might be injected with the isotope in a glucose solution. Either way it's pretty harmless."

"My God," she breathed quietly. "I wasn't expecting it to get this far when I let you take him in. How long is it all going to take before he's better?"

"My dear, must I repeat? We can't start the cure until we've found the cause. This is a particularly difficult one. I'd say one of the most difficult I've ever had to treat."

"But how *long*?"

"You must think in terms of weeks, if not months."

She drew in her breath sharply and bit her lip. The most

trivial implication was the one that first came to her mind. "I'd better arrange something with the school."

"I'll give you a note that will cover everything," he replied smoothly. He saw her to the door. "Believe me, it's the only way. Medicine works on cause and effect. One must eliminate the possibilities logically, one by one. We live in the age of reason."

She gave a slight shudder and didn't reply. She turned at the door. "I suppose I should be thanking you. Somehow I find that rather hard."

Lawrence held the door open for her. "I understand. It's not easy for you. But I'm glad you came in."

"You're a cool customer, Dr. Miller, aren't you," she said as she left. "I only hope to God you're right."

In the hospital corridor she found herself wondering why she didn't trust him. He was a man of great experience and considerable local reputation. Why shouldn't he solve a problem that she'd spent years unsuccessfully over? He'd called it difficult. Perhaps it was *that* difficult.

For the third night in a row Lawrence phoned Fiona to say he'd be home too late to say goodnight to the children. That went against principle and practice and was a measure of how taxing and yet enthralling was the problem Jonathan posed. Alone in his office and away from the immediate demands of the department and his outlying clinics, he could stop, take stock and think. Time and again he ran through the results of the tests and his puzzlement intensified. What the *hell* was going on? It defied reason and analysis. But he was determined to get there. He'd crack it somehow, or else it'd crack him.

Frank might have left it a month before returning to Buckingham had it not been for the shock when Jonathan cycled over almost two weeks later. It was hot in the mill-house and at first the boy refused to take off his balaclava. When he finally did, Frank understood why.

"I've had a haircut," said Jonathan with a strange, forced laugh.

Frank was shaken. What the hell was Lawrence up to, disfiguring the boy? Jonathan was sensitive and ashamed. His talk was rambling and veered on and off the point in the same way that his eyes never seemed to rest on any one thing for more than a second. In a garbled fashion Frank learned about the tests he'd been taking and the PET scan that he was due to undergo next. He was in a state Frank could only describe as chronic fright. Quite abruptly, before their accustomed walk by the river, he stood up and left, refusing a lift. Frank followed in his car, out of sight, to make sure he got safely home.

Furious and frustrated, he at once set about rearranging his week's program so that he'd be back in Buckingham as soon as possible.

The day he chose was an early February morning, bright and clear and with a hint of spring in the air. He enjoyed the drive through the crisp countryside. In the interim the registrar of deaths had managed to stave off *rigor mortis* and welcomed him warmly.

"I have the entry here for you," he said proudly. "It took me a considerable amount of searching. You said you believed the infant was deceased in March. The actual date was in June. You've picked a rather curious one. Look for yourself."

Frank examined the record of the death of Philip Andrew Hall. Under the heading marked *Name and Surname of Informant* the following was written: "Certificate received from Dr. Morrison, Coroner for Buckinghamshire County. Postmortem carried out by Dr. Bailey, pathologist. Report disclosed exact cause of death as unascertainable. Coroner's inquest held on June twentieth."

He turned to the registrar. "*Inquest?* I don't understand."

"The death cannot have been due to natural causes."

"But a coroner's inquest?"

"Dr. Bailey is from the Home Office. He's not the county pathologist. That means there must have been a suspicion of unlawful killing."

"But it says the cause of death couldn't be ascertained."

"Perhaps the body was in too bad a state."

"My God."

"Pardon?"

"My goodness."

The registrar inclined his head sympathetically. "If it's a family matter, you could always try the library of the *Chronicle*. I don't recall the case myself but the newspaper is sure to have written it up."

Frank came out of his momentary daze. "Of course. I'll do just that. Thank you. You've been most kind."

The back-numbers office of the *Chronicle* was less helpful. Two girls sat far away from the counter discussing a boyfriend and doing more filing of nails than of press-clippings. Frank rang the bell and one reluctantly came forward.

"The Junes are down in Rebinding, ain't they, Liz?" she called to her friend. It was obviously their standard routine.

"I'll go down to Rebinding then," said Frank. "It's very important."

He could see her weighing up the alternatives. "Hang on," she said. "Which year did you say?"

Fifteen minutes later she sauntered back, carrying a large-format folder in which the month's papers were clipped. Frank turned to the date closest to June the twentieth. A small front-page article was entitled "INQUEST HELD ON MISSING HALL BABY" and referred him to a quarter-page inside. He took it over to a table and read carefully. His pulse was rising.

He skimmed it quickly for the essential facts.

Philip Hall, a six-week-old baby, has been snatched from his pram in Victoria Road, Buckingham two months earlier.

His mother, Mrs. Sarah Hall, appeals for witnesses. The boy is one of twins. The search is extended to Oxfordshire and Berkshire. The police make door-to-door enquiries, frogmen dredge the gravel pits, volunteers comb the woods.

Then two girls, out exercising their dog, come upon a body under a plastic fertilizer sack in a small woodland. It is barely two miles from the snatch. The children receive a reward. The mother is unavailable for comment. The police treat the case as death by misadventure. And the coroner holds an inquest. The garments identify the body as that of Philip Andrew Hall. But after two months in the heat of early summer the body is too badly decomposed. . . .

Frank sat locked rigid until finally one of the girls called out to him that they were closing. Then he rose unsteadily to his feet, his muscles stiff and his jaw hurting where he'd been clenching it. He walked out into the fading sunlight and went to a coffee-bar. Things were falling into place.

Sarah. She was the key; he'd always sensed that. He imagined what she'd gone through: the guilt, the self-hate, the anxiety, the despair, the cruel wait and finally the appalling truth. No wonder she clutched Jonathan so tightly to her; no wonder she was so neurotic about defending her privacy from outsiders. What mother wouldn't be overprotective of her remaining son after all that? And to have to endure it alone, too, with a husband that left her. For what reason? he asked himself, thinking how attractive she was. When finally he returned to his car he felt his heart swell with pity and his feelings for Jonathan grow to embrace her too. At last he understood. No wonder she behaved towards him as she did.

And what about the effect on Jonathan? With all that pressure on him, a sensitive child like that could easily invent an *alter ego*. Especially if Sarah wouldn't talk about it, maybe even strongly repressed it.

This explained a lot. And it showed that Lawrence was barking up the wrong tree. It wasn't organic but psychological, however sophistically the man argued there was no real difference. The difference was real and tangible: the tests could now stop.

Yes, yes, yes! he exclaimed aloud. Throwing the car into gear he put his foot hard down on the accelerator. However, despite all his phone calls, he wasn't able to see Lawrence until three days later.

23

Jonathan turned his cheek aside as his mother kissed him goodbye in the waiting-room of Hammersmith Hospital, for he could already taste the bitter almonds. He asked the nurse for the lavatory. There he locked himself in a cubicle and kept flushing the toilet so as to drown the noise of his desperate humming.

Someone other than he opened the door and looked out cautiously. He was in a long corridor that smelled of carbolic and kitchens. A woman in nurse's uniform seemed to be waiting for him. Suddenly she pinioned him by the elbow and steered him away. People in white coats passed with trolleys. Everywhere he saw signs with long words he couldn't read properly. He felt like a trapped animal. He didn't belong here. He belonged in fields, on the farm.

The nurse marched him into a small, hot room where more

men in white coats made him take off his jacket, loosen his shirt and lie down on a hard, high bed. He didn't trust their smiles. This was punishment of some kind.

They taped a mask over his mouth and nose and told him to breathe normally. Then they pushed the bed so that his head was in the center of a huge ringlike machine with nozzles and pipes like the beam of a crop-sprayer. He became aware of a whirring noise and a rapid series of clicks. They were shooting rays into his head, to punish it for having thoughts.

He had to get free. Violently he ripped off the mask and struggled off the bed, landing on the floor on all fours. He shouted, he spat, he clawed. They came for him. He was strong and quick, but they were stronger still. They strapped his arms to his sides, forced his head into a brace and carried him back to the bed. He lay pinned down, the mask jammed roughly over his face, while the machine whirred and clicked and he could feel it atomizing his brain.

Three days later Lawrence was handed a large yellow hospital envelope bearing a London postmark. He cleared a space on his desk and pulled open the tag. The results of Jonathan's PET scan came in the form of eight large color plates, each showing a slice of brain looked at vertically downwards so that the two hemispheres and the ventrical cavities within them were clearly distinct. A color-separation technique represented in blue the areas where the brain's oxygen uptake had been low and the radioactive isotope had stayed concentrated. Tumors would show up in this color. By contrast, epileptic *foci*, having high metabolic rates, would show up in red.

Lawrence wasn't completely familiar with the new technology and spent some time examining each plate before turning his attention to the attached report. At first he didn't see the small bright red spot, no more than half a centimeter across, somewhat to the center-left of the sixth plate. The report only referred to it in passing, implying the neurologists at Hammersmith considered it just some kind of aberrant result. Its name, Hirschfield's ganglion, sent Lawrence leafing through his brain atlas. He could see it lay deep in the hippocampus, the oldest part of the brain, but its function was speculative; it had probably grown vestigial through evolution or it might merely be one of the many areas in which the brain was so surprisingly redundant. At all events it had no scientifically mapped function.

But that wasn't good enough: it was just such a rare abnormality that he was seeking. He took the plate over to the window and stared at the small bright red spot for a minute. Could this be it? A sense of elation crept over him. He called up the consultant neurologist downstairs and within a few minutes that normally dour man was infected with the same puzzled excitement. Lawrence went back to his office bearing a fat reference book on brain anatomy.

Arriving to find Frank waiting in his room, he felt a moment's annoyance.

"Frank, I must ask you not to drop in out of the blue like this. My professional time is my patients'. You can always get me at home. Let's try and keep business and pleasure apart, shall we?"

Frank stood with his back to the filing-cabinet. "This is business," he said.

"Don't tell me: another theory about Jonathan. I don't want to hear any more."

"This one you will, though. I've made a breakthrough. Here, look at this." He pulled a photocopy of a newspaper article out of his pocket and held it out. Lawrence sighed, looked at his watch and took the paper ill-humoredly. He read it quickly.

"Very nice, Frank. But what does it prove?"

"It's obvious! This explains everything—Sarah's suppressed

guilt feelings, all that neurotic protectiveness, Jonathan's need for a transference image, everything! Can't you see it?" He sounded incredulous.

"It doesn't prove a single bloody thing."

The psychiatrist saw the expression on Frank's face and said wearily, "Oh, Christ." He put his head around the door and asked his assistant to get two coffees from the machine, fumbling in his pockets for the right coins. "Frank, I'm giving you ten minutes. That's all. OK?"

"My God, you don't seem to *realize* . . ."

"Sit down, man, shut up and listen. You've got to realize you're out of your depth and you should stick to peddling books."

He opened the window a fraction; the room was stuffy and Frank's presence made him feel flustered. He should have expected this; twice, the day before, he'd received telephone messages from Frank and hadn't called back. The man was obsessive about this Jonathan business; it was coming between them. He waited until the assistant had brought the coffee, then took a breath and faced the truculent man before him.

"I have a theory and I've set about testing it. A theory's valid until it's proven wrong. The tests so far, until now, have shown nothing. But because I haven't found evidence *for* the theory doesn't mean there's any evidence *against* it. Until there's disproof, I'm bound to stick to it. That's the way science works, any schoolboy knows that."

Frank nodded, glaring.

"You have a naive, Cartesian view of the brain. You think of it as the ghost in the machine. For you, mental disorders are either psychological or mechanical. But it doesn't work like that: they are *both* things at the same time. The ghost isn't separate or distinct from the machine, nor the spirit from the body. The only difference is in the way you look at it. Your theory of an infantile trauma is just one view of the problem from one angle. It's no more valid than my theory which considers the problem fundamentally as an organic one, to do with the mechanics of the brain."

"Then yours isn't any more valid than mine, either," said Frank sourly.

"Except that I have concrete proof." Lawrence was becoming needled.

"What do you call *this*, then?" cried Frank and tapped the newspaper article.

"I'll show you what I call proof."

The psychiatrist picked up the yellow envelope and pulled out the plate showing the small red spot. He thrust it into the other man's hands and went on, "What you don't seem to appreciate is that there are levels of *hierarchy* in making diagnoses. Suppose you'd broken your leg and I asked you what was wrong. You'd tell me you fell off a ladder, you'd describe the pain or you'd demonstrate that you couldn't walk. Those are all perfectly valid responses. But if I offered you an X-ray showing the fracture itself, wouldn't you say that was a more compelling proof?"

Frank waved the plate in the air. "You're saying everything is physical. What about God and love and feelings?"

"If you're not being frivolous I'll answer you. Feelings could well exist as certain macromolecules in the brain. One day the experience of God might well turn out to be a network of amino-acids on a complex peptide chain. I don't know, I don't *have* to know. The principle's what counts."

"I don't understand what's come over you, Lawrence. You used to be the champion of psychotherapy. Are you now in favor of psycho*surgery*?"

"Look, the whole point of analysis and therapy is to get the brain to cure itself, and that means at the neuronal level. For God's sake, the brain is where it's all happening, and the brain is *matter*—neuronal, electrical, chemical matter."

Frank straightened. "OK, then, tell me what's the significance of this red splodge."

"I'm not prepared to discuss it with you. Anyway, it's too early to say."

"Too early to say? After all those EEGs and scans? After that PET thing you just did—I suppose these are the results?" He pointed to the yellow envelope. "Too bloody *late*, if you ask me."

Lawrence clenched his fists in his pockets. How the hell did Frank know it was a PET scan he'd done? He'd been talking to Jonathan. He reached for the color plate but Frank held it back and began examining it more closely. He turned it over; on the back were the notes Lawrence had made during his talk with the neurosurgeon.

"What's the Hirschfield ganglion?" he asked abruptly.

Christ, here we go, thought Lawrence. "Oh, that. Nobody really knows, actually: It's probably vestigial, like the appendix."

Lawrence laughed shortly. "The brain's not some kind of fuse-box: pull out this fuse and the lights go out in the living-room or wherever. You can take out a chunk of brain and apparently not lose any faculties. The system has an incredible amount of redundancy and duplication. Take memory, for example. You can't isolate a particular memory and cut it out. It's pretty much everywhere at the same time." He stopped, aware he'd been talking too much.

Frank's eyes hardened. "So this is where you think the boy's problem lies, in this Hirschfield thing. Don't you?"

"Forget it, Frank. It's only a theory. One of many possibilities."

"You're back-tracking. You're trying to keep me in the dark."

"Now you're being paranoid."

"Why won't anyone speak to me honestly?" cried Frank in

exasperation. "I'm not trying to make trouble. If everything's all right then I'll be the first person to be happy and shut up."

Lawrence went over to the door and held it open. "I hear you, Frank. But you'll just have to trust me for now."

Frank cast him a hard glance. "That's what you're always saying to Jonathan."

"Look, we're getting to the bottom of it all at last. Just please stop rocking the boat, OK?"

Frank stood in the doorway and said fervently, "You'll have to do better than you've been doing if you want *my* confidence."

Lawrence let the door slam behind him. Angrily he crushed the plastic cup and flung it into the bin. Damn the man, he thought. If he infects Jonathan with his mood, that'll make things really difficult. The boy's not going to like the next step and he'll need every bit of trust and goodwill he's got.

Sarah was extremely worried about Jonathan. He was taking far too long to recover from the tests in London. He was weak, demoralized, fearful and withdrawn. He could scarcely hold his food down and he lost the thread of conversations in mid-sentence. She kept him in bed, his cropped head a sorry sight above the bedclothes. He was too listless to play with his computer or the CB radio and fishing was out of the question. William delivered homework to the door, but she wouldn't let him in, saying the fever was catching. But Jonathan had missed too many classes to be able to keep up and, in a mood of helpless frustration, he seemed to be on the point of giving up the hopeless struggle.

Worse, he seemed to be losing his intellectual grip and sliding more often into a new kind of state, a penumbral world where the borderline between being Jonathan and Tommy was increasingly blurred and tenuous. He would switch between the two personalities at any second. This added to her anxiety; Lawrence had said that, in the event of a gross deterioration in intellect, brain surgery had to be considered. She tried to keep the boy alert and interested by reading to him a good deal, gleaning gossip about his school friends for him and generally appearing cheerful and lively.

But the strain was telling on her, too. Neither of them could take much more. And she felt increasingly bitter that Frank and Lawrence had betrayed her. All they'd achieved was to turn the clock back three years.

Lawrence had phoned her to report the anomaly in the Hirschfield area. The idea sounded most improbable to her. He was bent on doing still more tests: this time, a cerebrospinal tap. She asked around her colleagues at school and was horrified to be told the operation was unbelievably painful. How could Lawrence want to inflict this on the poor boy, after all he'd been through? Her faith in the psychiatrist plummeted.

At school it was no easier. Every day people inquired after Jonathan. The questions, at first kind and innocent, took on a sinister edge as she sensed her colleagues were talking behind her back. A hush seemed to fall over the staff-room when she entered. And then she learned that the first hint of truth was out. The Middle School's canteen manageress had a child in hospital and reported seeing Jonathan there, his head shaven.

When Frank called, wanting to see her, she couldn't face him again. He knew too much.

That night Jonathan's temperature rose. She sat for hours with him, reading to him when he was awake and holding his hand when he was asleep. Later she went to the bathroom, leaving his door slightly ajar. Her face was drawn and hollow in the mirror. In bed she lay rigid and tense, unable to sleep. Around her mind revolved continuously the memory Frank had provoked, the memory of that terrible day almost twelve years before.

. . .

The empty pram. That was the image on which it all focussed.

Remember Jonathan, just six weeks old, sniffling with a cold in the portable crib on the kitchen table? She recalled the odor of the house: home-baked bread, diapers, baby vomit. And the neighbor's boy, a teenager with needle punctures the length of his arms, forever coming around scrounging. The radio on full volume across the street, the windows open to let in the warm spring air. And Philip in the pram, Philip the odd one who didn't take to the nipple, out in the small strip of front garden.

It was a normal midday. The garbage truck had come to collect refuse. An ice-cream van pulled up two doors down. The children playing in the street were called in for lunch. Nothing out of the ordinary.

It was time Philip came in. She remembered tripping over a wooden toy by the front door. The day was bright and dazzled her. Half-way down the flagstones she noticed the front gate swinging gently in the wind. "I didn't leave that open," she thought. The pram's hood was towards her and she walked around to the front of it. She reached in for her baby boy, her child Achilles.

The pram was empty. Empty coverlet, empty blankets. A dent in the pillow where the head had been. Warmth where the body had lain. And the streets quite deserted, the world unseeing, the act unseen.

Her first thought: "This is a mistake, it's the wrong garden, the wrong pram." Then, "It's obvious: he's been crying and the neighbor's girl has taken him in next door."

Then, quite suddenly, with utter clarity, came the certitude of disaster. She remembered walking back indoors, breaking into a run, tearing up the stairs, rampaging through the house, howling *where is my baby boy, where has he got to?* And then screaming. The whole of her body turning inside out at the scream.

Later she was to see her baby everywhere, at supermarket

checkouts, on boards outside police stations, on bus shelters and telegraph poles. A thousand pictures of the boy, each bearing the single, hateful word, MISSING.

Then the long wait. Waiting for a ransom note pasted together from newspaper lettering. Waiting for clues from the local radio appeal. Waiting while one lead after another proved to be a hoax. During this time she couldn't let Jonathan out of her sight. She watched over him as he slept. She would not allow strangers near him. She scarcely slept herself, she lost weight and grew ill.

The news came finally.

The police officer in charge thought it better she didn't meet the two children who'd found the body, and he firmly discouraged her from seeing it; little remained after the foxes and sharp-toothed predators of the countryside had worked on it those long weeks. But she did identify the clothing: there was no mistaking the pale blue bonnet, the red jump-suit and the socks with white ribbon laces.

Her husband's drinking grew heavier and they fought frequently. One day he abruptly walked out. It was then that she packed two suitcases and took the folding pram on a bus and went to find a new life in Warwick. And, later, from there to find another new life in Bedford. Where would it all end?

24

The local library shelved the brain between arthritis and cancer; its stock comprised three titles. Only in one was the Hirschfield ganglion mentioned—a minor cell area in the hippocampus. Under "hippocampus" he read about Vinogradova's discovery of special cells which could count, and those Sokolov had identified which could retain a pattern of stimuli given to them, then repeat it endlessly. There were other cells in this area which gave the brain a spatial map of its surroundings and would only fire when the person was pointing in a particular direction. There was even a suggestion that traces of magnetite had been found there. Magnetite? Frank was driven to a scientific encyclopedia. This was an element that responded to magnetic fields. Pigeons possessed particles of magnetite just above their beaks; it was one of the things that gave them their extraordinary sense of direction. Humans possessed something similar, too, in the sinus bones of the nose. Hence the phrase, *follow your nose.*

Frank laughed curtly. "Christ, does the man think Jonathan's some bloody homing pigeon?" he said to himself. "*He's* the one who should be certified."

But the puzzle needled him for days afterwards. It wasn't until the first day of a quarterly sales meeting at head office in London that he decided he'd have one last attempt at it. If he failed this time, he'd take Lawrence's advice and stick to peddling books.

The reading-room of the British Museum library was stale with heat and the weight of learning. Frank was not a Reader; he posed as a visiting academic to get in. When his books arrived he was dismayed to find the Moscow studies incomprehensible. The only references to Hirschfield he could understand were in the context of phrenology and witchcraft. The man was, apparently, a nineteenth-century German religious fanatic who thought he'd found the source of Christ's miracle-making in the brain—in the tiny, vestigial ganglion to which he gave his name.

Frank was taken aback. "Does Lawrence fancy himself as some kind of John the Baptist, with Jonathan as the Second Coming?" he snorted. "This is crazy!"

Driving back to Oakley that night he came to the firm understanding that this absurd conclusion was the result of a fundamentally wrong approach of Lawrence's. His "scientific method" meant you took a theory and tested it until it was disproved. You'd end up with a great cure—but a dead patient, too. No, this was one of the areas where an intelligent, imaginative amateur might get there faster. Once home, Frank poured a large drink and took a sheet of paper and began to write down all the relevant facts. Maybe something would emerge from them.

· · ·

Jonathan knew Lawrence was only waiting for him to recover completely before he called him back to hospital. His fever had abated, but he was fighting to regain his spirits. He set himself to work on a new program on the Spectrum. He couldn't concentrate; everything seemed to distract and terrify him. He didn't like to stray too far from his bed, for the spells were striking now at random. Often he'd be scarcely aware of the transition in and out of the Tommy states, only his hands, numb and blue with cold, or a lingering pain in his back would remind him he'd been on the farm.

But night-times in particular were difficult, and the hour before bed worst of all. This was when the real fits now came, with their familiar pattern. And when he came out of them, sometimes on the floor but most often in bed with his mother calming him, he'd be left with a desperate sense of panic. It was a race with madness. Would he go over the edge altogether before they could get to him?

He grew to dread Lawrence's visits. One afternoon the man came and sat on the end of his bed, his forehead beaded with sweat and his small lips moist. He took Jonathan's chin in his hand and said, "You look unhappier each time I come, my boy. Cheer up. We'll soon be there."

How soon? was the question Jonathan asked himself. And in time?

With assumed cheerfulness the psychiatrist proceeded to draw a picture of the brain and spinal column. It wasn't a biology lesson: he'd come to prepare him for the next test, the cerebrospinal fluid sample.

"The whole brain is encased in a sack of fluid," he explained. "It acts as a kind of shock-absorber, as well as transporting chemicals and hormones around. The sack goes right on down inside the spine, so when we need a sample it's obviously simpler to take it from there. The procedure's quite simple. You lie curled up on your side and it's over in no time. I'm afraid it can hurt a bit, and you'll have a rotten headache for a day or two afterwards. But I'm hopeful we might find the answer there."

You're hopeful. I'm hopeful. But what hope is there?

Jonathan said nothing. When he was alone again he lay staring up at the cracks in the ceiling. It was a race. Lawrence against Tommy. *He* didn't think Lawrence was going to win.

Frank went about like a haunted man. His mind drifted off in the middle of writing up the office paperwork. Out jogging that Saturday morning, he stopped at a stile to catch his breath. The next thing he knew he was cold and stiff; he'd been staring into the misty middle-distance for five minutes. In the supermarket he stood detached and motionless in the center of an aisle with housewives and noisy children milling all around. He went to cash a check but forgot the banks were closed.

Twins, he kept thinking: *twins*. He re-read passages in Professor Bouchard's book, but they dealt only with the strange identities of habit and behavior, not with *communication*. What about those pairs of twins you read about who knew when the other was in trouble? But *this* twin was dead. So was it some weird case of communication with the dead? What on earth would it be like anyway, communicating with an infant? Or maybe the dead grew up too? What nonsense! There again, could it be a case of reincarnation: the soul of Philip entering another person? But it had clearly entered *Jonathan*, the other twin. It was as though, at the moment of death, Philip had somehow merged into Jonathan so that he now, quite literally, had two minds.

Frank's thoughts lurched to and fro, awash in a sea of unreason. Once you cast off from the raft of scientific logic, once you abandoned reason and common sense, what was there to cling to? Perhaps you just had to hope for a lucky intuitive leap.

To make matters worse in this case, he had no contact with the subject: Sarah and Lawrence had closed ranks against him, and Jonathan was out of touch.

Waiting until he guessed, from past experience, that Sarah would be at church, he phoned Jonathan's home. It rang for ages before the boy answered. His voice sounded far-off, flat, disembodied.

"Look, I want to talk to you," Frank began.

"OK."

"I mean, see you and talk."

"Mum won't like you coming here. And I don't like going outside."

"Just go to the end of the garden, into the field. I'll meet you there. Don't worry, I'll look after you. But wrap up. I'll see you in twenty minutes, all right?"

Jonathan arrived wearing his balaclava; he was pale and his face thin. Dog didn't greet him with her usual effusion but skirted him and sniffed the air around him uncertainly. For a while they walked in silence, the boy hugging close in the shelter of his overcoat. Finally he spoke and told him about Lawrence's visit. He was going in again the next day, this time for a CSF test.

"I'm afraid," he confessed quietly.

What could Frank say? He felt his temper rising: this agonizing test surely wasn't necessary. But there was nothing he could do except reassure Jonathan. "You've been this far," he offered. "I suppose you've got to see it through."

"I suppose so."

Frank stole a glance at him; his cheeks were hollow, his eyes ringed and gray, his manner nervous. Was it right to broach the subject on his mind now? He had to: he might not have the opportunity again.

"Jonathan," he began, "I've been thinking about your Tommy person. Don't you think it's strange that you also had a twin, as a baby? I mean, perhaps in a way you're inventing Tommy to replace Philip . . ."

The boy stopped and kicked at a fallen log. "I'm *not* inventing Tommy! I wish people understood. He's there, inside my head."

"Twins can be very close. They probably sometimes feel they're inside each other's head." Frank paused for a reaction, but he knew his logic was too weak to deserve a response. Philip was *dead*. He tried another angle. "Why did you call him Tommy?"

"I didn't. That's his name. He's Tommy because he just bloody *is*."

"I see. Tell me, does Lawrence talk to you about these things any more?"

Jonathan shook his head.

"I'm sorry he stopped the sessions. I thought that was going to be the way through. Are you feeling any better since then? I mean, are the spells getting better, or worse?"

"Worse. Specially at night. Different, too."

"Oh?"

"Sometimes I get stuck half-way. It's like a pulling feeling right inside my head."

Pulling feeling? Frank felt sweat breaking out under his arms. "Where? Between your eyes, at the top of your nose or somewhere?"

"No, deep, deep inside, right at the back."

"What's it *like*?"

"It's funny. Doesn't really hurt. Anyway, it's not half as bad as before. That time."

"What time?"

Jonathan kicked his way through the bedraggled grass.

"The time we had the accident with your car."

Frank's spine tingled. He tried to press for more, but the boy had said all he was going to. Instead, he tried to cheer him up and they played at throwing sticks in opposite directions simultaneously to tease Dog. When they finally returned to Jonathan's back gate, Frank gave him a firm hug.

"Good luck tomorrow. It'll be all right."

The boy shot him a brave, despairing look as he slipped back into the garden, with the expression of an innocent man going to the gallows. He seemed to know that Lawrence's way wasn't working but there was nothing he could do.

Frank's fury grew, fuelled by his impotence. By the time he was half-way home a storm was seething inside him. With sudden resolve he turned back towards Bedford and made for Lawrence's house. The man himself came to the door.

"It's me again," announced Frank. "I've got to talk."

"What about? You want to join the golf club at last? You've been fired? Come on in."

"You know bloody well what." He pushed on into the warm, noisy hallway and swung around to face the psychiatrist. "You never told me you were going to do a spinal tap on Jonathan."

"My dear chap . . ."

"You never mentioned *that*," he repeated. "It's wrong, it's unnecessary, it's unjustified, and I won't have it. You're not to do it. And don't give me all that crap about interfering."

"If that's what you've come to say, now you've said it you'd better leave." Lawrence put his hand on the doorhandle.

Frank was shaken by the hard indifference in his tone. He stepped forward and shook him by the shoulders.

"Damn it, can't you leave him alone? He doesn't deserve any more. It's monstrous!"

The psychiatrist freed himself. A cold draft swept in as he opened the door. "Don't be a fool, Frank. Just go home."

"I won't have it. I *forbid* it!"

"Out!"

Anger swelling within him, his muscles tensed for a fight.

Instead, he let out an oath and stormed out of the house. He pulled the car up around the corner and waited until his fury had subsided. He'd fired his last shot and he'd lost.

That night Frank composed a long letter to Sarah in which he opened his heart. He laid out the whole case as he saw it, concluding that, despite the Hirschfield evidence, by assuming the problem was organic Lawrence was going down a dangerous blind alley which could have terrible consequences for Jonathan. He ended the letter,

> I believe Lawrence blackmailed you into admitting Jonathan to hospital. I want you to know I had no part in that, no part at all. I was away when the fire occurred and I've always been utterly opposed to the tests—in fact, he and I are no longer friends as a result of our differences over this.
> Sarah, I've become very fond of Jonathan in these past months and that gives me a right to offer advice, whether you accept it or not. I beg you, think again! Get Jonathan out of there, before they really do some damage. Whatever you finally choose to do, I wish you and the lad all the very best in the future. With great affection, Frank

Late the following morning he dropped it through her letter-box, knowing Jonathan would already be in hospital and she'd be at school. Then he went about his week's business. He'd done all he could.

He was unprepared for her telephone call when he returned late that night. He'd been at supper with the sales manager and had drunk rather too much in an effort to clear his mind of the obsession. In a taut voice she asked if he'd mind if she came around to see him. Right then, if it wasn't too late. He agreed, anticipating a final and bitter showdown. He put out a bottle of brandy and poured himself a glass.

It was after midnight when she arrived. She hesitated on the doorstep until he drew her firmly in out of the cold. Her face, gaunt and lined, was tightly framed by a headscarf; her blue eyes stared out at him with unnatural brilliance. She let him take her coat and stood by the fire in a stiff pose, too self-absorbed to notice Dog sniffing at her shoes.

"Brandy or a liqueur?" asked Frank.

"Thank you."

Unsure of her meaning, he poured her a Benedictine and topped up his own brandy.

"I got your note," she said. She held his eye, scarcely blinking. "Parts of what you said I didn't quite understand. This Hirschfield thing. Explain."

"Surely Lawrence is the one to ask," he replied with a short laugh. He realized from her stony reaction that she wasn't getting very far with him either. "I'm afraid I told you all I know. I just did a bit of elementary reading, that's all. As I said, I think Lawrence is taking the wrong road. Analysis and therapy are what the boy needs, not lumbar punctures and brain scans."

Sarah sipped her drink and stared into the fire. After a while she replied, "I'm beginning to think you may be right."

"But I'm no expert, as Lawrence is forever reminding me. Don't take my opinion. I can't really offer an alternative."

"Jonathan seems to think you've got some ideas."

Frank hesitated to follow that up just yet. Instead he asked, "How did he get on today? Was it dreadful?"

"They hadn't quite warned him about the pain." She paused. "They give them a mirror so they can see what's going on to their backs. If you ask me, that only makes it worse."

He felt his hand tightening around his glass. "If Lawrence draws a blank there, he'll just go on with more tests, more scans, then biopsies. Christ knows what's at the end of the road. A temporal lobectomy? I'm sorry, it makes me furious."

She went on addressing the fire. "I wish to God you'd never

brought that man into all this. It's too late to change that now. Jonathan will just have to see it through."

Frank moved closer to her and put a hand lightly on her shoulder. "No! He's only in there voluntarily. You can put an end to it any time you like. Or insist on changing to another consultant. Go private: I'll pay."

She looked up and for the first time her face softened into a slight smile. "That's a sweet thing to say."

"Damn it," he exploded, "I don't mean to be *sweet*! I want to help. Listen, call the man's bluff. What's he going to do now, apply for a compulsory committal order? It's two months since the fire; Jonathan has had his spells but he hasn't done anything delinquent since then. Lawrence wouldn't have a leg to stand on."

"I'm not sure. There's the situation at school to think of, too . . ." She turned back towards the fire. The flickering flames cast a warm light on the side of her face and a wave of sympathy swelled within him. "It has been my fault all along. It started all those years ago. I still blame myself, you know. It's not easy to live with a thing like that."

"Sarah, you're not to punish yourself. Blaming yourself is counterproductive. I know. That was perhaps the one good thing Lawrence taught me."

She looked up.

Frank swirled his drink around the glass and spoke more quietly.

"I was married until a couple of years ago. My wife died of an incurable illness. I crucified myself with blame afterwards, so much so that I had a nervous breakdown. Lawrence pulled me through. By talking to me—chat therapy, he called it—not drugs or poking around inside my head. I owe him a lot for that. No, Sarah, self-blame is like self-pity. It eats you up."

Her eyes softened and she stretched out to touch his arm.

"I'm sorry. It must have been a terrible time for you." Then, with a smile, she added, "Might I have a drop more of this stuff? It works wonders."

"Of course, of course."

She stayed for another hour. She talked of her past as if it belonged to another person. Or, perhaps, as if she could not bear to look into the future.

When she finally left he insisted on driving behind her and seeing her safely to her front door. There she put a hand on his and pressed it.

"Thank you for being a friend, Frank," she said.

He drove away, elated. It was the law of destiny: when you wanted a thing too badly it ran away, and only casting off from it brought it back. Cut the metaphysical crap, he told himself curtly. The important thing was: would she act on his advice?

25

When Frank called Sarah the following evening she said, "They're keeping Jonathan in a bit longer."

"They've found something?"

"Well, no. That's the point."

"You mean . . . more tests?"

The silence at the other end was his answer.

"Right," he said decisively. "Now's the time to do something about it! Discharge him. Just get in your car, drive over to the hospital, see the ward sister, get him dressed and take him home. He's yours, after all, not theirs."

"I've been thinking . . ." she began. He didn't need to hear the rest; her tone said it all. She'd lost her nerve. It was useless to push her further, at least he'd learned *that* lesson.

In the morning he was out on the road. Finding a phone booth, he rang the hospital; Jonathan was "under observation" and couldn't be visited. He tracked Lawrence down to one of the clinics out of town but when he was on the line he heard the psychiatrist's voice in the background saying, "Tell him I'm not here."

He tried to turn his mind to the work in hand, but the daily trivia of the job were choking. At lunchtime he drove to a remote spot in the country. Locking Dog in the car, he planted his feet apart, loosened his tie and took a deep breath. For two full minutes he yelled out his rage to the winds. That got him through the afternoon.

Into the early hours of the night, like a knight keeping vigil on the eve of battle, he brooded quietly by himself. He sat staring into the fire, a bottle of malt whisky open on the table beside him. It wasn't that people didn't care, but they wouldn't *do* anything. And Jonathan was headed for the abyss. Dozing in the chair, he woke stiff from the draft and dry-mouthed from the alcohol.

The facts, what were the facts? He had to take stock. Fact: Jonathan is in an extreme psychotic state. Theory: he's a case of multiple personality. Fact: he had a twin he lost six weeks after birth. Theory: the Tommy *persona* may or may not be a subliminal echo of the dead twin. Counter-theory: both Jonathan and Lawrence, for their separate reasons, think there's no connection. Fact: twins do have extraordinary powers of communication—but with the *dead?* Rule out the para-normal.

Frank's head was aching. This was the same loop he'd been caught in all day. It revolved over and over in his mind; a maze without an exit. Wasn't there another approach? OK, begin at the beginning. How had it all started?

It had started on a country road one dark, wet evening half a year before. Fact. Jonathan had been running away from home. Fact? Frank's hand stopped with his glass half-raised to his lips. What had the boy said? *"It's like a pulling feeling right inside my head . . . not half as bad as before . . . the time we had the accident with the car.*" And into Frank's mind came the word, whispered repeatedly, Hirschfield.

He stood up, then sat down abruptly. He was visualizing the geography of the road that terrible night. Jonathan had been running down the hill when he'd struck him. Downhill was towards Bedford, towards his home. You can't be running away from home if you're running towards it. Maybe he'd changed his mind that very moment? Or maybe he was running towards something else. Being pulled by the pulling feeling.

Frank went to the sink and downed two tumblers of water. Either the whisky was making him hallucinate or else he'd stumbled on it. There was only one way to check.

It was six in the morning when, his hand shaking and his head throbbing, he finished the coffee and toast and put on his outdoor shoes. Adding an extra jersey against the dawn chill, he climbed into his car.

In the cold mist he nearly overshot the spot. He pulled into the side, switched on his hazard warning lights and climbed out of the car. He stood in the center of the empty country road and looked around. It rose, in the direction he was pointing, towards a small bus shelter on the crest, before bending away to the right. He shut his eyes for a moment and the whole picture came back to him: the boy running down the middle of the road, running right at him, right into the car. Then he recalled stamping on the brakes and wrenching the wheel, the car lurching to the side, a brief crumpling sound and the boy sheering off the fender. The car skidding, slewing around and finally coming to a stop broadside across the road. Then running down to the ditch, where he could hear choking, choking and then cursing. In the Tommy voice. And the fit, the storm of convulsions, wave upon wave of them.

Frank stood aside to let a bus pass. It crawled up the hill without pausing at the top, for there was no one to pick up. He strolled up the road and took a look inside the shelter; graffiti defaced the concrete walls and a smell of urine hung in the air. Had Jonathan stopped in there, maybe for a bus to take him on his first leg? But why then was he running in the opposite direction, downhill? He stepped into the road again; he checked his bearings. He'd been right: Bedford lay down the hill.

Slowly Frank's brain worked over the conundrum. *Pulling* suggested being drawn somewhere, not being driven *from* somewhere. Perhaps he *had* been going somewhere. But where? He recalled reading about magnetite. Pigeons partly derived their sense of direction from particles of the stuff just above their beaks. Humans had an equivalent, too. Or was it more obscure than that? If you called Biblical miracles "psychic phenomena" in today's language, perhaps that nineteenth-century religious crank Hirschfield hadn't been far from the mark after all. It wasn't as if Lawrence with all his aids of modern science and reason had come up with anything better.

He sat in the car, the fan heater whirring noisily, and fixed his eye on the crest of the country road. He felt suddenly light-headed and laughed abruptly. It was the lack of sleep, or the whisky, or the surreal dawn country scene. But his mind wouldn't be still, for the next question forced itself inexorably upon him: *what was Jonathan being drawn towards?*

The laughter died on Frank's lips and he suddenly felt very cold. It could be one thing only. The grave of his twin, Philip.

As soon as Jonathan recovered sufficiently, Lawrence returned him to the EEG room and had extra furniture, including a vase of flowers and a small television, brought in to give a more homey atmosphere. This was going to be his home for a while.

The CSF tests had shown no abnormalities. So the trouble didn't lie in the chemical and hormonal circulation system around the brain. That at least supported the diagnosis of a localized neurochemical malfunction such as in that small ganglion in the hippocampus, deep within the brain structure. Meanwhile, the boy's fugues and fits were intensifying at night, and even during the day when Lawrence paid him visits he'd never know whether to expect Jonathan or Tommy. The nursing staff had been asking difficult questions, as he'd feared; to isolate him in the EEG area on the second floor made both medical and diplomatic sense.

A muscle biopsy would be the next step. This involved excising a small portion of a peripheral nerve from his arm; it was naturally preferable to performing a biopsy direct on the brain, and, since the brain itself was neural tissue also, it could give good enough results. If not, however, it would mean drilling a tiny hole in the skull and directly sampling the brain cells in the affected area. The sample would go to Pathology; if they confirmed malignancy, the way would be opened for surgical ablation. It might yet come to that. The boy's general intellectual capacity was patently declining; that was a general sign of brain disease, a literal rotting of the brain, which normally justified direct surgery.

Meanwhile he continued running EEGs, but this was now in order to check that there were *no* abnormal readings. Before the results of the PET scan, he'd explained their absence by assuming that Jonathan's states were, in the phrase used of parapsychological phenomena, "laboratory shy": that is, they hid from scrutiny when instruments were trained upon them. But now that he'd localized the *focus* of the trouble and deduced the disorder was neurochemical, he found himself expecting that the tests would continue without positive results. Very soon he would have the chance of taking an actual look at this quirky Hirschfield area.

He picked up the internal phone and arranged the muscle biopsy for the following afternoon.

·   ·   ·

That afternoon Frank returned home early from work. Disturbed and off balance, he listened to the messages on his answering machine without taking them down. The voices sounded distanced, their concerns absurd.

Later he called Dog and told her they were going for a drive. "No, I don't know where," he answered her interrogative look. In the car he took out a map and spread it out on the seat next to him.

The realization hit him at once. If you drew a straight line from Jonathan's home to Buckingham—where Philip had presumably been buried or cremated—you'd find it went nowhere near the accident spot.

It hurt, that night, like a tooth they were wrestling to pull out. Jonathan couldn't sleep. The room was stuffy, the plastic smell of warm electronics made him feel sick and the taste in his mouth was sour. He got up from the low camp bed and, careful not to dislodge the electrode apparatus on his head, went over to the window. He craned his neck upwards to glimpse the sky. By cupping his hands against the pane he could see the bright swath of the Milky Way. The tugging in his head intensified. It was as if a force was beckoning him out there, trying to tease him through the window and up past the sides of the building and somewhere into the vast and open firmament.

Then, without warning, the headset turned into the octopus, its quick tentacles probing his thoughts and wrapping themselves in jerky spasms around his brain.

"Get off, off!" he cried.

In a frenzy he began wrestling with it, but the tape stuck firmly to his chin and cheek and tore his skin painfully when he ripped at it. He knelt on the bed and fought like a cat with its head stuck in a jar. At last it came free. He flung it into a corner with a shudder of nausea, realizing as he did so that the tentacles were not on the outside of his head, but on the inside.

Gripping the window-sill he stared out into the night and listened, his brain still seething. Had he heard something, a voice, a distant sound like a far cry for help?

Frank lay in bed, unable to sleep, his mind churning. An owl cried mournfully in the trees. At the foot of the bed Dog whined, perhaps sensing his unease or perhaps deep in a dream of her own. He dozed fitfully, waking only to find the time had moved on by minutes. At three o'clock he could stand it no longer. He went downstairs and made himself a mug of hot milk laced with whisky. Then, quite suddenly, it came to him. Cradling the mug at the kitchen table, he felt suddenly decisive, resolute; the fog had lifted and he was impelled to action. Why hadn't he thought of it before? He set to work.

The frost on the gravel crunched underfoot as, later, he made his way in the moonlight towards his car. He'd found a white jacket to wear—the nearest thing he had to a doctor's coat—and on an old company conference name-tag he'd written, in Dymo-tape, "Dr. Turner, Neurophysiology." Under his arm he carried a clipboard and in a carryall he'd brought emergency rations, which included whisky and cigarettes, and his tracksuit and running shoes, together with a thick fisherman's-knit jersey and some old clothes that had shrunk in the wash and he thought might fit Jonathan.

He arrived at the hospital sooner than he'd expected; the streets were empty at that late hour of night. He didn't feel prepared. He sat in his car, smoking, his stomach taut with apprehension. Was he *insane*? He smoked the cigarette until it burned his fingers and he couldn't delay the moment any longer. Taking a deep breath he walked briskly in through the main door, miming a yawn to cover his face as he passed the woman on Admissions, and headed for the wards. Chancing being challenged or recognized (by whom? by Lawrence, at that hour?), he followed the signs to the children's ward. His act was unscripted and he trusted to adrenalin and the whisky smoldering in his stomach to carry it off for him.

Fortunately he'd never seen the night sister before. Thin, brittle-faced, she looked up sharply from a book. "Can I help you?" she enquired.

Frank consulted his clipboard. "Jonathan Hall. Checking he's all prepared for his appointment tomorrow."

Absurd. Foolhardy. Unconvincing.

"Oh." She frowned, suspicious, then put the book face-down and looked at a wall-chart. "He's not back with us until the day after tomorrow. He's still on EEGs."

His throat went dry. "Ah, of course. Now, that's down in . . ."

"Hold on. I'll ring upstairs."

"Don't trouble." He backed away. "The exercise will do me good."

Shaking, he found himself back in the corridor. *The exercise will do me good*: an idiotic remark in an idiotic caper. But he'd gone too far now to back out. Where the hell were EEGs done? Upstairs, she'd said. On the second floor a sign pointed to Radiology. That sounded possible.

The radiology department was a honeycomb of small units off a corridor that led away from a reception area. There was no one around. Radiators gurgled; machines hummed in the background. A lavatory flushed nearby and he melted into a doorway as a nurse emerged, crossed the central area and disappeared into an office. Stealthily he opened the first door down the corridor: an X-ray developing laboratory. The second was some form of waiting-room. The third was lined floor-to-ceiling with large pieces of electronic equipment. Above the door of the fourth burned a small yellow light. As his hand closed over the doorhandle he heard the phone ringing back in the nurse's office.

The room was in darkness except for a low blue lamp and light coming in through the curtains. As he stepped inside a figure sat up sharply in a bed against the far wall. It was Jonathan: wide awake and startled. His cropped hair gleamed pale in the low light.

"Ssh!" said Frank, a finger to his lips. "It's me. Frank."

"Frank?" exclaimed the boy. "What are you doing here?"

Footsteps were approaching. He couldn't bluff his way out of this one. He felt the door: there was no lock or key. Reaching for a chair he wedged it under the doorhandle and went over to Jonathan.

"You've got to get out of here!" he whispered urgently. "Come on, I'm taking you with me. Get ready. Quick!"

"But Mum . . ."

"She's waiting for you at home." It wasn't true.

"But I've got a big test tomorrow."

Frank took the boy by the shoulder. "Listen, those tests are crap. You've got to leave this place, with me, now."

The doorhandle turned but wouldn't open. At the other side the nurse tapped and called Jonathan's name.

"You mean, *escape*?"

"Yes. Now. Grab your dressing-gown and any clothes."

The boy looked at the door. "But how?"

Frank opened the window. They were perhaps thirty feet from the ground. His eye at once sought out a line of descent among the ledges, drainpipes and lintels. By now the nurse was rattling the door harder; any moment it would give. Jonathan stood there in his dressing-gown and track shoes, a bundle of clothes under his arm. "What do we *do*?"

Frank looked him directly in his blue eyes. "You've got to trust me with your life, Jonathan."

The boy bit his lip, then nodded. "OK."

Frank tossed the clothes out of the window, took Jonathan's wrist in one hand and the opposite ankle in the other and swung him onto his back in a fireman's lift. "Just hold on bloody tight," he hissed and put his right leg out of the window. By now the nurse was hammering with her fists and shouting; the door was bowing in against the chair. They had to move fast.

Foot-hold, finger-hold, foot-hold, finger-hold. Test the next before giving up the first. Jonathan clung to his back like a limpet. Frank whispered, "We're doing fine. Almost there. Don't look down. Keep your eyes shut. Just hang on to me."

Finally he dropped onto the grass and Jonathan slid off his back, retrieved his clothes and scrambled for cover. The nurse's face appeared briefly at the window, then went away. She'd have gone to raise the alarm. They ran over to where the car was parked. Frank started it up and was through the gateway before anyone could stop them. Pulling out into the empty street, he set course towards the west with the first hint of dawn glimmering in his rear-view mirror.

"Get dressed," he ordered. "Put that sweater on, too."

"But we'll soon be home."

"Do as I say."

Jonathan was shivering despite the sweater and the heat in the car. He kept twitching his head and scratching one hand with the other. When they'd left the street-lights behind and were in dark open country, he turned to Frank. His voice was jerky, nervous.

"Hey, where are we going?"

"Your place isn't safe. We're going to mine instead—the long way around, that's all."

When they reached the spot where they'd had the accident all those months before, Frank slowed to a halt and turned off the engine. The twilight silence of the countryside invaded the car. Jonathan turned abruptly to him.

"What's going on? Why are we stopping here? I want to go home."

"Jonathan," said Frank, staring hard into the boy's darting eyes, "this is where we had the accident that time. Do you remember?"

"No."

"The accident," he repeated. "When you had that pulling feeling."

"I want to go home."

Oh Christ, thought Frank. This is all going wrong, badly wrong. He'd somehow assumed the place itself would do it. He'd have to provoke him. How would Lawrence do it? By counting to three or hypnotizing him? His pulse racing, he began in a soft, low voice, almost below his breath, scarcely moving his lips and trying to keep the desperate urgency from his expression.

"Can't you feel the pull, Jonathan? Think, listen, let it come to you."

The boy grew agitated. In the rear seat Dog whimpered.

"You weren't running away, were you. You were going somewhere. Well, this time you're going to get there."

Jonathan's eyes widened into a stare and he inclined his head slightly as if listening to a soft, far-off sound. Frank persisted, the still small voice of persuasion.

"It's calling you, Jonathan. It's giving you the pulling feeling."

The boy let out a small shudder. He began blinking fast and his head jerked in an uncontrolled *tic*. Frank watched his eyes carefully and intervened to stop the progression the moment he saw they began to roll upwards. The boy had to be stuck half-way.

"Jonathan? Jonathan, keep listening to me. You can hear the voice, can't you? You can feel the pull, can't you? Hold it there, just there. You're going to go now. Go where you were going."

He reached across and opened the passenger door. The crisp country air knifed in. Jonathan hesitated but gradually, like a sleep-walker, he got out of the car and stood in the middle of the road. For a moment he stayed there, cocking his head from side to side, then quite abruptly he began walking up the hill in small stumbling steps that grew faster as he seemed to pick up his sense of direction, until he was running like a hounded rabbit, darting in short spurts and only pausing to incline his head before breaking into a run again.

He ran past the bus shelter and left the road where it bent to the right, jumped a ditch and ran on in a straight line through a row of trees and into a wide field beyond. Frank watched until he was out of sight. Then, parking the car in the entrance to a field, he changed into his tracksuit and running shoes. Into a knapsack went the car keys, the emergency rations, a map and a compass. And a minute or two later he was jogging across the same field, Dog at his heels, following the unerringly straight line that was traced by the speck of a boy ahead in the thick white fisherman–knit sweater.

26

*H*old on, hold on, hold on, he chanted in rhythm to his step.

The cold dawn wind bit numbingly through the sweater sleeves he'd pulled down over his hands and his ankles were raw where he'd kicked them running. He didn't know where he was or where he was going, only that he had to carry on, on along the same straight line he'd taken all the way from the car. He was following the pull.

The fields were rough and hard with a heavy frost. He constantly tripped and fell; the days in hospital had weakened him and his weary legs rebelled. The taste of bitter almonds kept rising in his mouth and he had to use his strongest will-power to stave it off. He mustn't give in now! He must keep going, steering his course by the distant beacon and its resonance inside his head. This was his chance to finish what he'd begun before. He had to. Somewhere deep in his blurry consciousness he knew the answer to his madness lay out there, at the end of the line.

By mid-morning, in the steely sunlight of an early spring day, he grew hot and took off the sweater, tying the arms around his waist. Thirsty, he drank from a stream but spat the water out as soon as he saw a herd of sheep upstream. He was ravenously hungry. From the crest of an escarpment he surveyed the country ahead of him. A reservoir lay directly across the line; he'd have to make a detour. At one end stood a small building, probably a pumping station; could he take a chance and ask for food? He decided against it. The men would be officials and maybe the word was already out that he'd escaped. It was risk enough to be crossing the country in broad daylight.

He went on, his pace now dwindling to a shuffling trot. When he came to roads he was careful to hide himself until the cars had passed. At mid-day he reached a small town. Everyone seemed to be looking at him, into him, reading his mind. They could tell he was on the run. At the edge of the town was a field full of garden plots. He found a rainwater barrel and he dug up young scallions and carrots. His stomach, strained by the exertion, refused to hold the food down. Giddy and weak, he stumbled on.

He had to eat something or he'd expire. In the next village he went into a small corner grocery shop and bought a bag of pies and sweets. Saying his mother was outside with the money, he ran out of the shop with the food. A mile further on he slowed down and found a safe spot behind a shed in a railway siding where he sat down and tried to eat, chewing every mouthful slowly. Gradually his strength returned with the nourishment. He dozed for a while in the sun before setting off again. How much further? The signal in his head was growing stronger. Sometimes it faded, when he crossed under a power cable or the overhead electric wires for the railway, but always it beckoned him on.

Frank maintained a distance of half a mile, though he allowed the gap to close as they approached the town. Whenever he gained ground and had Jonathan clearly in his sights he paused and marked his bearings on his map. As he took the second fix a jolt of excitement shot through him, and the third was conclusive. His hunch was paying off. They were travelling towards Buckinghamshire, where the twins had been born. More chilling still, the path the boy was taking was a straight line.

A dead straight line.

Among the small backstreets of the town he lost him. Only then did he realize the implications of what he was doing. This was kidnapping. How could he stand up in court and explain? He didn't even understand it himself; it was a crazy, half-baked theory. He took a desperate chance. Extending the line on the map, he found a spot several miles beyond the town that promised a wide panorama of the surrounding country. Pausing only for a slug of whisky and a cheese roll from the emergency rations, he set off at a fast, steady pace.

He arrived there an hour later. The days were lengthening and the afternoon was bright and clear. He took up position under a spreading beech tree and scoured the fields ahead that sloped away into the bluish distance. Several times he thought he'd spotted the boy but each time the figure was heading in the wrong direction. How the hell could he have let him slip?

Maybe he'd arrived too late. He set off along the line once again. Half a mile further on he halted by a tall barn and turned to look back. There was Jonathan, profiled against the skyline, just to one side of the very beech tree he'd been standing under. And coming towards him. Quickly he took Dog into the barn and hid high up in the bales of straw. He clamped a hand over her muzzle as Jonathan stepped inside the barn, paused to catch his breath, then quite abruptly disappeared. Frank waited for fifteen minutes before coming out into the open. There, several fields away, he spotted the small running figure again. With mounting excitement he hitched his knapsack on his back and continued the pursuit. But where, where was the boy leading him?

For Sarah the day at school was interminably long and painful. A woman police officer had visited her before breakfast. By the description Lawrence had identified the abductor as Frank. The police fully expected man and boy to turn up at one or the other of their houses; why hadn't they yet? Sarah quickly realized that he'd sprung the boy not to return him home, but to test out some crazy theory of his own. She went over their last conversation in her mind, trying to glean clues, but got nowhere. She was dealing with a maniac, a madman. She'd seen it from the outset, but lately she'd allowed herself to be seduced into trusting him. Now she hated him.

During the morning break she received a call from Lawrence. He told her the police had found Frank's car. Abandoned at the precise spot where he'd first knocked the boy down.

"So what does our psychiatrist make of that?" she demanded, but she got no satisfactory answer.

Several of the staff were away with flu and she couldn't stay at home because there was no one to replace her. The police had posted a watch, anyway. She tried to behave as if nothing had happened, but the worry paralyzed her and made teaching impossible. Finally, as she was leaving for the day, another call came through. It was Frank, from a phone booth. He sounded far away. She was convinced now that the man was unhinged.

"Jonathan's OK," he said urgently, speaking close to the

mouthpiece. He repeated, "He's OK. I've got my eye on him. That's all I want you to know. Try not to worry."

Try not to worry? She was frantic. Where was her son? She'd drive out at once. What did Frank think he was doing? This was criminal, unforgivable.

"I'll bring him back safe and sound. I promise. Trust me."

"*Trust* you?" she cried.

He broke in, "I'm not saying any more. Jonathan's OK, he's fine. You're not to worry. Believe me. It's our only chance . . ."

"Frank! I *demand* . . ."

"I'm hanging up now. Goodbye, Sarah."

"*Frank!*"

The line went dead. The others in the staff room had been listening. She snatched up her bag and ran out of the room. Driving home, she had to fight to concentrate on the road. Inside she was quaking with worry and anger. The bastard, she would *kill* him.

He'd lost sense of time and self. A penumbral light had settled over the landscape, but was it dawn or dusk? Was it the same day as when he'd started out? Frost had formed on the hedgerows and he felt giddy with exhaustion and hunger. Oh, stop, please stop this tugging. He was a fish with a hook lodged deep in his brain and someone far, far away was playing him in. Writhing and fighting free was no use; the pull was getting stronger. A strange warmth suffused his chest. Any mile now, any minute now. . . .

A small village. Its name on the signpost seemed dimly familiar. He followed the line through the village, along the main street flanked on each side by squat, impoverished cottages. It swung in a loop, making him cross a churchyard. He ran through it quickly. The gravestones seemed to be moving, twitching; at any minute hands might reach up from under the earth and catch him by the ankles. Meeting the lane again on

the other side he stopped to catch his breath. A woman was com‑
ing out of the front gate opposite. She seemed to recognize him.
She cast him a reproving look at if to say, "I know you, youn
lad. You shouldn't be out and about." Then a girl on a pon
came hacking past in the opposite direction and gave him
small familiar wave.

He was known here.

His spine prickled as he realized one other thing: he kne
this place, too.

The village ended at a small bridge over a brook. He lurche
along the side, his hands grazing the stone. He was going pai
fully slowly now, putting one foot floppily before the other, n
longer feeling his shoe-tops nicking his ankles. He was dete
mined to make it, even if he had to crawl there. And *there* w
very close.

The houses came to an end and the road began to clim
Half a mile on he came upon a line of rotten wooden railin;
that led to a dilapidated iron gate lying off its hinges. A po
holed, flinty path stretched into the grounds and wound awa
around two large evergreen bushes. Coils of barbed wire la
rusting by the side. On the left a jumble of old tires and (
drums were scattered over a paddock. He was exhausted. F
wanted to give up, to sink down deep into the earth. Perhaps I
was meant to die here.

The moment he let go, it all came upon him so suddenly th
he had no time to fight it off.

He was locked in, trapped. Night was falling; he could smell
it falling. He yearned to be out there in the dark underworld,
among the animals that only stirred at the hour that dog be‑
came wolf and he came into his own.

The moon was full. It beckoned him through the bars of the
attic window. Over the weeks he had loosened them. No one
could have guessed what he was going to do, silently, bloodily,
under cover of this night. He reached for the first bar.

When Frank reached the village he halted outside the wicket gate leading to the churchyard. His heart was pounding. This *must* be it! The twin, Philip, must be buried here!

Keeping Dog close at heel he cautiously went in. Twilight had absorbed the low-lying ground and mist hung lightly over the gravestones, their top edges illuminated coldly in the risen moonlight. Up the lane outside roared a small unsilenced motorcycle, but the churchyard itself was empty and quiet. Where was Jonathan? Had he found the grave already, in this dim light?

But the boy had gone on. Frank broke into a cold sweat. His hunch had been mistaken. God alive, what had he started? Would he be able to undo it, to bring the boy down off this weird flight-path? He had to put a stop to this before it was too late: he had to find him and shatter the spell. The boy's mind was at stake.

He broke into a run. Beyond the churchyard the lane doubled back on itself and led in a straight line to a small bridge where the street lighting ended and dark country began again. His feet and shoulders hurt beyond all limits of pain. All the while he ran he muttered to himself. Was he going mad, too?

The lane rose in a gentle incline, flanked by a broken white fence, before bending sharply to the right. A direct line would take him down a rough driveway into a farm. He checked the map in the light of a match. This was the way. Crows cawed high in the bare trees and a squirrel hurled itself from branch to branch as he walked down the drive. A light wind stirred two tall evergreen bushes standing sentinel to the farm buildings. There Frank paused. Ahead, beyond a muddy yard lined with barns and sheds, stood a farmhouse. Lights burned downstairs; he could see the figure of a burly man moving about inside. A single wall-lamp lit the yard, making the trees and sky seem darker. From the sheds he could hear cattle shifting and heaving. At his heel, Dog growled. Then he, too, saw the movement.

The boy stood in the shadow of the barn wall. In the d light Frank could see he was wearing a raincoat; he must ha stolen it. He'd seen Frank too. But he didn't move.

"Jonathan!" he whispered and went forward, skirting t pool of light from the wall-lamp. "It's me. Frank."

Dog bared her teeth. The boy let him get within a few fe then pulled out a knife. The clumsiness of the movement a the angle of his head and shoulders told Frank that he'd laps into one of his states. He began calling his name, softly, in tently. That was the usual way to bring him back, he knew.

But the boy's voice remained coarse and rough and his wo came out in a jerky, incoherent gabble. He jabbed the air tween them with the knife. Frank had never seen him that b Christ, the boy had flipped for good.

Dog's bark made him turn.

Standing in the center of the pool of light was the very sa boy, Jonathan again, *another* Jonathan, but this time wear the fisherman-knit sweater. Involuntarily, Frank drew in breath and stepped back. He stared at the first boy.

"Philip?" he asked hoarsely, dry-throated.

But he ignored him. He'd seen the other one. Cautiously, li a wild cat, he moved out into the yard. At the rim of light held back. Then suddenly he stepped forward until the two b stood merely feet apart and Frank could see them clearly.

Their faces were identical.

The one on the left was burlier; his body swayed in an coordinated way, he was dressed in a raincoat and his hair v long. The other one, who was standing still and rigid as statue, was clothed in Frank's jersey and his hair was clo cropped. But their faces were one face: the same squar mandibles, the same cast of forehead and eyes, the same co of hair, the same mouth. Mirror images.

The first boy shuffled forward, his jaw now slack and mou agape. Tentatively he put out a finger and touched Jonathan the cheek, then let out a grunt and snatched it back as if he'd received an electric shock. Jonathan came to life and reached out his arm. The other boy shrank further back and slipped to a crouch, growling and grinding his teeth. Frank caught a flash from the knife-blade in his hand, but he was too late. As Jonathan came closer, the boy suddenly lunged upwards. Jonathan let out a cry and drew back. His hand flew to his side and his face filled with shock and fright. By then Frank had grabbed the first boy by the wrist and wrested the knife from him. It clattered to the ground.

"Who the fuck *are* you?"

The boy spat an obscenity and broke free. He went back to Jonathan, circling him like a gladiator. Suddenly he sprang on him, going for the throat. In a rage Frank burst between them, tore them apart and flung the boy backwards onto the concrete yard.

Tears were streaming down Jonathan's face.

"You bloody bastard, Tommy," he yelled. "You lousy rotten bastard!" And he went for him.

27

The door of the farmhouse flew open. Outlined again[st]
the light stood the farmer, broad-shouldered, short-necked a[nd]
burly. His voice was surprisingly high.

"What's going on?" he demanded. Jonathan stood still in t[he]
center of the yard, Frank's grip tight on his shoulder. The ot[her]
boy had slipped off into the shadows. The farmer pointed [at]
Frank. "You! Get your hands off my lad!"

Frank found his throat dry. What he wanted to say was: t[his]
one isn't your lad. But no words would come out.

The farmer bore down across the yard and pulled Jonat[han]
roughly by the sleeve.

"Tommy, get back indoors!"

"Now, wait . . ." Frank managed to get out.

"Who in the name of buggery are *you*? What d'you wan[t]

He shoved him hard in the chest. "You're trespassing. Get out! Get off my land!"

But as he spoke the other boy, his own boy, emerged from the shadow of the barn. For a long second he stood frozen in the pool of light, then made a dash down the driveway. The man couldn't believe what he saw. He swung his head crazily from one boy to the other. He let go of Jonathan, stepped forward with an oath, then staggered a step back. One hand went to his heart, the other pointed straight at Jonathan. He coughed out the words.

"Holy Mary, who are you, boy? Ha! You'll catch it, son. Just let me get a hand on you."

Frank stood squarely in front of him.

"His name is Jonathan Hall. What I want to know is, who in God's name is that one over there?"

The farmer's eyes widened and his jaw dropped. At first only a dry, strangled rattle came from his throat.

"Hall?" he said. "*Hall?*"

"Jonathan Hall."

"Oh God. Oh Holy Mother of Christ."

Horrified awareness spread across his face. He stared long and hard at Jonathan. Then slowly he backed away. "You've got it wrong, man. Get out. Go away. Leave us alone."

Even as he spoke, from the darkness of the driveway came a single long-drawn-out cry, an animal howl from a human throat. It echoed eerily into the night. Dog bristled. Jonathan jerked his head in its direction and his body began to shake. Filling his lungs, he let out an answering cry, a replica of the animal howl. Then, as if mesmerized, he started out towards the sound.

"No! Jonathan, *no!*" shouted Frank. He threw out an arm to stop him.

But the boy dodged past and was quickly lost in the dark.

Frank followed, but the naked courtyard light had blinded him and he had only the boy's footsteps pelting down the drive to guide him. Behind, the farmer was yelling and cursing. The front door of the farmhouse slammed and a few seconds later a car engine burst into life. Before Frank was more than half-way down the drive a Land Rover was bearing down on him, its lights scouring the darkness. He flung himself for safety onto the shoulder and it passed, gears crashing and tires ripping the gravel of the drive. Then it swung violently off the track and broke through a gap in the fence into the paddock. Suddenly the headlights picked out the figure of Jonathan, the boy in the pale sweater, darting crazily in and out of the oil drums and piles of tires. A moment later he was out of sight, running through a hedge at the far side and into a tightly planted copse.

Unable to penetrate the wood, the farmer drew the Land Rover to a skidding halt and jumped out. As he passed through the beam of its headlights Frank saw he carried, under his arm, a shotgun.

He followed on behind, plunging clumsily around in the dark, but the farmer, knowing the pathways, easily outstripped him. As Frank's eyes grew accustomed to the low light he made better headway through the dense undergrowth, until he could see, through a barrier of thick dead brambles, a clearing. In the center of the clearing the two boys were fighting viciously. One had dragged the other to the ground and was throttling him. And suddenly the farmer was there, standing over them. With a single kick he separated them so that they rolled apart onto the ground and he raised the shotgun to his shoulder.

Frank yelled to Jonathan, "Watch out!"

As he lunged wildly through the brambles he heard the report of the gun. The noise ricocheted around the wood, to be drowned by the shriek that followed. Almost at once came a second shot. Breaking through at last, he threw himself on the farmer and brought him down with a flying tackle. He grabbed the gun and raised it over his head. He'd crack the man's skull open.

He could hear coughing. He spun around. One of the boys was on his knees, vomiting. Christ, which one was he? Despite the mudstains he recognized his own sweater.

"Jonathan!"

He flung the gun into the brambles and rushed over to the boy. Grabbing him by the shoulders he turned him around. He was coughing and choking, but where was the wound? Frank looked for the other one: there he lay, face-down, his fair head lying in a ragged, misshapen tangle and a dark wet black patch spreading on the grass around.

Frank grasped Jonathan to his chest, trembling, gasping. Thank God, thank God. Out of the corner of his eye he could see the farmer, his face in his hands, sobbing. He hugged the boy tighter.

"It's all right. It's all over now."

Jonathan was shivering uncontrollably.

"Are you hurt?"

The boy shook his head. Frank forced him to look him in the face. It had changed. Quite suddenly something had been lifted. Gray, bloodied, scratched, exhausted, his features nevertheless revealed something different: a strange, resolved glow. Frank recognized it. He'd seen it once before—on Cathy's face, moments before she passed away. She'd been at peace with herself.

"Are you sure you're OK, Jonathan?" he insisted.

The boy took a while to reply. His voice was low and quiet. "I think I'm going to be all right now," he said.

28

"Where's Jonathan? What the hell's going on?"

Lawrence stormed into the farmhouse, shaking the rain off his car-coat. Bags swelled under his eyes and angry red blotches tinged his smooth cheeks. Rain and sweat beaded his forehead and glistened in the roots of his wild dark hair.

"He's upstairs, sleeping. He's exhausted, a bit cut about but he's OK. Now *wait*," Frank commanded, gripping the psychiatrist by the arm. "I said he's OK. I want you to see to this fellow first."

He pointed to the figure of a man in a moth-holed cardigan sitting huddled in an armchair by the dying fire. His head was buried in his arm and his stout back, turned away from the room, heaved and shook with the tide of internal emotions. "Who is he?" demanded Lawrence, "and what in God's name is wrong with him?"

"His name is Croome. He owns this farm. He needs something to calm him down. He's in shock."

"Christ, what kind of circus is this? Don't speak: I don't want to hear. I'm going up to see Jonathan."

"All right. But don't wake him up."

Frank waited downstairs while Lawrence assured himself the boy was safe and undamaged. He put more coal on the fire and drew up another chair. From time to time Croome came to life and babbled a few incomprehensible words, then hid his face further in the chair. He was a broken man. Frank understood why: he'd drawn the whole story out of him before phoning Lawrence. He helped himself to another whisky from the sideboard and set it down on a coaster.

Lawrence returned, his expression relieved but his eyes red and raw. It was almost two o'clock in the morning and he'd been dragged out of bed. He now picked up the phone to dial the police. Frank came up behind him and put his finger down on the cradle.

"Still no fuzz. Not yet."

"Get out of the way, Frank. You're in deep trouble. I advise you not to make it worse."

But Frank forced the receiver out of his hands and set it down.

"No, Lawrence," he said roughly. "*You're* the one who's got things to answer for. You won't be so eager to call the police when you've heard what this man's got to say. I suggest you just hold on and listen. Have a drink. You'll need it."

He took Croome by the shoulder and forced him to face the room. The man's hands fluttered and twitched and he found difficulty in speaking. His ruddy, outdoors skin had turned gray white, cadaverous.

"Give him a jab to wind him up," said Frank tersely. "I want you to hear it from the horse's mouth."

Lawrence took Croome's wrist and felt his pulse. "Ticker,"

he pronounced and added, "You must be proud, Frank. Quite a bag for a night's work."

"Shut up and see to him."

The psychiatrist drew a syringe from his bag, filled it swiftly and fed it into Croome's arm. "He's ready for interrogation," he said sourly, dabbing the pinprick with cotton. He withdrew to the window.

Frank held a drink to the farmer's lips and explained who Lawrence was and what he wanted him to do.

"Just tell him exactly what you told me. Begin at the beginning. There's no hurry. Take your time."

At first the farmer wouldn't speak, suspicious of the psychiatrist, but after several minutes of cajoling he broke. Hanging his head, he spoke into the carpet in short, hesitant bursts. Eleven years he'd lived with the secret; every day for eleven years he'd looked at Tommy and heard the boy's subnormal gabbling and was reminded of his guilt. Now it was over. What was done was done. He was ruined, finished; the center of his life had collapsed. He was ready to make his confession.

"We tried, Mary and I," he began. "We tried for ten, fifteen years, but we couldn't have any. We tried adopting, but, well, they turned us down. Too poor. They all get given to the nobs."

Croome shook his head, still staring down at the carpet. He hesitated before continuing.

"Then it happened. All of a sudden our prayers were answered. Mary got pregnant. She carried it like a dream and she dropped it in the spring, eleven years ago. Bloody beautiful it was, a right little howler, healthy and strong as a baby bullock. We called him Tommy. She said he took after his dad. Took after his dad," he repeated, his shoulders shaking in distress.

Frank looked across at Lawrence; his face wore a weary smirk. Outside, the wind drove the rain against the small panes and the electric lights flickered momentarily. Croome went on.

"Then one morning, I'd been out at market. I sold an Angus bull, big bugger, and a good price too. I came back and there was Mary screaming the place down, 'It's Tommy! He's dead!' A crib death. I'd read about them. One moment he was alive and kicking, the next he'd snuffed it. Just like that. I didn't need to call the doctor; I know a dead 'un when I see it. Our own little Tommy, after all we'd done and prayed for! It wasn't right.

"Mary went crazy. She wouldn't be quietened. She got hold of the van—I couldn't stop her—and she drove into Buckingham. She wasn't gone long. And when she came back . . ."

Lawrence's expression had changed. Now he was alert, penetrating. Frank murmured, "Go on."

"When she came back it was like she'd brought our little Tommy back with her. Brought him back from the dead, a right miracle. I didn't go along with the idea at first, but they looked so alike . . . well, I gave in. We kept him. Then I saw the papers; that was terrible. It got headlines at first. I felt really bad about the mother, the Hall woman, but the baby was one of a pair, wasn't he, she having two and us having none, and I reckoned she still had one left . . ."

He stopped, uncertain how his defense was being received. Frank prompted gently, "Tell Dr. Miller what happened next. Tell us what you did with your own child."

This wasn't the absolution Croome had been wanting. A look of betrayal came over his face and he turned away from the room. Frank knew he'd been pushed too far. He faced the psychiatrist himself.

"OK, I'll tell him, then."

"Yes, Frank? I'm listening."

Lawrence's small, close-set eyes and thin lips had hardened and his whole expression was that of a scientist reserving judgment. But it was clear he didn't like the evidence so far at all.

"It was quite simple really. They exchanged the babies' clothes. Philip Hall became Tommy Croome. The dead Tommy was taken out in the van and dumped not far from where Philip had been snatched. As it happened, it took the police weeks to find the body. By then it had decomposed beyond recognition. There was an inquest but the coroner couldn't say how it had died. But the clothes identified it: there was never any doubt in anyone's mind *who* the child was. Everyone, including the mother, quite reasonably assumed that this was the missing Hall child."

"My God," breathed Lawrence finally. But his frown deepened; he hadn't been sold on the story yet.

Croome now looked up, a sudden look of urgency flushing his face. He had to be understood, he had to be reprieved.

"It wasn't like you think! We brought him up as our own. We gave him everything we could: love, a home, animals around him. We tried to think of him as our Tommy. But he wasn't. He was different. Strange. We both saw it early on but we pretended nothing was wrong. We thought it would pass, but it didn't, it only got worse. And then we realized: we'd picked a bad 'un, a simpleton, the village idiot."

Lawrence's hand had frozen mid-way to his lips. He spoke but had to clear his throat and repeat the word.

"Descr . . . describe."

The farmer dropped his eyes again.

"The boy was backward. He couldn't read or write properly. Clumsy, too. Always spilling things and knocking into things. He'd never learn unless you clouted him. I didn't like doing it, but you had to. When there was only one of us about you had to keep him locked up in his room. He was wild, violent, a little animal. You never knew what he'd do next. Like the time he set the place on fire . . ."

"Set the place on fire?" snapped Lawrence. "When, exactly?"

"Sunday after Christmas, of all times."

A dense silence filled the room. Upstairs, a floorboard

creaked. Frank exchanged a glance with Lawrence but neither moved.

"Sometimes I had to be really firm," Croome repeated, justifying himself. "Mary was dead against using the strap, but it was the only way to deal with him. I mean, he was a right *moron*. But we loved him. Or we tried to. Till Mary fell ill."

"His wife died a short while ago," Frank explained quietly.

"He'd got into the tool-shed where I keep the paraquat. I didn't find out till later, till it was too late. I'd taught him about poison but maybe he didn't remember, or maybe he did; I don't know. I can't prove he did it—there wasn't a post-mortem or the like—but he took her life, I know he did. He was growing up and growing evil." He clutched his face in his hands. "Oh, Mary, my poor dove, Mary. God forgive us."

Lawrence stood up. "Where is the boy now? I want to examine him right away."

Croome turned away once again, buried his head in the chair and refused to reply. Frank supplied the answer.

"He's dead. Croome shot him. The body's in the back of the Land Rover. I think you'd better take a look at it, Lawrence." His tone hardened. "There's enough of the face left for you to come to your own conclusions."

"Where is the Land Rover?"

"In the yard. I'm going to call the police now." Frank picked up the telephone.

Lawrence laughed harshly from the doorway. "You're a screwball. Do you expect them to believe all this? It's the craziest load of bull I've ever heard in all my professional years."

"Take a torch with you. One thing: if I were you, when the police arrive don't start shouting about abduction and kidnapping and so on. You'll understand why when you look in the Land Rover. You don't get much credit out of it; nor does medicine, for that matter. As for Jonathan, there's no question of sending him back to hospital. He's going home, to his mother. I'll be seeing to that. In fact, I'll drop you off and take your car. OK?"

Lawrence scowled. Without replying, he reached for his bag and slammed the front door behind him.

The light from Lawrence's torch flickered over the lumpy sacking on which a light frost had already fallen. A foot shod in a muddy boot stuck out at an awkward angle. The under-layers of sacking glowed dark and wet as he peeled them back, guessing where the head would be. He steeled himself for the sight of blood.

Even so, he wasn't ready for what he saw. His stomach welled up with a lurch. Dropping the sacking, he gripped the side of the jeep, riding down the rising vomit. But he'd seen enough; it was Jonathan lying there.

But Jonathan was upstairs.

Maddened, confused, disbelieving, he gripped his bag and went back to the house. He'd take a proper look at the boy upstairs.

He was surfacing from a nightmare. A maniac with a gun had been hunting him down in a forest. Every time he thought he'd escaped he would run into a tree which would come alive and turn into his double. Then he'd have to fight it, to smash it, to kill it, but as soon as he'd killed it he'd turn around only to find the next tree melting into the image again, his own image, and it too would come alive and its branches would become arms stretching out to throttle him. . . .

He half-opened his eyes. Where was he? Instinctively he swallowed, expecting to taste the bitter almonds. But he didn't. No blood in his mouth either: he hadn't bitten his tongue in a seizure. Where was this room, this bed? He sat up on an elbow but winced. His muscles howled in agony and a sharp pain stabbed at his side. He waited. This was when it often came, at weak and vulnerable moments like this. Did he have the strength to try and stave it off by humming or reciting or something like that?

He lay back on the pillow and waited for the invasion.

Nothing came. No bitter taste on the palate, no brief tugging feeling inside his head, no stirrings of the tentacled animal beneath his skull, none of the slip of focus that heralded his occupation by his other person. Nothing.

Perhaps it was hiding, lying in wait, preparing to pounce when he least expected. Dimly he recalled the confused events of the night, unsure which were real and which were dreams. He'd found Tommy (had he?), then Tommy was real (was he?). They'd fought to the death, to wipe each other out. He gradually began to understand. That evil bastard, Tommy, he thought; he'd been responsible for the years of pain and madness. But Tommy was dead, dead, dead! That meant he was free, cured!

Was he?

After several minutes he got out of bed. The room was unfamiliar at first and the floorboards creaked under his step. He went to the window and drew back the curtain. In the dull, drizzly moonlight he gradually began to recognize it all: the garden with its broken trellis, the rusting wreck of the tractor abandoned in the field beyond and the line of ash trees stretching away to the stream. He'd built the bridge over that stream. Around the corner, out of sight, was the flat stone on which he'd sacrificed Puck.

He tiptoed down the corridor, knowing the places where the boards creaked. He climbed the stairs to the attic room. A shiver of dread shook him as he touched the doorhandle. Did he dare go in? As he opened the door his hand automatically found the light-switch in the dark. He hesitated, tasting his spit for the sign. This was the moment it would choose to pounce.

He snapped on the light.

His room, his familiar room. The iron bedstead and the lumpy mattress. The boxes of broken crayons and the slashed wallboard with a child's first vocabulary written up. The books and magazines which he couldn't read but enjoyed for the anatomical pictures of animals. The plastic giraffes and lions used for torture in his make-believe zoo. The wooden desk with rabbits' feet and the jaw-bones of crows and sheep hidden away in the drawer along with the forbidden matches. The bars from the skylight.

He started: there were sounds behind him. Brother! he thought. Then, Dad? What Dad? Jonathan had no father, and yet dimly he remembered that long ago, in far-off days, he might have had a dad. But he didn't any longer. He was Jonathan. Jonathan was an only child.

In the doorway stood Lawrence, a doctor's bag in his hand. He was watching him, his eyebrows raised in astonishment.

Jonathan smiled.

"Oh, hello. How did *you* get here?"

29

The briefest statements were taken, confirming Croome's confession to murder, and he was taken off to Buckingham police station, an aged, white-faced ruin of a man. Jonathan was put in Lawrence's charge and the police telephoned Sarah to say he'd been found; he was in his doctor's hands and was being returned home. Frank was told to report to the Bedford police in the morning. The matter of the abduction was being handled in their jurisdiction; it would be up to them to decide whether to press charges or not. At four-thirty the ambulance left with Tommy's body and Lawrence started out back to Bedford. Frank sat beside him and Jonathan lay asleep under a rug in the back.

Ahead of them, as they drove through the waterlogged countryside, a reluctant dawn was breaking. Frank found his mind shifting in and out of focus as waves of exhaustion swept over him. The world had taken on the surreal quality that came with lack of sleep. He was too numb to feel anything, let alone wish to tackle the swarm of questions the past hours had raised. Instead he slumped back in the passenger seat, aware of the tension in the silence but indifferent to it.

"Of course, this changes everything," Lawrence began at last, in a tight voice, keeping his eyes on the road.

"I should bloody think so," murmured Frank. "For one thing you won't be seeing Jonathan in your wards again."

"On the contrary."

"What the hell do you mean?"

"He's still my patient. He's not been discharged. I'll have to check him thoroughly before certifying him fit to go home. And I doubt if after tonight I could give him a clean bill of health. No, I'll need to be seeing a good deal more of Master Hall."

"You'll do nothing of the sort!" Frank now sat up.

"We may have been slightly off the track, but the events of the night prove he does have a serious clinical condition." The psychiatrist paused to change gear. "If anything, we'll find the shock has set him back."

"For Christ's sake, you dumb scientists, can't you see beyond the warts on the end of your noses? This 'clinical condition' of yours is simply a psychic empathy with his twin. Of course you reject that; you call it paranormal. I call it normal. Science is completely blind to what's obvious to the rest of us. How do you think it was that the truth came out? By my hunch, my lateral thinking, my intuitive, inductive idea. *Your* methods would certainly never have brought it to light. You'd still be treating Jonathan for disorders he hasn't got. Temporal lobe epilepsy, indeed! Minimal brain dysfunction! You've misdiagnosed it the whole way through. Frankly, in your shoes I'd be worried as hell. It's nothing but criminal negligence."

"Don't let's get into a row, please," said Lawrence in the tone of indulging a child. "Not just right this minute."

"All right. Then tell me how *you* explain what you've seen tonight. Come on: give me a nice, hard, logical account based on deductive reasoning."

"I'm not prepared to."

"You can't, that's why."

"I could advance a theory."

"Go on, then. Try."

The psychiatrist sighed before launching out.

"We seem, *prima facie*, to be looking at a sensory faculty that functions outside the five we recognize. Now, either we've made an error in analyzing the evidence, or the hypothesis that we mammals possess five senses is itself wrong."

"Great. That's what I call really smart."

"Each of the alternatives must be tested," Lawrence went on, ignoring the sarcasm. "Regrettably, one half of the useful evidence is on its way to the mortuary at this moment. The other half is in the back of this car. That's what I meant by saying this changes everything. It changes the reason I need Jonathan. He's more vital than ever now."

"Tough."

"I don't think you know quite what you're saying, Frank. I am his consultant. What I say goes. I could section him."

"Section him?"

"Under Section Twenty-five of the Mental Health Act, 1959, I can have him compulsorily admitted to hospital. It only takes another signature, his GP's, and I already happen to know the man's very obliging."

"You sod, Lawrence!"

"Now, now, Frank. That's an emotional reaction."

"Of course it's bloody emotional! Being emotional is being a human being. You've forgotten. You see Jonathan as a case, a syndrome, an interesting experiment. You've lit on a theory, this week's pet theory, and you poke around inside his brain or his psyche to test it out. If that doesn't work, you'll poke around some more until you find one that sticks—or else the kid snuffs it."

"Rubbish."

"Admit that's how the scientific method works. But you can't do that with Jonathan! He's not clinically disturbed, he's not mad. The whole point of getting you over to that godforsaken farm was to prove that. Jonathan's not mad and he never has been. To the extent he is, it's you that's made him it. You and the other quacks who've dealt with him. You shrinks are all the same: if the boy doesn't conform to your idea of normal behavior you start out with the hypothesis that he's mad and then you set out to prove it. Only in Jonathan's case it wasn't so easy. Oh no. You tried analysis, then EEGs, then scans, then spinal fluid tests. Soon it was going to be, 'We'd better take out a few actual brain cells,' and then a few more. . . . You can afford to play around with metals or chemicals or inert things, but not with living beings, not with *people!*"

Angrily Lawrence slewed the car sharply around a corner and looked across at the other man. "You're sentimental and naive, Frank. And you're insultingly hypocritical. You take the benefits that science and medicine bring while knocking all that has to be done to get there."

Frank lowered his voice, suddenly remembering Jonathan asleep in the back.

"Ends do not justify means, Lawrence. That's all civilization is about. To say they do is to condone torture, animal experiments . . ."

"Listen! *If* this is twin telepathy, *if* it's a dormant faculty that has somehow come awake and *if* it has a specific physical location in the brain—say, in the Hirschfield area, as one might suppose—then think of the implications. We'd be on the brink of an absolutely phenomenal scientific breakthrough."

Frank snorted derisively.

"Look, man," continued the psychiatrist, "there has never

been one single paranormal event that has ever, *ever*, stood up to scrutiny. They've never been properly recorded or convincingly repeated under controlled conditions. Now if this is the first, think what that means. It will overturn the entire way we think of ourselves, the whole basis for our actions, our behavior, our very purpose in being here in the first place. The implications are prodigious. Don't tell me a slight inconvenience to one small boy outweighs the value of progress of that order!"

"Sacrifice the one for the many?"

"If you must put it that way, yes."

"Fascist."

"What does that make you, then: naive, ingenuous, infantile?"

Frank felt flushed with fatigue and anger. He'd lost the power to argue. Perhaps the two of them started out with such opposing assumptions that any ultimate dialogue wasn't really possible. He weighed in again, annoyed and slightly lost.

"And of course your role is entirely altruistic. No sniff of Nobel prizes in the air? Lawrence at the service of humanity . . ."

"Wise up, Frank."

He clenched his teeth. He knew he'd argued with too much feeling and too little logic. But what was wrong with that? Finally, all issues were moral issues. Morality was merely a form in which people's basic feelings about life and behavior were coded. Scientists of Lawrence's type believed knowledge was pure in itself and that moral issues arose only when their work was put to use. But times and views had changed. Did anybody today believe that the man who built the Hiroshima bomb was any less to blame than the man who dropped it? Lawrence Pontius-Pilate Miller was the one who should wise up.

He looked out of the window to calm himself down. Milkmen and newspaper boys were already on their delivery rounds and hazy figures wrapped deep in coats and scarves were cycling off to work. His throat was dry. Lawrence sickened him.

"I quite simply will not allow it to happen," he said quietly. "This is the end of the hospital tests for Jonathan."

Lawrence snorted, suggesting that Frank was wasting his breath.

But from behind them came Jonathan's voice. The boy was wide awake and he'd heard everything.

"Frank's right. No more tests," he said.

Lawrence dropped Frank and Jonathan at the boy's home and drove off in an angry mood, telling Sarah that Frank would explain everything and he'd call her later in the day.

Although it was early morning Sarah was already dressed. All the house lights were on and she had a hot bath all ready for Jonathan. Her eyes were heavily ringed and the agony of the past hours had left her complexion lined and gray. She grasped him to her and examined the battered, limp child. Stripping off his filthy clothes, she half-walked and half-carried him upstairs. Frank started to follow but she repelled him with a glance.

He searched the cupboards for alcohol but finding only sweet sherry made himself a strong coffee instead. He struggled to keep on his feet, knowing that if he sat down he'd fall asleep. Fatigue washed over him in blurry waves.

When Sarah came down at last she kept her distance. She spread her hands on her skirt and said, "At least I should offer you breakfast."

"Breakfast?" Of course, it was morning. The day was today. This was the here and now. "Thanks. I could use some food."

"Bacon, eggs, the works?"

"The works."

Breakfast revived him and restabilized his sense of being.

"You'd better call the school, Sarah," he said when he'd finished. "Take the morning off. I have a lot to tell you. And it'll probably come as an awful shock."

"Jonathan's told me everything. He found Tommy, and Tommy's dead."

"Jonathan doesn't know everything. One thing he doesn't understand is that Tommy *was* Philip, your other son, his twin."

Sarah sat down abruptly. She put her mug of tea down so as not to spill it and sat, digging the nails of one hand into the palm of the other, as Frank told her the truth about Philip, about Croome, about Tommy and the farm. She listened without speaking, sitting bolt upright, with scarcely an expression passing across her features. It was mid-morning by the time he felt he'd said it all and he could leave. He telephoned a taxi, then stood over her, a hand on her shoulder. She didn't withdraw.

"Dear Sarah," he said quietly and tenderly.

She lifted her eyes from her lap. They were full of tears: tears of anger.

"All those years! All those years she stole from me! And my poor Jonathan! The bitch!"

"She's dead, Sarah."

"I'd stopped thinking about the future; I couldn't bear it. I killed myself inside," she sobbed, now leaning against Frank. "Do you think Jonathan really *is* going to be all right? I was waiting for him to explode. He was going to explode. And me, God forgive me, I *wanted* it to happen! I wanted it to be over! Oh, *God*," she moaned. "What a mother I am!"

"Hush, Sarah, hush," Frank comforted her. "It's going to be all right." He held her, waiting for the sobbing to subside, and then gently pushed her back into the chair. Her face was utterly naked to him, for the first time.

"In the first place, you've been a wonderful mother. What Jonathan needed was self-control, and you taught him it. You protected him from the world; you could not protect him from something inside himself."

"Ah," she cried in self-disgust, "I did nothing for him. I tried to teach him to be blind, as I have made myself."

"It's not that simple, Sarah," said Frank. "In fact," he added, "nothing is that simple. Think, for instance, what would have happened if that woman had not taken Philip."

She sat up a little and stared at him.

"The boy was mad. He was violent and dangerous. You saw it; but you saw it in Jonathan. Jonathan had what many people call a gift, a psychic gift. He probably still has it. In his case, it was a curse. As he grew into adolescence he grew more receptive to everything Tommy—Philip—saw, heard and felt. *Think* what it would have been like to live with the real thing, how much worse it might have been for Jonathan, and for you."

Sarah's eyes, unfocussed, had turned inward; a look of faint horror was on her face.

"Yes," he went on, "you've got quite a lot of thinking to do. Not about what might have been, but what was. And about how things are going to be. Jonathan," he said, desperately wanting to believe it himself, "is going to be all right. You are going to have to start inventing a future for him."

He held himself together in the taxi going home. It hit him as he closed the front door. He leaned against the wall and wept like a child.

30

Sarah brought Jonathan lunch in bed. On the tray, beside the milk, she'd put out his pill as usual. She drew the curtains quietly, careful not to wake him too quickly, knowing this was one of his most vulnerable moments. The crisp light of the first real day of spring poured into the room; the may tree was in bud and the lawn had taken on a bright new green.

"What time is it, Mum?"

Jonathan was sitting up, rubbing his eyes. Instinctively she searched his face for the signs but found none.

"It's almost two, darling. You've been asleep for a good eight hours. How do you feel?"

"Different. But my tummy hurts at the side."

"Here, let me see. I'll change the dressing." She drew back the covers; the wound was already healing. "What do you mean by *different*?"

He shrugged. "What have you brought? I'm starving."

She handed him the milk and his pill. He shook his head.

"No, not those. I'm not going to take them any more. I don't need them."

"Lawrence hasn't said anything about that. He's phoning later and I'll ask him then. In the meantime, you've had a terrible shock and we don't want to take chances, do we?"

"Oh, Mum, don't you understand anything? I feel different. I haven't had the slightest twinge since that farmer . . ."

"No! Don't think about that, my sweet."

Holding his hand, she automatically checked his eyes; they were bright, alert, intelligent, quick: just as they used to be, all that time ago.

"Stop looking at me like that," he said crossly. "I'm not loony any more, Mum. I know I'm not. I'm better, I can *feel* it."

"Oh, darling, I do so hope so."

His simple faith pained her. How could he imagine a lifetime's mental disturbance could be reversed in one night? She drew him to her. If only she, with her adult's cynicism, could believe he was right. Frank believed, of course, but she hadn't heard Lawrence's view, though she could make a guess.

As for the police, when they came around earlier that morning they had adopted a pragmatic attitude. Croome had murdered his son and Jonathan was a witness: that was all they were interested in. The boy had broken out of hospital and gone on the run . . . but to say he'd been summoned across forty miles of country by a telepathic signal was too improbable, too farfetched for any officer of the law or any court in the land to take seriously. No, concluded the detective constable, the file on Philip Hall was to remain on the shelf.

"Mum?"

She stroked his cropped, fair hair. "Yes?"

"Holidays start the week after next. Let's go away some-where."

"The sea's far too cold at this time of year."

"Abroad, I mean. William's dad takes them to France."

She was about to say he knew they couldn't stray too far from home, to remind him of their pact and to ask him what they'd do if he had a bad spell in some foreign country. But she held back. He was looking intently at her, his gaze firm, an almost quizzical, teasing light in his blue eyes.

"I think that's a wonderful idea," she replied at last. "We could take the car and explore. Brittany's lovely. I've got an old friend from school we could look up. Oh, don't let me forget, I'll have to add you to my passport."

Lawrence had gone home to bathe, shave and change. He was in his office in the psychiatric ward long before the day staff arrived. He brought four mugs of heavily sugared coffee from the vending machine and set them out in a row on his desk. From his drawer he took out a pad and began planning his course of action. By the time his secretary came in he was ready. He called her in at once and began dictating instructions.

First, he wanted everything ever published, written or re-searched on the Hirschfield ganglion. The British Medical Association would supply a bibliography and between the In-stitute of Neurology and the main London teaching hospitals he'd be able to track down anyone working in this area. Next, he wanted an urgent meeting with the hospital's consultant neurologist; he had to develop a simple, effective and easily administered means of scanning this small center in the hippo-campus. Time on the PET scanner was too expensive and the machines too few and far between; this had to be something that could slip readily in alongside the normal, standard brain tests. As for test subjects, there was no problem of shortage: in hospitals and clinics up and down the country there were literally thousands of patients suffering from various forms of brain damage. This would be his catchment pool.

Then he planned his own research into twins. On Dr. Cameron's ward there was a child, one of a pair of identical twins. As soon as he had developed a reliable H-test—as he now referred to the Hirschfield scan—it would be easy to arrange for the twin to be brought in and run through it. Ideally, he'd do this to every pair of identical twins in the county. He planned to contact all the local health authorities, adoption societies and university researchers for pairs of normals. The beauty of his position was that he could do all of this in his own right as area chief consultant psychiatrist, without having to get permission from the board.

And yet. Was he starting at the right end?

He took the fourth cup of coffee, now cold, and poured it down the small basin in the corner, then went over to the window. Of the alternatives he'd mentioned to Frank in the car, was he not perhaps examining the wrong one? He should be scrutinizing the evidence first. But the evidence was Jonathan, and Jonathan wasn't going to co-operate. Damn the boy; damn Frank's interference. In Jonathan's present mood there was simply no point in trying to section him, whether he could do so legally or not.

But there again. The ESP business.

He frowned. The very hypothesis he was setting out to test rested on one assumption: that there was such a thing as extrasensory perception. His mind rebelled at the idea. Here was Dr. Lawrence Miller actually *assuming* the existence of telepathy! Absurd. Just think for a moment: how *could* it possibly work? Like radio waves? No: formidable power would be required, far beyond the scope of the human brain, whose entire electrical current was hardly enough to light a flashlight bulb. Besides, radio waves degraded with distance and required constant boosting, while all studies of telepathy agreed that it worked, if it worked at all, irrespective of distance.

He scratched his wiry dark hair and snorted impatiently. OK, then, he said to himself, what else could it be? We know the brain operates chemically as well as electrically—but the telepathic conductor can't be chemical since that would demand a physical medium of transport. So, does the brain work in *another* way too? Perhaps magnetically? Are there some kind of force fields—as it were, ley-lines of the mind—lying in strips across the surface of the globe and bending with its curvature, into which a specially tuned human brain like Jonathan's could key its messages and which would carry them across great distances, instantaneously, without degradation, without power consumption?

He turned away from the window in disgust. He was dipping his toe into all that hocus-pocus. He had to keep thinking as a *scientist*, within the four walls of logic, experiment, reason and measurement.

And then an idea came to him, the perfect, scientific starting-point. He reached for the telephone. In a short while he was speaking to the surgeon in charge of the Buckingham mortuary.

"The Tommy Croome body," he said. "When you've done with it, would you keep the brain aside for me?"

"The cranium's hardly intact." The surgeon's tone suggested this was a considerable understatement. "A good part of the cortex and occipital lobe is missing."

"But the hippocampus?"

"You might be in luck there."

Telling his secretary to ignore his instruction about a meeting with the consultant neurosurgeon, he put on a white coat and went to visit the man at once. He'd need the facilities of Neurology to examine the tissue when it arrived from the mortuary.

As he stepped out of the lift he shook his head. It was regrettable that the brain would of course be dead. There was, to his knowledge, only one living brain with an active Hirschfield ganglion. He stopped half-way down the corridor. Once again he came to the realization that all avenues ultimately led back to the same point: Jonathan.

Frank woke stiff and cold. He crawled out of bed and heard voices shouting downstairs. Two police officers stood at the foot of the stairs; he'd forgotten to check in at the station that morning. Bleary-eyed and unshaven, he dictated a statement admitting to what they called "unauthorized discharge"; he noted they weren't referring to abduction or kidnap. He skirted anything to do with the twin link. When they left he was reasonably certain that the matter would be allowed to drop.

He strolled to the village shop to buy food. The early spring air was rich and young. He thought of Jonathan and Sarah, and found himself considering the mother more than the child. It was going to be harder for her.

After making himself a late brunch he turned his attention to his neglected business. Among his mail was a holiday card from Tangier; his friend, the bookseller in Deanshanger, was investing some of his quarter's profits in a well-earned cruise. Head office memos reported that his sales figures were down, but he knew he could make them up next quarter. On impulse he telephoned three real estate agents and put the mill-house on the market. The home still held too many memories of his life with Cathy; he needed a fresh start. There was a large stone barn in the next village, with planning permission, on which he'd always had his eye. He'd build something from scratch. Its crest would be a fox and he'd call it Fuller's Earth.

It was Friday afternoon and there was no work that couldn't wait until the following week. The day cried out to be enjoyed. Calling Dog, he set off down the garden and into the fields beyond. By the river the willows were putting out the first catkins and from the sedges came the mating cries of moorhens and ducks. Across the pale, cloudless sky flew high flocks of birds on their return passage and all around on earth he could smell the sap rising.

"Frank! Wait for me!"

He recognized Jonathan's voice at once. Dog bounded towards the running boy and jumped up to lick his face.

"I cycled over," he said. "I had to see you."

He put his hand over the boy's shoulder but he winced. "Bruises," he said with a laugh. Then, "Which way shall we go?"

"Let's take the towpath."

He nodded.

They didn't mention Tommy or the events of the previous night. In the bright daylight it was hard to believe they existed in the same realm. They spoke of their plans for the future. Jonathan was off to France soon, his first trip abroad. When he got back he'd be keen to help with rebuilding the old barn. Frank noticed a mature, almost adult note in the boy's conversation.

After a while Jonathan grew serious.

"Frank," he asked, "Where do you think Tommy, I mean Philip, is now?"

"It depends if you believe in an afterlife."

"Oh, of course there is."

"How can you be so sure?"

Jonathan shrugged. He was sure, that was all.

"Well," continued Frank, "it can't exactly be a place with rivers and trees and skies. I don't suppose he's fishing right this minute."

"Could he still talk?"

"Talk?" Frank paused to examine the boy's expression. He was meaning all this very intensely. "Personally, I find it hard to imagine he could. Clairvoyants and mediums think they can call up the dead and communicate with them. Literally, talk to them. Maybe the soul lives on as energy without substance. In that case I suppose it's possible that energy can create thought and thought can create speech."

Jonathan pondered this.

"When I was getting Tommy's thoughts," he said slowly, almost to himself, "that was energy without substance, wasn't it?"

Frank felt a shiver pass through him. "What are you trying to say, Jonathan?"

"Oh, nothing."

They walked on in silence, then quite abruptly they stopped in their tracks at the same moment. Jonathan looked up at Frank with an intense, puzzled frown. To ease the tension Frank threw Dog's stick far across the field and waited for the boy to continue. For a moment he seemed about to go on again, but then his face relaxed and he smiled. He fixed his blue eyes on Frank and said,

"Shall we turn back now?"

The ginger cake was sweet but not sweet enough to cover the faint trace of bitterness in Jonathan's mouth. Sweat broke out under his arms. Oh Christ, he thought.

Suddenly he had to be alone. He got up and said he was going to the lavatory. He locked himself in and stared out of the small window. The garden led to the fields, the fields to the river, the river to more fields, and so to infinity. If he wasn't *there*, where was he?

The almonds weren't so bitter; they bore a strange, sweet overtone. Clenching his fists, he waited for the first writhings within his head, then the overwhelming sense of invasion. But nothing came.

Nothing?

There *was* something there, something trying to come

through, something made partly of words and partly of thoughts, floating like skeins of whispers through his mind.

"Tommy?"

He wasn't sure if he heard a reply. But even as he strained to listen, he sensed a gentle flood of release, a vast sigh of a spirit's ease. This was no invasion, but the sweet comfort of a brother's touch. He was still himself, still Jonathan Hall, and it didn't hurt.

FREE!!
BOOKS BY MAIL
CATALOGUE

BOOKS BY MAIL will share with you our current bestselling books as well as hard to find specialty titles in areas that will match your interests. You will be updated on what's new in books at no cost to you. Just fill in the coupon below and discover the convenience of having books delivered to your home.

PLEASE ADD $1.00 TO COVER THE COST OF POSTAGE & HANDLING.